NOIR BY NOIR WEST

NOIR BY NOIR WEST

Dark Fiction from the West of Ireland

James Martyn Joyce

Editor

ARLEN
HOUSE

NOIR BY NOIR WEST

is published in 2014 by
ARLEN HOUSE
42 Grange Abbey Road
Baldoyle
Dublin 13
Ireland
Phone: +353 86 8207617
Email: arlenhouse@gmail.com
www.arlenhouse.blogspot.com

978–1–85132–077–6, paperback
978–1–85132–078–3, hardback

International distribution by
SYRACUSE UNIVERSITY PRESS
621 Skytop Road, Suite 110
Syracuse, New York
USA 13244–5290
Phone: 315–443–5534/Fax: 315–443–5545
Email: supress@syr.edu
www.syracuseuniversitypress.syr.edu

Typesetting by Arlen House
Cover image by Dagmar Drabent
www.dagmardrabent.com

CONTENTS

ACKNOWLEDGEMENTS

Dagmar Drabent, www.dagmardrabent.com
Paul Callanan, www.designassociates.ie

'Hellkite' by Geraldine Mills was previously published in *Hellkite* (Arlen House, 2014).

'Snagged' by Aideen Henry was previously published in *Hugging Thistles* (Arlen House, 2013).

'Death at a Funeral' by Micheál Ó Conghaile was previously published in *The Colours of Man*, edited by Alan Hayes (Cló Iar-Chonnacht, 2012).

'Full-Sized Life' by Susan Millar Dumars was first published online on the website *Irish Left Review*.

'Angel of Hospitality' by Ken Bruen was first published online in *The Big Click* electronic magazine.

An earlier version of 'Murder and Self-Harm' by James Martyn Joyce was published in *ROPES*.

In memory of Gerry Galvin (1942–2013)

and in honour of all the Galway writers
who have finished telling their stories

… and for those who are just beginning

NOIR BY NOIR WEST

FISHING

Gerry Galvin

Listen to this, from *Fishing Ireland*, the brochure I picked up in a tourist office: 'a network of lakes connected by man-made canals, teeming with life, a fisherman's paradise. Nowhere else in Ireland has been blessed by such a rich tapestry of waterways famed in song and story'. There's a section on schmaltzy fishing ballads and poems that 'lap and ruffle in the wind'. Advertiser's claptrap. I'd shoot the fuckers.

These are pike lakes, always were. I keep my boat in a cul-de-sac off one of the canals, completely hidden in summer tunnels of overgrowing myrtle and sycamore. Fished and swam here as a kid, know all the hazards. Greatest hazards of all are fishermen. Not so bad now since the drownings. Ten last summer. I blame prosperity. Everything gets out of hand. English and Continentals as well as the city fellas, with enough equipment for a moon landing. They pack the pike into frozen containers. There's as big a demand for them as there is for frogs and truffles. Wouldn't touch them myself but that's not the point.

I live on the boat Easter to October. Moonlight is the best time on the Corrib. I like to glide in the shallows, pike nuzzling up to the boat. They know me. Beautiful creatures. Big buggers, binocular vision, ambush experts. Sprint, kill and swallow. Your average pike devours two hundred times his size in a lifetime. So they say. Teeth like saws.

Tourists take liberties, get lines tangled, wade into pools deeper than they think. Rubber boots slip on the rocks. Swimming's no good with all that gear. There was a fella last year, big German with a belly. Fell off the jetty. I could see the cut above his eye. Kept shouting and clawing at the side of my boat, gasping, trying to say something. Couldn't make out what, don't speak German.

That American couple last week, they knew a bit about pike alright. We talked about the great pike lakes of Nevada. Never been myself but I've done the reading. I showed them my books, maps and pictures of pike lakes in Germany and Russia. There's a lake inland from Murmansk where pike are sold in the local market for their skins. They make waistcoats and shoes for the children.

Cleo and Bob, the Americans, they caught a twenty pounder on the first day, hauled it in, washed off the green slime and cut the head off. Knife like a razor, couldn't keep my eyes off it. They invited me to lunch in a clearing off one of the jetties. Roast pike. Never eaten it before. I didn't like myself for that, breaking my own rules. They should have known better.

Night fishermen are even more stupid. They behave like teenagers out for a night on the town. Hyped up with booze and drugs they think they have nature by the balls. If anything goes wrong there's nobody around to save them.

THE KING OF GALWAY

Séamus Scanlon

The man waited in Crow's pub on Sea Road.

The local drinkers told wide-eyed American tourists that it was named after the crow's nests of Spanish sailing ships that crowded bow to bow in the docks of medieval Galway waiting for Atlantic swells and gale force winds to abate. Centuries back when Galway actually liked foreigners. Centuries back when the mayor of Galway hanged his own son for killing a Spanish sailor. Centuries back when Galway girls picked tanned smooth-skinned Spaniards to be their lovers and the fathers of their black-haired handsome children. The Yanks loved it. And bought drinks for the raconteurs. Romanticism is Galway's middle name. Followed closely by mendacity. The real reason was prosaic – the painter misspelt the owner's name, Martin Crowe.

Dusk was close. The streets were sleek with drizzle. Fog horns sent deep laments back out into the narrow channels of Galway Bay. Soon rain would fly in off the Atlantic.

A man sat a table with a mobile phone and a drink in front of him. An ice bucket with beads of condensation on its shiny surface sat close to his elbow on the cigarette-burn-scarred tabletop. He was in his early sixties but his vitality shone through to anyone who noticed such things. His eyes were the colour of grey Connemara flint. His skin was unlined and blemish free. He was called Baby Face by Galway girls when he was a teenager. Galway boys knew not to say it.

The pub was almost empty. The annual Galway Novena was on in the Abbey Church. A few agnostics rested their arms on the counter and leant over the dark stained altar as if their drinks would be their last. Behind the bar a ceiling-high mirror ran the length of the counter. In the high corners the glass was blurred by chemicals leaching out to the surface. Impurities always break through. Men watched themselves as they drank and brooded. They looked away quickly whenever they noticed their distorted grey alter-egos staring back.

The door opened. A man in his late thirties in a fine tailored Magee suit hesitated for a moment. Three bodyguards crowded behind him. He looked around and then strode across the wooden floor and sat down beside the older man. His three minders followed throwing off scowls and sat at an adjacent table. They had violence and poverty hard-wired into their bodies and minds. The newcomer smiled.

Hello there, Daddy. Long time no see.

The older man didn't look up. He just kept sipping his drink.

Hello Daddy, I said.

Don't fucken hello Daddy me.

Hostility radar, Daddy!

You are a fucken joke.

Temper, temper, Daddy!

I would not call this here a temper.

Temper fugit!

It's *tempis fugit* dummy. It's Latin. Time flies.

Is it? Does it? Who knew?

Fucken everyone in the universe basically. Except Yanks. And you. Time flies, except around you.

Now, Daddy, don't be like that.

The son points at the mobile phone.

Waiting for a call to say your truck has made it, I suppose?

The father shrugs.

Early alert warning. It may not happen!

You happened, that's bad enough. You are a disgrace to the criminal classes. Not to mention our family.

Let bygones be bygones, Daddy, I always say.

You would since you are just a snivelling cur. You should be fucken dead sure. That rhymes.

The father gestured at the three bodyguards at the adjacent table.

I see you got your boyfriends with you to protect you, is it?

I can handle myself.

Autodictat dick wise just about. You can't handle anything. Why don't you just fuck off and join those scabs over there? They are your type. Suppurating wounds on the criminal body.

Jesus – autodicwhatever – suppurating – I'll have to look them up.

Look up fuck off as well.

Daddy, Daddy, such hostility! Hey that rhymes.

Barely. Only the 'y' rhymes – it is pure weak. Like you.

Change the track. Or the old 78 in your case.

Very droll.

Droll – ok, will have to check that one as well. You are an educator at large. That degree you did in Mountjoy worked out.

I would not call ten years inside worked out. Also that degree was simple. I could have done five of them simultaneously. That means at the same time.

Very D.R.O.L.L. (he spells it out from his mobile phone screen). Anyway you got off easy with ten years – you were at it for forty years and not one scratch.

It's S.T.R.E.T.C.H. not scratch.

Whatever. Anyway I have bad news for you.

You mean you don't have colon cancer?

Too-chet.

It's fucken *touché.*

Is it? Who knew?

Same answer as above.

Above what? I don't get it. Anyway you won't be getting a call about the latest shipment into Ross A Mhíl.

Why is that?

We are intercepting it as soon as it lands, which should be any minute. It's fucken windy out there so your boat must be behind schedule.

I factor in possible delays to cover mishaps, acts of God, weather, Gardaí, customs, mermaids, giant sea squid. You should try it.

Always a jokester!

Easy to be a jokester compared to you – you are quip less.

Well I think I will have the last laugh here. Your last big deal is about to go east.

It's south.

What?

The shit went south – like down the toilet. Or migrating birds fly south. Down Africa way.

Africa. I am kinda lost.

Don't you know anything? It's bad enough you being a snitch, but being stupid is somehow worse. You are as dim as a British toff.

Toff – toffee? I don't get it. Like Scots Clan is it?

Never fucken mind. Life is too short to be explaining the toff-toffee impasse. You here to gloat, is it?

Well, Daddy, you are over, let's face it. I am the next big thing. Soon everyone will know it. You will stand on the bridge over Lough Atalia like a broken reed of a man. People will say he used to be the one. Now no more. His son runs things.

You couldn't run diarrhoea out of your arse if you had dysentery.

Wow that smarts, Daddy.

Unlike yourself!

Tres bun.

It is *tres bon*.

Is it? Whatever. No one can stop me now. I have guys all over Galway ready to join my team.

Like those dolts, is it?

At least mine are here. Where are yours then? At the Novena? They abandon ship already? Since it is a leaky currach already I am not surprised.

They are on a job. No one abandons ship.

Is that so? Well it looks like I didn't need to bring my boys with me tonight so.

You could have brought six more of them and you wouldn't be safe.

You are all talk, Daddy.

You are the one with the talk tic. As soon as you got picked up by the Guards you couldn't stop shopping everyone. The Church of Stop Shopping is the only religion that counts in this family. You were spewing your guts out like a leveret – that's a fucken baby rabbit before you ask – as soon as they closed the cell door. It was just a pick up on something minor. Routine. The guards had some overtime. Let's hit the Laffeys, they decided. Yes let's go. It should be fun. We might get lucky. And they did. They found you. They had no evidence. They couldn't charge anyone with anything.

Well, I'm afraid there's been a change of plan …

I see your ADD is still in full effect.

What?

You can't listen to anything of consequence. I was just explaining your yellow belly antics.

Whatever – ok, your truck won't make it to Galway.

You're bleating on about a truck. Fuck a truck. Am I there in the truck? Or am I there on the high seas waiting to be hijacked? Am I on the quay side avoiding miserable squalls and fucking customs' patrols? Am I crying my eyes out like a scalded baby rat? I'm here in Galway where I started drinking in the sixties. When I wore gear that was all shiny and new. When I was all shiny and new. When the high summers of the sixties made me great. That's me. The King of Galway. I remember girls crying in the dark. And lithe bodies cooling after fist fights. And the cool fine feel of steel knuckle dusters finding their mark.

Jesus – it sounds like *Love Story*. I'll be crying soon.

You usually are.

The sixties is far away now, Daddy.

Not that far.

My name's Jack in case you don't remember.

I remember well. I try to forget it. I try to forget you. We named you after my uncle Jack. He won a Military Cross in the Great War. He had more bullet holes than Bonnie and Clyde. His torso was puckered for ever after. He walked around with limps in both legs so they cancelled each other out so he was able to walk straight. He even liked Germans because they made great belt-fed machine guns.

Give me a break, another family nut-job.

You're the total opposite – a snivelling cur who sold us out, who killed his mother with shame. She was one of the Rabbits. She had guts, she had beauty, she had brains. You lack all three. I met her when she was sixteen. She didn't carry a Luger for me and burnish steel in her tote bag so the likes of you could undo us all in one fell swoop. A speculative police swoop that was minor. That sent you into a major league spiral. That imbued you with verbal diarrhoea as soon as you saw the inside of a cop shop. MCs and Lugers and Sheffield Steel should have steeled your backbone. Instead you turned out to be a supine serpent.

Supine serpent – great alliter-something there, I must say. That Open University degree really expanded your vocabulary.

Fuck the Open University. I had more literary exposure than five professors. I am self taught. My grandfather knew Nora Barnacle's boyfriend who waited for her all night in the heavy rain falling from a black sky. She was another Galway girl worth waiting for. Died he did from consumption. And then Joyce was consumed by her and her accent and her love for Johnny Mulqueen and he forged that obsession into a beautiful blade that cut through the English language to make something immortal and dangerous.

Jesus – you have a thing about blades.

I have a thing about blood-tainted rats.

Daddy – you know what – when you got out of jail you should have called it quits.

The only downside about being out is knowing you're slithering around somewhere in the long grass. And having to look at your yellow rat whiskers sprouting from that face of yours. You ever hear of soap or plastic surgery or skin grafting? Or laying your neck down on the smooth steel of the railway line over Lough Atalia or lying akimbo so you end up in five or more pieces?

Akimbo. Jesus, another jaw breaker. I don't remember that you talked so much.

Well you won't have to worry about that for long.

What?

Can't you ever follow a conversation? Or does that only happen when you are crying your eyes out in a police station? Spilling your guts onto the floor like a baby projectile-vomiting tainted formula across a room?

You have a thing about vomiting as well.

The father looks over at the other table.

Those dummies of bodyguards are former boot boys gone to seed. I used to slash their faces with razors while they were still assessing the situation. You can spot the carvings on some of them if you look closely. You can see their foreheads glistening with sweat now even from here.

The son looks over. The minute hand of the clock over his head marks time in jerking motions as if it was afraid to move on. Blue-white cigarette smoke trails across the room reaching for the ceiling.

Did they know who you were meeting tonight? I doubt it. Do they think they are the Krays with those suits and black ties and surly looks and attitude? They have a better chance of being mistaken for super-computers and that chance is fucken zero.

They look fine.

They look slothful. They have camel faces. They look like thick fuckers. They smell like the underbelly of slow moving river tugs. They are not thugs. I'm a thug. A literary thug. A wise-cracking thug. A Mensa-minded thug. I have no clue where you came from. You are a throwback, a spew-back, a rotten yellow-back.

You are all talk. Let's get back to the truck. I don't …

Is this another one of your grand schemes? Hijacking other people's jobs? No change there then. Can't you figure out any capers on your own?

Why would I, Daddy? When you set them up and I walk in? You never learn – you were asking for it. This shipment must be worth a fortune. I like doing it this way. Especially when it's you. The guards told me about this one. So I am doing you a favour really. Otherwise they would have nicked you.

I doubt it. You still a tout then? Still in witless protection?

Don't be like that, Daddy. It's on the QT – just me and my handler. He has expensive tastes as well.

Yes I suppose porcine brain transplants are expensive.

Porcine – shit, another dictionary lookup for me. This smart phone is working overtime.

He looks over at his bodyguards.

I hope one of you is taking notes.

He turns around to face his father again.

I am doing you a favour – there are too many thugs out there that will run you into the ground. A lot's changed since you went inside.

Father appreciation day, is it?

Sure. You don't seem too bothered about your early retirement, starting today.

What about your early demise, starting soon?

What? What can you do? You are outnumbered 4 to 1.

Well at least you can count.

You don't seem too bothered by the loss of that truck and the merchandise.

I'm never bothered by anything.

Well you're bothered by me. Well now's your chance, Daddy-o. Big Bad Daddy. Give me your best shot. You barely talked before you went to prison. And now you can't stop.

It was in The Talk of the Town I met your mother. I was a doorman. Me and Chick Gillen. Chick could knock you into the middle of next week. We worked every Sunday. The rest of the week I robbed houses, cars, shops, factories, laundries, petrol stations. We punched culchies from Tuam and Headford out of their dancing shoes when they started arguing with us. We were skinny but lethal and lithe. That means ... never mind. No one could stop me. Everything slowed down when a fight started. It was like a blue light went through me then into the ground. I could hear everything – I could see everything. I could see myself from above. I could see the culchies going for razors in slow motion. I could hit them before they even knew about it. I was as sure-footed as a mountain goat on a precipice. I felt I had infinite time to hit them – to move in – to move back – to take the next guy. I can still hear the song that the showbands were playing during fights. I can see every guy I hit. I can see the spirit behind their eyes waver in fear. Their irises contract. I can feel their skin on my knuckles. I can smell the fear. And smell the spilt lemonade and the sweet sweat of women and their shrieks as they ran to get away and the crowd on the balcony standing up to see what was happening and the band playing louder to distract the crowd.

Jesus – *Come Dancing* is it? So what? It's ancient history.

I still have that.

Scary! Great. Spirit possession. Good for you. So no call I see from your boys in Ross A Mhíl, Daddy. I guess you lose.

That phone looks dented and scratched. Did you bleed on it when you were shaving? You might have Parkinson's. Next stop, the old criminals' retirement home for you, Daddy. You should join the 21st century and upgrade to a smart phone. Look at this phone, all shiny and new.

I used that already.

What?

All shiny and new. I suppose you have to steal everything?

Sure it is flattery if you look at it that way. Fair use, I think they call it. Whatever, Daddy. Last chance to cry before I call my boys.

Call away.

The son looks over to the bodyguards.

Keep an eye on him. Stay alert.

They nod and sit up straight. They crush out their cigarettes.

Ok smile, Daddy!

The son raises the phone and takes a photo.

For the archives, Daddy.

He examines the result.

It's a good one.

He shows it to his father who doesn't look at it. He shows it to the bodyguards. They lean in to look. And then they sit back.

The son raises his phone in an ostentatious manner.

Ok get ready, Daddy. Standby to be gravely disappointed. 5. 4. 3. 2. 1.

The son hits quick dial. The hesitant jerking motion of the clock's hands on the wall is audible.

The battered mobile on the table in front of his father rings sharply. The ringtone of *Galway Girl* by Steve Earle fills the silence. The son looks uncomprehendingly at the phone and back at his own. Then he jumps up.

That's a fucken classic, you know, sonny boy? The song as well.

The father pulls a Luger that is taped under the table and levels it one-handed at the three bodyguards.

Don't move fuck-heads. This is a Luger. Finest German engineering.

They stop in mid-movement of standing up and going for guns, but sit down reluctantly.

He points to his son.

How stupid are ye morons. This guy is the finest congenital fuckup on the planet. He would not be able to lead the Sioux at Custer's Last Stand. He could not drop a bomb on Hiroshima. He could not catch syphilis from your mothers. He could not clean his arse if he had two hands.

The father grabs his son's left hand and cuts it off with the Sheffield Steel knife he pulls from a neck scabbard. The light shines off the blade as it moves in its sure pure arc.

The bodyguards look at it in motion. The son doesn't see it coming. The son screams – he tries to struggle. Blood spurts onto the table. The father holds the hand up. He does a ventriloquist's voice.

I kwan kwen my arse, Addy, so I can. I owly weed one 'and, Addy. The woke is on you, Addy, ha ha ha!

Not really.

The father grabs the other arm and cuts off the right hand. He holds both up. He mimics a Mexican wave.

Come on Galway United. You can do it again. Be bottom of the league as usual.

The father drops both hands in the ice bucket. He arranges them so they point upwards as if in prayer.

The son has passed out from pain and shock.

After a few minutes the father slaps the son across the face with one of the severed hands and then throws it back in the ice bucket.

The father sings quietly.

Wake up mister sleepy head – wake up – come on now – wake up.

Name that song.

The son regains consciousness. Moans. He looks at the stubs.

I am ruined. Please.

The father sings: *Please release me let me go – for I can't love you anymore.*

Name that song. No quips left I see Sonny?

What exactly is a quip?

Well that fucken sums it all up there! You don't even know what a fucken quip is. As you can see your hands are in the ice bucket, so all is not lost yet. Maybe we can sow them back on? Did you not wonder why there was an ice bucket on the table when I am drinking Pernod? You need to be more alert. I am just saying. The Regional is great at reattaching limbs. There seems to have been a rash of that lately for some reason! It was written up in the *Irish Medical Journal*. You should read more than the Evening Herpes I mean *Herald*.

I am your son.

That's the only reason you are still alive. I wish you were fucking adopted. I wish I could explain you away. I wish you were anyone else. I wish you were one of the Kray's there. They are stupid but loyal. They are stupid but brave. They are stupid but have reasons to be. How they follow you is a mystery? It's the eighth wonder of the world.

We bought you *The World of Wonder* every week. No good.

We bought you the *Encyclopaedia of Executions*. No good.

We bought you a silver flick knife. No good.

We bought you kung fu lessons from the skinny lithe chefs in the Golden Rickshaw in Dominick Street. No good.

We got boxing lessons for you from Chick. No good.

We sent you to the Bish so you could learn Latin and how to fight. No good.

We sent you to Paris to stay with your uncle Tommy 'The Gun' McGowan so you could learn French. T*rès fucken malade.*

We deprived you of nothing. And you are nothing. How can I fix you being a tout? The hands are symbolic. You can't call the fucken guards now, can you?

The son begins to cry.

I am sorry.

Blubber me not. Are you not forgetting something?

I don't know.

What about your Ma? You killed her stone dead.

I am sorry about Ma.

Can you see the error of your ways?

I can.

Remember 'symbolic', ok?

The father slashes the knife across both eyes of his son. The light flashes off the blade. Again! Blood and vitreous liquids flow out behind the son's arm stubs which he has raised to his eyes. He screams. His bodyguards watch. The father wipes the blade on the son's suit.

The father then lifts the phone and takes a photo of his son.

Smile Sonny.

He looks at it, holds it up to show the bodyguards.

It's a good one.

THE BLUE FLAMINGO

Cristina Galvin

She doesn't know why the blue flamingo has chosen her garden to nest in. But it has. Already six weeks it has been there. Came in August and now it is October. There it is perched on the tip-top branch of the beech tree down by the old wood-shed with the mossy roof that sags in the middle. The past half hour while she brushed her teeth, washed and blow-dried her hair, pinned her curls in a tidy bun and applied her make-up, it has spent preening itself. Now it has taken to sharpening its beak against the branch, which swings over and back in the wind.

There's something consoling about the fact that it has built its home in hers. She's taken to gazing at the blue flamingo in the mornings before work. She's been drawn especially by the dignified way it holds itself, standing there on one leg with its knobbly knee, its feathers full, effulgent, periwinkle blue. Still it stands there, despite the wind that chortles chill through darkening mornings and the rain that comes slant-ways at the house. Still it stands in frozen arabesque although it never appears to shiver. It roosts there on the topmost branch, perfectly balanced on one leg, absolutely still, as if it may as well have found itself on the shores of an African waterhole where heatwaves shimmer the surface of the water. And when she watches it, she too becomes still and if there were someone watching her watching the blue flamingo they in turn would feel a certain awe. The watcher watching her would notice that in the act of watching the blue flamingo she has completely changed. Her eyes have lit up lantern-like, as if from within, her posture alert, chin lifted, shoulders dropped so her chest lightens, her heart opens, expectant. And the watcher of the watcher of the blue flamingo would also become still, all tension dissolving. The watcher of the watching woman would perhaps conclude that she looked happy as she stood there at the patio doors looking out at the strange bird in the tree, oblivious to her pensive reflection in the glass.

And then the beep-beep-beep alerting listeners to early morning news-time on the radio in the background reminds her of the fact that routine has to be attended to, and with a deep sigh she turns, no backward glance, picks up the pouch that contains her iPad and slips it in her briefcase. Her coat she whips up from the back of the chair, and stretching one arm into a sleeve, she hurriedly pulls it on before grabbing her bag. The pink wool hat with the marshmallow bobble she unhooks from the coat rack over the umbrella stand in the hall, and once she tucks the stray curls in under the edge of her hat with her free hand, adjusts it, tugs it down over her ears, she's out the door. It's hard to walk quickly in a tight skirt, but she manages. The cold propels her. No time for ambling on a chill morning like this.

If you just met her on the street you wouldn't notice anything untoward. You would just walk right by the thirty-something woman hastening down the street in the pink hat with the marshmallow bobble, a woman with shapely legs in nude, sheer gloss tights. This is a woman heading for somewhere else, somewhere important, a woman with a point to her life. But if you were watching her watching the bird a moment before you would notice the energy of quiet reverence has stayed with her. There is a spring in her step, ever so slight, but it's there. Definitely it's there. And while she appears to be in a rush, there seems to be a distance between her and that rush, that need to get some place other than where she is. There is something about her eyes – steadiness, something about the lightness of step, and the fact that her economy of pace does not translate to a furrowed brow.

If you follow her you will find yourself on a tour of the seedier parts of town. So you do. You follow her past the boarded up pubs, the once-upon-a-time grocery store with produce still moulding on rusting shelves – hairy orange, wizened turnip, tomatoes gone a-mush with maggots. Rats scuttle across half-eaten lino to holes in the skirting board below a cash register that will likely never ping again. And you wonder perhaps whether this is the neighbourhood where she grew up, although you find yourself almost immediately discounting the notion. For this is a woman with the poise and self-assurance of one who came from an elsewhere where mission and meaning in life were a given along with fluffed feather pillows and sit-down family dinners of roast duck with ginger-infused oriental gravy.

What is she doing here? She has the aura of one who knows this place and her own place in it. But how is it that the drabness doesn't get to her? You follow her on past the deserted school with high security razor coil fencing – whether originally erected to fence trespassers in or out has never been entirely clear. There is only one shop left open on this street. Mr Patel's newsagents, which sells everything from Fruitfield's apricot jam to porn magazines, hard or soft, take your pick, and papayas of just the right squishiness. She smiles, greets him, *Hello, Mr Patel*, but she never stops. And he calls back, *Good morning, Miss*. And that is the only time you hear her voice.

She is quite adept at dodging the overladen wheelie-bins, spilling half-eaten ketchup-encrusted chips, soiled nappies and smashed glass on the pavement. The smell of fetid matter assaults you and you clasp your belly and heave, emptying the contents of your stomach onto a pile of empty beer bottles and Diet Coke cans outside a beat-up chippy. Wiping your mouth on the back of your sleeve you wonder how she can keep on walking. Maybe she is one of those lucky people who can't smell? The taste and smell of sick lingers, makes you grimace. It's on your clothes. It's in your mouth, inside your nostrils. You want to scream. You can't get it off.

Pigeons squabble among the scraps, pecker at the mess, oblivious to the clip-clop of passing heels. Only when the mangy dog with the septic ear yaps and springs at them out of a graffitied doorway do they take flight, littering the air with yips and hisses. Moments later, they're descending again to nibble at lumps of raw chicken the pallor of wet cement, and the dog, having quickly realised the injustice of being trapped in a body without wings, limps off down an alleyway in search of fairer fights for breakfast.

She could avoid the path through the park, but she never does, though it is full of waist-high nettles and great poofs of brambles choked by bindweed which threaten to smother the trail and sting or stab anyone who ventures through. A broken swing dangles from a chain that yelps in pain with each sudden blast of wind. She pulls her hat down, scrunches the ungloved fingers of her free hand in a fist which she stuffs in her pocket. Her other hand has turned pasty white with cold. The young saplings that border the path and which had been planted in the spring in a rare burst of community collaboration were months ago snapped in two. The pointy spears remaining cut cruel silhouettes against a grey day still struggling to dawn. A skreek as the steel security screen sealing the light from a mechanic's work-shed opposite the rusty park gate jiggers and lifts. The woman's gait and pace remain smooth, do not betray whether her heart has skipped a beat. This is her place and she is utterly at home in it. Or so it appears as you follow her.

You slow your pace when she stops at the entrance to a building, which, with its black, bullet-proof doors and grating covering porthole windows, has all the welcoming features of a soviet barracks. She jabs at the numbers below the intercom and a low drone buzzer sounds. She pushes the door in and is gone.

You look up and imagine an airplane trailing a banner headline across the sky: *Woman with Soul Swallowed by Concrete*. You stand across the road at the corner by the old warehouse with the buckling walls that months ago was earmarked for demolition and you wait. For what else is there to do? If life is a series of waiting rooms we pass through on the way to somewhere else, you might as well get curious while you're standing here: make waiting interesting. Right now, though, you're not just curious, you're intrigued. Who is she, this woman? Why does she work here? How can she work here? You want to know. But the air is cold and you have to keep moving. You tramp around the back. There's a hilly patch of waste ground with a dumpsite behind. You clamber up, look down on the walled scrap of grass that has been cleared for an allotment. There are lettuces growing and some scraggy yellow dahlias on which slugs are feasting. At least the effort's being made, you think, though you have a sudden urge to buy a canister of slug pellets.

And then you see the queue of men gathering out front by another door of the same bullet-proof black steel as the one the woman went in. Men with grizzled chins, stony expressions and holes in their shoes, who have tramped from the direction of the estate which, the tabloids say, has the country's highest murder rate. The man at the top of the line presses the buzzer and a disembodied voice with a cold, keep-away tone replies: *Number?* The man addresses the intercom, says something you can't hear. He shoves the door in and disappears. The other men stare at the black door and wait.

At the other end of the building a group of women are gathering. Black, white, Asian. Aged fifteen to sixty-odd. Women with tear-stained faces are holding their children in their arms, others are pushing buggies. Buggies with babies – a few of whom are gabbling and waving their hands and legs about, while others kick vigorously and crease the air with cries. A banshee keening rises, competing with the babies' screams. If you hadn't already seen the women you would imagine that this was the terrible noise of women having their bellies slashed. The cries dissipate to snuffling, finally. All that's left is the sound of telephone wires twanging in the wind.

Your eyes are drawn to a slender girl in green hot-pants and leopard-skin top holding the bar of her buggie with both hands and doing plies. She's rising on tiptoes now, then squatting down, before shooting into the air like a bullet, striking a blow at an invisible punch-bag with her fist and performing a scissors kick.

'Have you no shame? Cut it out, Shania!' the woman behind her spits, her hands clasped across a bulging belly held in by a dodgy cardigan zip. 'You're giving up your baby and all you can think of doing is gymnastics? Show some respect – if not for your own child, then for ours'.

'Quit your whinging, Bridget', says the hot-pants girl. 'I spend all my life in queues. I have to do my boxercise or my joints will seize up'.

'What's that?' says a woman wiping her eyes, blinking and pointing at the strange-looking bird which has alighted with slow-motion grace on the roof of the barracks.

'Probably a stork', says the woman called Bridget. 'Though I never saw a blue stork before'.

Titters reverberate through the queue. The girl named Shania has momentarily quit her work-out to gaze at the bird whose plumage is bluer than her own eyes. 'Storks are meant to deliver babies, not take them away', she says.

One at a time the women press the buzzer. One at a time they enter, fifteen minutes between them. It takes all day before the last woman in the queue vanishes into the grey hulk of the building. The scene triggers a memory of a piece you saw on the news a few weeks ago regarding the surfeit of children in the country.

It's 5pm and raining. A door opens. Men trail out, stuffing money in their pockets. Unspeaking, they file down the rain-thrashed street. After the last man has rounded the corner by the warehouse, another door clicks ajar. There's a pause then before the air outside allows space for small voices. The women leave. Buggy-less and weary-looking, they make their way back towards the estate.

You follow the men for a bit, past the *For Sale* signs, the derelict premises, the chippy with no-one in it that reeks of burnt oil and killer vinegar. The men don't walk, they slump. Heads cowering in hunched shoulders, they trudge past like they're heading for a funeral. You break into a run, cut through an alleyway where the stray dog lies wet and lifeless in a bloody puddle, a feast of black flies crowding around its ear. You sprint back towards the estate. The women plod despite the cloudburst. It's hard to know whether it's tears they wipe from their eyes or rain. Some smile, link arms, give each other friendly digs, like they've offloaded something. The deluge dwindles to a drizzle. The sky's still grey, the air nippier than this morning.

You're rounding the perimeter of the barracks. The woman you followed here reappears. She looks harried now. Glancing left and right, she hurries towards the rusty park gate. The pinned-up curls she'd tucked under her hat have come undone. Her lipstick's smudged. There's a rip in her tights. She's got something hidden under her coat. A little gurgling thing – a baby. She hugs it close. You follow her as she traces the same route back through the nettled park, past the derelict school with the scrolls of razor wire, past the wheelie-bins, one of which is dripping green gunk that flows an unctuous rivulet across the pavement into a gutter. She pauses then. You hear her laboured breathing. She dives down an alleyway, waits by the wall, her thumb vaguely stroking the baby's cheek. It's as if she senses she is being followed. Minutes pass. A man in a black business suit, dark glasses and grey wool fedora hat with the brim snapped down, back snapped up, is hastening along the street from the direction of the barracks where the door has just clicked shut. He has the pallor of one who has just vacated a morgue and the sharpened step of one who intends to put others in it.

The woman hears, quits breathing. A hush descends. And then the rising sound of wings. Standing rigid in the shadows of the alleyway the woman's eyes light on a rectangle of cinereal sky far above, where she spies a fugitive flicker of blue. The baby burbles. She clamps a hand over its mouth.

When next she peers around the corner the street is empty. All clear. But the darting fear in her eyes indicates she's not convinced. She hurries back towards the wheelie-bin, stops, glances around again and lifts the lid on the one that's leaking green goo across the footpath. Setting the baby in a damp, half-mashed cardboard box, she lets down the cover. Already overstuffed, it doesn't close. Squeals, some muffled whimpering. 'Shhh', she whispers. 'I'm sorry. This was not meant to happen'.

Edging backwards, she wipes her hands on her coat, face puckering as if she's just been forced to eat the stuff that's made her fingers sticky. Stepping over the slimy stream she makes off down the street.

Time stalls. You wait. And wait. The man in the fedora hat never reappears. You wonder about him, about the fate of the other babies in the barracks. Dusk has still not given in to dark when you finally approach the bin. You lift the lid, take the baby in your arms, hold it close. It gulps, lets out a long wail that knifes your eardrums, scatters pigeons. You pat its head. The little body heaves and screams.

Your whole life you've been a watcher. Getting involved was never meant to be your intention. But now you're making little cooing noises. And after a time you hear yourself hum. The space between the baby's wails lengthens, howls becoming less heartfelt as you track your way through no-name parts of town. A snaggy breeze nips your cheeks and fingertips. You pause, unzip your old down jacket, pulling one half around the baby to keep it snug. It's sleeping now, nestled in the downy warmth. On a splintered telephone pole in the corner of a patch of wasteland, feathers shimmering against the sky's indomitable grey, the blue flamingo sits.

Im Niemandsland

Kernan Andrews

With great reluctance, the first strains of dawn begin to break. A thin band of mellow, sickly orange light stretches across the horizon. It casts a weak glow over fields decimated and engorged into an undulating swamp of mud and craters, scarred throughout by the trenches in which we have spent much of the last two and half years of our lives.

The light is not strong enough to penetrate the burrow in the trench we call our sleeping quarters. Despite this, I awake before my comrades, before any bugler or officer rouses us from slumbers that can be fitful and nervous, troubled by recurring visions of what we have endured, or from that state most desired by the soldier – the deep, dreamless sleep of sheer exhaustion.

I awake from force of habit, from a sense of duty. As silently as possible I get up, there is not enough room to stand at my full height – six feet, three inches – I am constantly stooped. I wonder if I will develop a hunched back by the time the war ends.

From the inside pocket of my coat I take a match, feeling for the head to make sure it is the right way up, before striking it along the side of the little box in which it was kept. A tiny, warm light flickers into being. It is enough by which to see the candle placed on a small, rickety table in the corner of our bunker.

I light the wick. The candle crackles into life, emitting a halo around itself, enough for me to perform the Shaharit. 'It should be after the sun rises and when there is enough light to see a man six feet from you', my Grandfather always advised. He would not approve of my timing, would question whether the sun could truly said to be risen. I can barely see my hands unless I hold them close to my face, but I have my reasons and I apologise to none for them.

I take my Tefillin, wrapping one carefully around my arm, the other around my head, and begin reciting my morning prayers, keeping the Lord's words as a sign on my hand and a memorial between my eyes. I recite the prayers silently, rocking backwards and forwards.

These moments before the others rise is my time, when even in the forsaken, ravaged fields of Northern France, I find a space where God somehow manages to be.

It is easier at this time. I do not want to endure any comments from those who resent my presence in our battalion. They are by no means the majority, yet I remain wary of them. It takes so little to set them off.

The bugle sounds and shouts go up for the men to rise. The sentries return from their nightshifts. Gerhard, his eyes heavy, his face pale, enters our dugout and finds me already dressed even as the others try to remember where they left their boots. He looks me up and down. I say

'Guten Morgen'. He makes no reply, simply drops onto his makeshift bed, and is asleep within seconds.

I take my helmet and place it on my head, tying the leather straps around my jaws. It may be a small comfort but the Stahlhelm makes you feel safer, that your head has some protection, some chance, even if the rest of your body remains as vulnerable as it was at the start of the war.

I remember the ridiculous Pickelhaube we once wore – a cap of boiled leather that barely covered the top of your head. The Stahlhelm's peaked rim and sloping flared skirt cover the entire sides and back of your head in a case of steel. I almost feel sorry for the Tommie with their tin hats, which leaves so much of their heads exposed to bullets and shrapnel. At home in Leipzig my mother has a photograph of me in full uniform, not long after we were issued with the new helmets. It hangs in pride of place in our living room. I cannot help but fear that one day it may become a memento and no longer a portrait of a son.

I cannot linger on such thoughts as we are being called out on parade duty. Our battalion stands in a row, while our commander, a large, broad man, with a thick grey moustache that curls at the ends, inspects us, the vaguest hint of contempt, or is it weariness, in his eyes.

The morning light has increased to a dull grey. It bears a look which decrees there will be no variation in its makeup until the darkness begins to encroach in the evening.

Our orders are given. Lothar and I will be on watch at one of the farthest sections of our trench. We take our Gewhar 98 rifles, binoculars, P08 pistols, and a couple of mortars. Lothar is from Bavaria. He is small and squat and prefers to stay silent, answering only in monosyllabic utterances when he has to. In our two and a half years on the front we still know next to nothing about him. 'Die ruhige ein', 'the quiet one', we call him. We make our way to the appointed sector.

No matter how long I have been and will remain in these trenches I will never get used to the stench. Putrid, fetid water clogs the sides of the trench walls, the smell of vomit, urine and waste never fades. We do what we can to keep such filth at bay but it is a Sisyphean struggle.

Sentry duty is long and often dull, but with a taciturn companion, the hours drag on even more. Not a word has passed between Lothar and I. Maybe this is no harm. Our concentration needs to be high as we have heard rumblings that the British are preparing a major offensive and even more than usual we must keep our eyes open for enemy activity.

The winds of the last few days have died down but the chill they brought remains. I pull up the collar of my Feldgrau coat around me. I look across no man's land, across the entanglement of barbed wire, the scarred, pockmarked fields, the charred hunks of a couple of trees which stubbornly remain. So far we have seen no activity worth reporting.

I do not take Lothar's silence personally, yet my surprise is immense when I hear him utter the first complete sentence during our time at the front.

'What are we doing here?'

I turn around to look at him. Part of me wonders if I imagined him speak.

'We're here because we have been ordered to sentry duty at this point'.

Lothar emits a 'Hurumph' thinly disguised as an exhale of breath.

'You know well what I mean! What are we doing fighting in France? Why are we in this war?'

Keeping my eyes on the British lines in the distance I reply: 'You might remember that Britain has declared war on us and before that the Archduke of Austria was assassinated by Serbian separatists ...'

For a moment I am unsettled by how easily I have slipped into trotting out the official line like a good and obedient lapdog.

'Then why don't the Austrians and Serbians fight it out among themselves and leave the rest of us out of it?'

'Austria is our ally', I reply. 'We have a duty to stand by our allies'.

'Duty! Duty!' spits Lothar. 'I'm sick of hearing about duty!'

'Be careful what you say', I tell him, 'if any of our superiors hear you, you know what they'll do'.

A wry smile spreads across Lothar's wide mouth revealing his protruding teeth. 'Huh! I'm sure they've often thought the same themselves'.

'I'm sure they haven't', I say. 'Besides, we need the Austrians. They're keeping the Italians at bay, stopping them crossing into Austria and our southern borders'.

I place special emphasis on 'southern borders'. If the Italians do break through, Lothar's native Baviara will be the first part of the Reich to see them.

'The Italians?' he says, a mild contempt in his voice. 'Last time they were any good as a fighting force was the days of the Roman Empire and even then they never got past the Rhine or Danube!'

We smile and permit ourselves a shared laugh.

As the evening draws in, the subdued grey of the day dims before the oncoming darkness. We rejoin the others for food. Each man receives a helping from a large pot of vegetable stew, a small bowl of beans and a hunk of bread as hard as stone. It hardly becomes softer when dunked in the stew which is tasteless. Yet to feel the stew's warmth coursing down through my chest as I take the first mouthful, turns it into something like luxury. Tinned sausage is also on offer but I refuse. The sight of pork almost makes me sick.

Lothar and I sit together and he devours the sausage first, relishing every morsel. As he wipes his mouth with his sleeve, two soldiers pass by. One of them laughing, glances in my direction: 'I suppose it's as well there are Jews in the army, at least they'll leave the pork for the rest of us'.

His companion, with a leering smile, makes porcine grunting sounds. 'Judenschwein', he said, not too loud, but enough to make sure I heard him.

I ignore them and continue to eat, but I still hear their laughter. Suddenly it is cut short. Lothar has cast a filthy look at the two men, a look even I find unsettling. They hurry away, out of sight. The Bavarian scoops a pile of beans with his spoon. As he eats them a smile crosses his mouth and a dribble of sauce trickles down his chin. I notice for the first time how large and expressive are his eyes, set in that square head with its close-cropped bristle of hair. I do not know his religion, but I feel closer to him today.

For the first time in two weeks, post has arrived. Letters from home are precious, a lifeline to the world outside the trenches. They also make us nostalgic for life before August 1914. How jubilant we were parading through the streets to cheering crowds, all of us believing 'It will be over by Christmas'.

Some of my comrades are reading and re-reading letters from wives and sweethearts back in Germany. I both envy and do not envy them. I would like to think there is potentially a woman for me back in Leipzig. Yet should I die in combat, this hypothetical girl would be but one more to add to the list of those who would mourn my passing. Her father, her brothers, may also be at the front, she does not need another soul to add to her worries.

When we win this war and I return to the Fatherland I hope it is then I shall meet her, and in time we may become man and wife.

Out here it is not good to let your mind stray too far into the future when at any moment you can die from an enemy's bullet or from an accident, unplanned and unforeseen, during training and manoeuvres. Yet sometimes I need to let my mind paint pictures of how I hope it will be. I see myself on a spring day in Leipzig, perhaps on the way to the Synagogue, the first leaves have appeared on the trees and the early flowers are in bloom. I stroll along, dressed in my army uniform with her, whoever she is yet to be, beside me. Passersby will point and say, 'There is Abraham Rubenstein's son who served his country with distinction in the war'.

Whatever my occasional doubts or misgivings, I have never lost faith that to stand and fight for Germany was the right thing to do and that thousands of German Jews like myself have shown – proved – that we were not found wanting during a time of crisis, despite what some have, and continue, to say about us.

There is one letter for me. From the elegant curve of the handwriting on the envelope I know it is from my brother Emil on the Eastern Front.

He tells me he is well and the army is making good progress against the Russians. Morale is high and there are prospects for further advances. Trouble is also brewing in Russia and their leadership is divided and suffering a lack of confidence.

I smile as I read this. Emil is a military censor's dream come true. There is no need to edit this letter, it is just the kind of information the high military command want those of us on the Western Front to hear and take inspiration from.

I am being unfair on Emil to some extent. His information tallies with what we have been hearing informally through various channels. If victory can be achieved speedily in the east, it would free many of our soldiers to come to our aid and help deliver a knockout blow to the French and the British. Yet none of this is as remarkable or as astounding as what Emil has discovered in Russia:

My dearest brother,

I am writing to you from the westernmost regions of Russia, and there I have come across a world I scarcely thought possible to exist. In the regions we have passed through, there are numerous villages, and even some towns, where the inhabitants are almost entirely Jewish – not parts of towns like back home, but entire villages. I see synagogues, menorahs in the windows, mezuzahs on doorposts. I hear snatches of Hebrew amidst the Russian and Yiddish. And yet it feels as foreign as any other part of Russia I have seen. It is strange to be confronted by something at once so familiar to both heart and mind and yet so alien.

The Jews here live mostly rural lives characterised by poverty, hardship, and the mercy of nature. Educational standards are poor, and nearly all live and die with no hope of straying any farther than the area into which they were born. Yet how could it be otherwise? In one town where we were stationed for a time, the chief Rabbi spoke to both me and our regiment's Fieldrabbiner, telling us of the restrictions placed on Jews in Russia, the daily discrimination, and the constant threat of pogroms which come with official sanction from the regional or national authorities.

This is why, brother, they are so glad to see the German Army. Time and again people take to the streets as we march through their towns and villages. They cheer us, they wish us well against the Tsarists, girls come out holding bunches of flowers in their hands and they give them to us. They see us as liberators, a force repulsing the hated Tsarists, and when they find some among us are fellow Jews their joy is overwhelming, and they shower us with blessings.

It makes me immensely proud to be both Jewish and a German soldier, playing a role, however small, in alleviating the suffering of Russian Jews, one Ashkenazic aiding another.

My dearest Hans, tomorrow we are on the march again and I ask you, if you can find the time, to offer a Tefillat HaDerekh for me, so that our progress may go well, and that I may be safe on my journeys.

Your brother and friend always.

Emil.

I let the words sink into my mind and imagine and re-imagine the scenes of Russian Jews greeting Emil and his comrades. I feel proud of him and wonder what our Grandfather would think of this. I wonder if he has sent him a similar letter. Grandfather has not been critical of Emil for taking part in the war as Emil is a conscript, but he has never understood my reasons, as I volunteered to join the Deutsches Heer even before the outbreak of war.

On one occasion, during a brief leave from the front, he asked me how I reconciled my faith and belief in the Sixth Commandment with what I had to do on the fields of battle. In reply I asked him, if by his logic, David was wrong to fire his slingshot at Goliath or Samson wrong to pull down the pillars, when both found themselves and their country in danger from aggressive enemies.

'But the German Army are the aggressors in this war', he said, jabbing a finger in my direction. 'It was they – and this includes you – who invaded neutral Belgium, and need I remind you of what happened in Leuven, the war barely a month old? And it was Germany that declared war on France, so who is the aggressive enemy, tell me?'

Checkmate, or stalemate, yet the issues run deeper than politics. My Grandfather is Jewish first and only then, by a distant margin, a German. He does not doubt my commitment to my faith but disapproves of my feeling that I am German first and foremost.

II

A scratching, shuffling sound, and the feel of something against my face, rouses me from a sleep already disturbed. My eyes twitch open, and by the faint light of a lamp held in the hand of passing sentry outside our sleeping quarters, I see the outline of a rat. I do not move. The rat's eyes stare directly into mine, before the bristles of its wet tail hit me in the face as it scurries towards the diminishing light from the door, and out of sight. I spit, gather more saliva in my mouth and spit again, anything to lessen the feeling of the disgusting creature's former presence.

How long had it been there? Had it crawled over my blankets and across my face? Was it that what made my sleep so fitful? The rats are something we are used to but it is still repulsive to see and feel them. None of us thought when this war started we would be sharing our beds with rodents. The only animals we want to see are the cavalry horses and the Schäferhunds we use for communication. Yet the horses and dogs are more than just practical additions to the army, they can be friends and companions, a reminder of home comforts. Every other kind of animal is either a threat or the sort no one ever wants to see dead, especially not as a casualty of war.

Death is something we live with each day. We accept it, yet are not immune to the pain it causes, the anxiety it brings. But in these trenches it does no good to be paralysed with fear. Emotions must wait until there is a safe time for them to have an outlet. It is the only way to endure being confronted by the returning dead of our former comrades. I do not mean the bodies brought back from the battlefield in the immediate aftermath of a confrontation, but from after the time we buried them in hastily-constructed plots.

When new trenches are created, or, as happens from time to time, trench walls collapse, some improvised resting places are disturbed and the rotting remains of the dead emerge through the mud walls. It terrifies and disturbs the new conscripts to see these deceased faces leering at them. The corpses seem to wear deranged smiles on what is left of their faces. I wonder if they are laughing at us because we are still here, enduring what they no longer have to, or if their laughter says, this too is what awaits you.

Rumours circulate that the British offensive will come within days. Originally it was thought to have been some weeks away but our spies inform us the Tommies are further ahead in their preparations than we realised.

The men are animated with talk and speculation about what will happen.

'I'm sure part of their preparations will involve them writing poetry about it all', laughs Otto, a tall, burly man, with a bristling beard.

'We'll give them plenty to write about', joins in Becker, a Saxon.

The British may have the poets but we have the painters, or had – August Mack and Franz Marc, two of the leading lights of modern German art. I came across an obituary Marc wrote for Mack who was killed almost as soon as the war began: 'His death means that a head has been cut off a nation's culture ... German art will become paler by several shades'.

I found the Expressionists the most exciting thing to happen in German art for years. I admired their boldness, their daring, how they take reality and the world around them and use it, not to copy nature but to give voice to their inner realities; the colours and forms of the everyday world become twisted and exaggerated to make real spiritual truths; they deemed emotions higher than reality and made their art an outlet for, and rebellion against, a nation where conformity, duty and order were prized as the highest virtues.

I would often take the train from Leipzig to Berlin to view Expressionist exhibitions. Sometimes it seemed I was the first into those galleries and the last to leave, so captivated was I by these artists' works.

However the admiration they arouse in me would equally arouse the ire of others. In our battalion is Heinz with whom I was in university in Leipzig.

'This is not art! This is the product of a diseased and idle youth', he declared on one occasion. I argued that this was a new flowering of German culture, a new mode of painting in which we were leading the world.

'It's not German! There's nothing German about these pictures except their titles', he complained. 'They're contaminated by French indolence and subversive ideas from Russia, and don't deny there aren't Russians involved in that Der Blaue Reiter group!'

'But Heinz!' I said, 'Ideas travel. It's the nature of things, but these works are how the *German* imagination interprets and refashions them into something no Frenchman could ever have come up with. This is how they become uniquely German'.

'But look Hans', he said, pointing to Erick Heckel and Karl Schmidt-Rottluff streetscapes, hanging side by side.

'Buildings don't lean like that. They don't lean at such obtuse angles without falling over, and look at how crudely they are rendered!'

'The camera has made redundant accurate descriptions of nature', I replied. 'Artists have to look for new ways to record and interpret reality'.

'Photographs can't capture colour, they can't capture what a sunset looks like'.

'But the academic style you favour cannot tell you how the sunset made the artist feel, how a sunset makes you feel', I said.

Such debates dominated our conversations. At the front, such divergences must be put to the back of our minds. In the face of the reality we are enduring they seem trifling, although I cannot help feeling something else underlies our differences of opinion, as if in their own way, they point to divisions over the future direction of Germany once this war is over.

Our worst fears have been confirmed.

The commanding officer addresses us and gives confirmation that the British attack will come at 6am on Tuesday, starting with a massive artillery bombardment.

The next few hours and days are spent in preparation for the attack. Rolls of barbed wire are laid across our first and second lines of trench, mines are placed, new trenches are constructed and reinforced with sandbags. Manoeuvres, strategies and counter-attacks are discussed and readied, and drills carried out so each and every man knows what he is to do when and where. We polish, clean and check our weapons. We cannot afford a gun to jam or malfunction.

Lothar and I are one of the teams assigned to machine gun duty. We practice assembling, disassembling, reassembling, moving and readying to fire our Maschinengewehr 08 while Otto times us. We are able to do it in twelve to fifteen seconds. We are pleased by this, but know it only takes five seconds for a gunshot from the enemy to kill us both.

That night I pray fervently, begging The Lord for the courage to face what we must face; for the mercy that will see as few of us killed as possible and for our victory in this engagement. Unlike the other nights, there is no comment, no sly remark, no hostile word upon seeing a Jew pray.

Each man in our battalion has too much on his mind and each man knows I pray for him as well as me.

III

The bombardment does not start at six as had been expected, it begins half-an-hour earlier. Mercifully our commanders have learned from bitter experience that soldiers killed are not easily replenished and our resources are thin enough as it is not to waste. Last night they ordered us to fall back to our second and third line of trenches, just enough to put a safe distance between us and the shells which now rain down in torrents from the British guns. Yet it does not lesson the excruciating terror of the shells exploding where only hours before we had been.

Explosion after explosion after explosion, the sound of a thousand thunderstorms upon a thousand thunderstorms, a dense wall of raging sound echoing throughout the early morning.

Mathias crouches in a corner, his eyes scrunched tight as if in pain, the palms of his hands pressed tightly against his ears, yet I doubt it in any way reduces, much less blocks, this awful noise to any degree.

'It's like the jaws of hell have opened up and screamed', he roars. The agitation and panic in his voice is unmistakable.

I think back to my days as a child, being taught to read the Tanakh by my Father and Grandfather, and my early, faltering attempts to pronounce Hebrew correctly. I remember the passage from the *Sefer Y'Hoshua*, with Joshua's priests riding around the walls of Jericho, blowing their horns and the army issuing their war cry. On that day it was enough to cause the mighty walls of the city to come crashing down. Yet the soldiers defending Jericho never heard a sound as terrible as we do now.

The bombardment does not stop, it goes on and on, echoing endlessly from the darkness into the first rays of the new rising sun. Metal and explosives erupt into clay and rock for five relentless, nerve-shredding hours. How any of us have not lost our minds in this rage I do not know, but our fortitude is a product of the instinct to survive. For all their horrifying sounds, the shells do not touch us, and indeed the more the pounding goes on, the more I feel within myself, within the men around me, the resolve growing to deliver a counter punch to the British they will not forget. Even Mathias has gathered himself together.

When the bombardment finally ceases, it almost comes as a shock. The surprise of silence takes us unawares, but only for a moment. We know we have to prepare rapidly for the oncoming charge.

Our first line of trench will have been completely destroyed by the shellfire and be indistinguishable from any other charred and desecrated region of no man's land.

The men fix the bayonets to their rifles. We take our positions along our second line of trench and check our magazine supplies. Behind us boxes of mortars are opened, ready to be thrown at the advancing British.

Lothar and I quickly set up our Maschinengewehr 08 machine gun, I behind the trigger, while he feeds the magazine into the gun.

Now we wait.

We can see no more than a few feet in front of us. Smoke, dense and grey, like a thick fog, floods across no man's land. Clay particles, uprooted and disrupted from the earth by the bombardment, hang in the air, obscuring everything. Eventually we begin hearing shouts and the tread of boots. The British are near, very near.

'FEUERN!'

Upon our commanders' order, we unleash a hail of bullets at the enemy. I squeeze the trigger and keep it held down. The Maschinengewehr shakes as it spews out its cartridges. Our worry is that it will overheat and cut out at the wrong moment. Lothar continues to feed in the long magazine belts, while on either side of us our comrades fire, fire, fire, and reload, and fire, fire, fire.

The dense smoke is beginning to clear, slowly and stubbornly, but enough for us to see, for the first time, the silhouettes of the oncoming British. Now we have something definite to aim at. The intensity of our fire becomes more unrelenting. Each enemy I hit is in revenge for a fallen comrade, each enemy I hit I ask God to forgive me for the life I have been forced to take.

'How many of them are there?' shouts Lothar.

Though I am beside him, I can only just hear him, the noise of the Maschinengewehr, the rifle blasts and mortar explosions drown out almost everything else.

'I don't know! Never mind that now, just keep the gun fed!' I yell.

Wave upon wave of British come, but they run into a hail of bullets. Wave upon wave of them fall dead onto the ruptured earth.

Those behind must fight their way through the heavy smoke, clamber over and around the growing piles of bodies, and then face our unforgiving gunfire.

This is not war, this is a massacre.

Half a day of fighting passes before silence falls on this field in Northern France. What is left of the British has retreated in haste. Victory has been ours today and only now do we breathe easy. The men begin to whoop and cheer, there is laughter and smiles and some even begin singing.

Lothar and I stare at the battlefield.

Stretching out in front of us is a near endless panorama of khaki-clothed corpses, some in piles, former comrades slumped over each other, others impaled upon the barbed wire or face down in the mud. Many more lie singly. I see one man lying curled up as if only asleep.

These are my sworn enemy.

These are my brother humans.

I do not know how I feel.

I lean back against the mud and wood-lined wall of the trench. Lothar checks the Maschinengewehr, pulling out the last half-used magazine belt. I close my eyes and gather myself, allowing my breath to steady and my pulse to slow to a normal pace. I light a cigarette and with the tips of the fingers of my left hand touch the rim of the visor on my Stahlhelm. I offer a silent prayer of thanks to The Lord that I have been spared this day.

It is then we hear the insane roar.

A lone British soldier appears from nowhere, his bayoneted rifle clasped tightly between his hands, his eyes wide and ablaze. A look of insanity inhabits his entire face as he charges at us. He must have been knocked momentarily unconscious and having recovered to see his comrades dead, been driven into a frenzy.

He thrusts his bayonet forward and reaches the lip of our trench, lunging forward at Lothar who is isolated from the rest of us and exposed on the machine gun platform. Only inches separate the tip of the bayonet from the Bavarian's chest. Without thinking I reach for my pistol and fire.

The gunshot destroys the silence that had settled over the battlefield. As its noise dies away and is absorbed back into the stillness, the Briton stands on the edge of our trench, still clutching his bayonet. From the corner of his head a thick flow of blood courses down his cheeks and neck onto his khaki uniform.

The manic look is frozen on the Briton's face. Moments pass before he drops to his knees. The rifle falls from his grasp, and his whole body tumbles forward onto the floor of the trench. He lands with a sickening thump, face up. His large, dark eyes glare up at us from his lifeless face and a kind of rigor mortis keeps his teeth bared, clenched in fury.

'Good shot Hans!' declares Otto.

'You saved my life! My friend you saved my life', gasps Lothar, who has scrambled back beside me. 'I am forever in your debt'.

He shakes my hand but I tell him he would have done the same for me had our positions been reversed.

Some of the men are examining the body. Mathias is on his knees, going through the pockets. He pulls out what I take to be identification papers and looks through them.

'From what it says here', he declares 'This man was of the Royal Irish Regiment. So he wasn't a Briton, he was an Irishman'.

'Huh! Irish, British, what's the difference?' says Becker in a surly voice.

'Try saying that to an Irishman's face and see how far you get', Otto says, a huge laugh and smile emerging through his thick, bristling, ruddy beard.

'I think Hans already did', Becker replies.

Becker's naïvety, were it not so crass would be almost charming. In 1914 it seemed it would be Ireland, and not Europe, that would erupt into full-scale war – one side determined to remain under British rule, the other wanting to break the link with the crown. How instead had an entire continent sleepwalked into this war?

'That was one hell of a shot Hans', said Mathias. 'You might even get a medal for this. Imagine an Iron Cross!'

'You might even get to meet the Kaiser! He might even give it to you himself!'

It was Becker again. We all laugh. His face shows he has no idea we are laughing at the very idea of such a suggestion. The Kaiser has no love for Jews and would probably baulk when put face to face with someone like me, with the name Rubenstein.

The exhibition is over. The men begin to disperse, except Lothar who remains by my side. I have no regrets about my action. My friend's life was in danger and I would not stand by and let him be killed. Yet I also curse those who put me and the Irishman in a position where perfect strangers must try to take one another's life.

The medical orderlies arrive and carry off the Irishman's body. As they do so my mind returns to my childhood lessons in the Torah with my Father and Grandfather, and reading the passage from the Book of Exodus:

'Thou shalt not oppress a stranger: for ye know the heart of a stranger, seeing ye were strangers in the land of Egypt'.

And I cannot help but think of how every one of us in these wretched fields of Northern France, whether friend or foe, are like 'strangers in the land of Egypt', looking for the path that will lead us away from the wilderness and towards home.

MUTANT

Órfhlaith Foyle

Barbara the tattoo artist sat her dumpy breasts astride my arm and examined my right bicep.

I told her I wanted it plain. I didn't want any fantastical decoration.

A large red strawberry pockmarked with green pips squeezed and stretched on her torso as she sketched out a cheetah's head.

'Small ears', she remarked. 'Not a lion … not a leopard … a cougar or a puma?'

'Cheetah', I insisted.

She shivered all the way down to her hips. 'Cheetahs look too female, don't you think?'

I glanced at her gallery of tattoos. There were Chinese and Celtic symbols. There was an American Indian headdress fixed onto Geronimo's head. There were snakes of various colours and there were women ready made for men's muscles.

'I want it exact', I told her.

Barbara looked at me. 'I'm an artist', she said. She smiled. 'You must make room for my imagination'.

She sat up straight and pulled down the neckline of her long-sleeved vest top. An Iris flower petal fluted out. I stared at its blueness. I imagined its roots lay near her nipple.

The iris twisted as she breathed. The more I looked, the more its blue colour disseminated into individual lines, like veins, looping, gnashing, popping and pooling.

I shook my eyes away.

'And this', Barbara said.

She slipped one foot from her high-class sandal and arched her toes on a small cushioned stool.

The whole of her left sole was covered in multi-coloured fish scales. Bronze, platinum, gold, taupe, purple, orange, green and red scales that scooped and dizzied from the base of her toes to the deep lines at her ankle bone.

She turned her foot to face me. It was blank with ordinary flesh.

'I'm an expert', she promised.

I glanced down at my bicep. It twitched slightly. Barbara brushed her fingers over my skin.

'It's good', she said. 'Tight'. She pursed her lips and turned my arm to its left, then its right. 'I'm seeing how the cheetah will move on you', she said.

She outlined the cheetah from the top of my bicep, across my muscle and its tail flowed into the concave at my elbow. Its haunches stood on the lower rise of my bicep. Its own muscle reached across mine. Its belly, its paws, then its jaw at the rim of my shoulder, and black felt-tip smudges for its markings.

Barbara put down her pen and examined her work so far. She shook her head.

'Cheetah yellow will not be a good colour against your skin', she said. She snapped her fingers trying to think of a description to explain why. 'Your skin is too pasty to begin with … too bleh'.

She brushed the back of her hand along the outline of my cheetah. 'His yellow will be lost on you. It won't stand out'.

'I want it exact', I reminded her.

Barbara glanced up at her gallery of tattoo beasts and pointed at a large orange-bristled dragon. It had blue fins and a long Day-Glo green moustache.

'I don't believe in dragons', I said.

Barbara rolled out a laugh. 'Jesus … no one does'. She patted her chest. 'A tattoo says something about you'.

Cheetah, I thought. Cheetah.

Barbara pointed at a woman wearing a leather bikini and carrying a fur-trimmed spear.

'Maybe you're into that', she suggested.

'I just want the cheetah', I said. 'I want it exactly as it is in the book'.

Barbara concentrated on the animal's back, and as she inlaid the detail for its paws, she mentioned, 'maybe this is too big for you?'

She ran her eyes over my torso and other arm. 'Maybe try something neat? Something that would fit on your hip or the back of your wrist?'

'No', I insisted. 'A cheetah is what I want'.

She sat back and admired the black stencil on my bicep.

'You've got good arms for ink', she said. 'Work out much?'

I looked down at her drawing. The cheetah's eyes stared at me.

'You forgot its tear lines', I said.

Barbara bit open her felt-tip pen. 'Sorry', she said. She leaned over my arm. She had a smell of apple and sweat. I watched her draw in the tear lines.

'During the day they can see up to five kilometres', I said.

'Uh huh', Barbara said.

'The tear lines help them focus'.

Barbara shifted on her chair and ran her fingers over a standing tray of ink bowls.

'I like your …' her fingers flashed out in a wide fan, '… your plainness'. She nodded over at her tattoo galleries. 'Sometimes people want weird things, you know?

I nodded that I knew.

Barbara tapped the middle of her forehead. 'I've got imagination, you know?'

I nodded that I knew that as well.

'My yellow is going to look foul on your skin', she told me.

'I don't mind', I said.

'Well I mind', she said. 'That's my creation on your arm. It has to look so damn good, other people will want it for themselves'.

I looked at her. 'It's a bet', I said.

'Oh God', Barbara said. 'I hate doing bets'. She glanced at her needles. 'You probably don't want the cheetah after all. You're just stuck with some bet with the lads down at the pub'.

She picked up a needle packet and rolled it between her fingers. She smiled at me.

'But bets are my bread and butter'.

She touched my skin.

'I can make him mutant though', she said.

I shifted in my chair. The cheetah's ears seemed to turn.

'A bet, eh?' Barbara encouraged.

I didn't want to tell her, but the soft buzz of the tattoo gun, the sensation of smoke rising from my skin, made me confess.

'I'm not a real man'.

She lifted her gun, stared at me for a second, then blew away the small bubbles of blood and extra ink on my bicep.

'Sure you are', she said professionally.

I nodded at the cheetah. 'Too female', I reminded her.

She laughed, shook her head.

'You have great muscles'.

She placed her gun's needle into a shallow bowl of blue ink.

'My favourite colour', she added. She pressed the needle into the cheetah's ears.

'I want shadowing', I said.

Barbara looked up at me.

'You did one of the lads a couple of weeks ago, and he wasn't happy with your shadowing. He said his tattoo didn't move'.

Barbara stopped her work. 'Who was that?'

'Terry'.

Barbara put down her gun, wiped her hands and took out a cigarette packet.

'If you don't smoke, you can sue me'.

I laughed. I liked Barbara. I liked her heavy hips, her tight and rippled waist, the squat strawberry on her torso, the tiny iris beneath her vest and underneath her ordinary foot, her brilliant fish sole with its rasp of scales. I breathed in, almost feeling those scales.

I said, 'I'll have one of those'.

She watched me smoke.

'Terry', she said. 'He tried it on. Squirt of a man. Not in my wildest nightmares'.

I laughed. She stared at me.

'You shouldn't laugh so much. It makes you too nice'.

She blew out her smoke, then pulled up her vest sleeve to show a large bruise like a splattered green flower on the inside of her lower arm.

'You ever give a woman something like this?'

'No', I said.

'Then you're fine as a man', she said.

She got off her chair, went over to her coffee machine, filled two cups and handed me one.

'Tell me about the bet', she said and sat back in her chair.

'The cheetah', I said.

'He'll wait'. She smiled at me. 'I like stories', she explained.

Terry caught sight of my penis in the pub's urinals.

'Not much there, is there fella?'

He hit my shoulder. 'Just joking', he said.

I wiped my hands dry with paper towels. 'Ok', I said.

'Ok', he mimicked.

I said nothing then. Terry stared at my face.

'Come on, come on', he whispered. 'Come on, come on'.

I hit him then. My fist crunched on his nose. He went down, clutching and catching blood.

I had to wash my hands again. Terry was still on the floor, so I stepped over him on my way out to the bar. The others had bought more drinks.

I sat down.

'Ok?' they said.

'Fine', I said.

They looked over my head. 'Where's Terry?' they said.

'Mopping blood', I said.

They laughed a little bit, then went back to their drinks. When Terry joined us, there was only a blush of pink on his nose.

'I'm glad you hit him', Barbara said.

She put down her coffee and resumed tattooing me. She was working on the cheetah's head. I watched its flesh stand out from my own. The faint blue seeped darker.

Terry had flexed his arm and the tattoo of a woman just lay there, doing nothing.

'Her belly is supposed to move', he complained.

I looked at the woman on his skin.

'Not a great choice', I said.

Terry looked at me. 'What would you know?'

Surrounded by his friends, he was brave.

I sucked up my lager. 'Fifties pin up', I said. 'Cheap and plenty'.

Terry smiled. 'You'd do better, I suppose'.

I nodded.

'What with?' Terry sneered.

I thought for the next few seconds. Then I said, 'A cheetah'.

Terry laughed, 'A fucking cheetah?' He looked at the others, giving them permission to laugh also. I finished my lager.

'A cheetah is a ponce's tattoo', Terry said.

I shrugged. 'I like cheetah's. I like how they run'. I stared at Terry. 'Mine will move so damn good, you'll want it for yourself'.

Barbara smiled when I told her that.

I thought of her fish sole. And thinking of it, I could feel water against my skin.

'You cold?' she asked. 'Goose pimples aren't good for my work'.

She turned and switched her electric heater on. She smiled at me. Her hair was in her eyes. I brushed it off.

'Thanks', she said.

Her apple sweat was delicious.

Cheetahs would like apples, I thought. I imagined lying in a tree in an African savannah, training my five kilometre stare on the grass and water, watching for Thompson gazelles or wildebeest.

My skin warmed up.

'Thanks', Barbara said.

She nodded at my cheetah.

'It's a great blue'.

I looked at my bicep. The cheetah moved. Its jaw flexed at my shoulder. It's tail switched inside my elbow. Its spots jostled as I tightened and released. Its mutant blue looked like the sky near its belly, then deepened over its haunches and back.

A night sky behind its ears and an almost felt-dark fur on its tear lines and the rim of its jaw, while its teeth brightened with white, whiter than my pasty skin.

'Grrrrrr', Barbara growled.

She finished the paws and the tip of the tail.

'Done', she said.

She reached for her cold coffee and another cigarette.

'Show me your foot', I said. 'Please'.

She lifted her foot out of its sandal and I crouched forward to align my cheetah with her fish sole.

'Mutants', I said.

Terry said he was uncomfortable in my presence.

'You've got this female vibe', he said.

The others smiled and looked from me to him.

'It's your hair', Terry said. 'It flops about too much'.

I cut my hair. I razored it to my skull.

'Your muscles aren't so good either', Terry said.

I muscled up. I graded their thickness and practiced in front of a mirror.

And still Terry didn't love me.

I found him in the pub. He was sitting alone.

'I've something to show you', I said.

He nodded and I worked up my shirtsleeve.

My cheetah gleamed in the pub's window light. She nuzzled my shoulder and eased her limbs over my flesh. Her blueness swallowed up my skin.

'Jesus', Terry said.

He reached and touched her.

'I want her', he said after a while.

I said nothing. I ate some crisps and drank some lager. He followed me out into the street. He followed me to my door.

He said, 'Let me sleep with your cheetah'.

I sat him in my kitchen then I opened my knife drawer and handed him a small carving knife.

I said, 'Get rid of the cheap bitch on your bicep'.

He started to cry and I sat in front of him and watched for as long as it took, and I thought of my cheetah lying in her tree, her eyes on her prey, slowly working out the one she wanted.

THIS PLAGUE OF SOULS
an excerpt

Mike McCormack

Opening the door and crossing the threshold in the dark triggered Scanlon's phone.

He dropped his bag to the floor and with the same hand drew the phone from his pocket and flicked it open. Instantly the side of his head was bathed in the blue forensic glow of the digital diode.

'Yes?'

'Welcome home'.

The voice at the other end was male, downbeat and hollow, just the sort of voice you did not want to listen to in the dark. Scanlon was immediately aware of himself in two minds – the sudden insistence of the voice on the phone drawing against his immediate instinct to orient himself in the hallway into which he had just stepped.

He made a swift decision to take the phone call standing with his back to the wall.

'You know I'm home?'

'I'd know a lot less'.

'What do you want?'

Two paces to his left Scanlon spotted a switch. He reached out with his spare hand and threw it, threw it back, then threw it again. Nothing. The side of his head remained shrouded in blue light.

'The disc is on the table', the voice said. 'It's a one off that cannot be copied and it has an inbuilt detiorant which will destroy its code in three days. So that's your time span, seventy-two hours after you open it up'.

Scanlon opened a door and passed into what he sensed was a wide-open room. A low, horizontal shadow revealed itself to be a table; he drew out a chair and took the rest of the phone call sitting in the dark.

'Seventy-two hours isn't much time'.

'We have every confidence in you', the voice drawled, 'but you will need some background. So listen carefully, you will only get this once'.

A sweep of his arm across the table found the disc. He held up the clear case in the blue light; the disc floated like an imprisoned moon. The voice continued.

'It's a turn-based strategy game built on a simple scenario. The game opens with your avatar – a community warden – finding a cache of HSE files dumped on a bog. This find enables you to hack into a database of medical insurance files and steal the identity and the bank accounts of the owners. What you do with this information is up to you, the player – there are multiple uses to which, for good or bad, you can put it. You could decide to sell off the identities to someone who wants to access some very expensive treatments or you might just auction the accounts to the highest bidder. Or you may just access the bank accounts and make off with the money to Latin America with a mistress. On the other hand you might choose to underwrite a breast-feeding clinic in Mumbai.

The choice is yours – good or bad; in effect you are playing against yourself'.

'And playing against myself, how am I supposed to win a game like that?'

'It's not about winning or losing – there are other considerations. External circumstances will reveal what they might be. You start with ten identities – that is all you have'.

'And my mission, should I choose to accept it, is what exactly?'

'You just run the usual diagnostic, playability, aesthetic unity and logical coherence, a three-page report will suffice'.

'And what do I get for slaving away at this game?'

'You get to meet me'.

'And who are you?'

'Let's say I'm someone with information'.

'Let's say you be more specific'.

'This isn't the time for specifics. One last thing'.

'Yes?'

'Stop blundering around there in the dark – the mains switch is over the back door to your left'.

And with that his phone went dead.

Holding the phone ahead of him Scanlon opened the door which led off the room and found himself in a small scullery which he calculated to be barely five feet in width. Sweeping the phone around he found a solid door to his left, over which there was a white junction box with a complex array of meters and fuses. The mains switch was the largest at the end of two rows but was too high to reach; he had to return to the bigger room and drag the chair from the table to the back door.

He stepped up and threw the switch; light flooded from the hallway.

It appeared that he was in a small back kitchen, a type of scullery. There was a four-ring cooker, a small fridge and a couple of shelves along the wall opposite the door. One step back into the kitchen brought him back to the table he had been sitting at. It was a long table beneath a large window that was closed with blinds.

Beyond the table was a sink unit with white cupboards and a brown countertop, all cheap décor from sometime in the early eighties. To his left was a three-seater couch above which hung a picture of the Sacred Heart and beneath which glowed a small orange cross. He reached out and flicked the switch and the walls of the room came up in a cool mint-green glow against which the blonde, pine table seemed warm and homely.

Back into the hall then from which he'd come. To his left four doors opened, two on each side. The first was a bathroom; tiled walls and floor with a peach bathroom suite and a shower cubicle tucked in behind the door. Behind each of the remaining doors he found three bedrooms of equal size with a double bed in each and built-in wardrobes squaring off each space. There were pillows and duvets on each of the beds but all the wardrobes were empty.

Out into the front hall then where one final room remained – the sitting room inside the front door. A laminate floor ran to a small marble fireplace beneath a low mantelpiece. Beside it a set of empty bookshelves reached to the ceiling. In the middle of the floor was a single leather armchair, an obvious partner to the couch in the kitchen. It was angled towards a large flatscreen television under which sat a white game console and a single wireless controller.

The décor and layout of the place suggested family life somewhere in the lower-working-class demographic. The general impression was that it was clean, not the raw cleanliness of a last-minute blitz before a visitor's arrival but the cleanliness of on-going effort which made it presentable at sudden need. It had been carefully maintained. Scanlon felt all his senses opening up and attuning themselves to this new environment. Now he was aware of a low hum throughout the house and he stood listening for a moment.

His hand on the radiator told him that the heat had come on.

To complete his survey he opened the front door to walk outside. A globe-light over the lintel illumined a small gravel frontage inside a pair of black gates. Beyond lay a quiet road. To the left, the gravel frontage gave onto an uneven grassed area which was swallowed up in the darkness beyond. At the other end it was obvious that the house was offset to one end of its site, a tall hedge leaned into the gable of the house. A cement walk took him around the back. He passed by the back door and the light from the kitchen, past the central heating generator at the opposite gable and back once more to the front door.

His survey complete he stood there and it took less than a moment to clear his mind and rearrange all the information he had gathered so far. He experienced it as a seamless morph of sense to structure, a complete ordering of the house's layout and detail. A gift he had not called on in five years and yet it flew to him seemingly unimpeded.

The old demands, the old gifts.

'Twelve minutes', he said, to no one but himself.

A glance at his phone confirmed that he had been in the house less than twelve minutes.

Next morning he tried to make breakfast.

A simple enough task but these new surroundings and five years of having his meals handed to him on a tray had apparently thrown him completely out of the flow of such a simple task. Although the house was well provisioned his stumbling efforts involved much opening and closing of cupboards and return journeys to and from the small back kitchen, before finally he had the toast and scrambled eggs on the plate.

The fifteen-minute task took him almost half an hour.

From his place at the head of the table he had a clear view through the window at the stretch of grass which made up the back garden. He saw now that in the darkness he had missed a few things. The house was set on a slight rise from which a long garden ran down to a sod fence; off to one side a grey galvanise shed butted up to this fence. Its door was padlocked. Running at right angles to the house was a clothesline which was fastened at its furthest end to the crooked limb of a hawthorn bush. The whole area was otherwise an open expanse of grass laid out with an eye to minimum upkeep.

The day was wet, this November weather drawing on gusts of rain which drifted by and obscured his view; the very light itself torpid, reluctant. One of those days saturated with rain, time swollen in its bleak embrace. Looking out on it Scanlon felt like a child once more, up on his knees on a chair with his nose pressed to the glass, his plans for the day spoiled by …

He caught hold of himself abruptly, the sudden reverie had almost displaced him from the here-and-now and this, as he well knew, was not the time to be dwelling on the past. It was a dangerous mood and Scanlon knew that if he succumbed to it he was fully capable of sitting there all day, looking out the window at nothing at all.

A quick search confirmed there was nothing by way of entertainment in the house – no books or DVDs, no reception on the TV. A quick scan through the cupboards failed to turn up the radio which was a fixture of every kitchen.

So he had to face it – there was nothing before him now but the game.

The thought filled him with a yawning emptiness. He had no expectations or curiosity about it, no trepidation either. Contrary to what he felt he might expect, he was not sure that any engagement with it would improve his current position – whatever that was – or illumine it. For the moment, everything was suspended in a stagnant timelessness. Everything about him was locked in freeze-frame and he sat there with his hands flat on the table.

He might have drifted off completely had the phone not rang at that precise moment.

He stood watching it vibrate in the middle of the table for a long moment, conscious of himself resisting the urge to pounce and answer it. The screen registered nothing save *private number*. It continued to ring, the moment now drawing out and he began to feel foolish, realising that his hesitation was nothing but a childish waiting game.

But for the moment, this waiting was all he had.

And then the waiting was over.

The voice at the other end was determined to overlook his little stubbornness; the tone was fatigued, matter of fact.

'So your belly is full and you've had a full eight-hours sleep behind you. Time for a day's work don't you think?'

'I'm a free man', Scanlon countered. 'I hadn't planned on doing anything'.

A sour chuckle came down the line. 'Your plans are neither here nor there. All plans derive from me from now on. The sooner we come to an understanding of this the better for both of us'.

The blunt clarity of the assertion riled Scanlon. Things had evidently moved on overnight.

'I have questions', he said.

'I'm not surprised, make them quick'.

'Suppose I refuse this game, suppose I open the door and walk away from here?'

'You won't do that'.

'How do you know?'

'The same way I know that you're sitting at that table with this phone in your left hand'.

Scanlon clenched in the chair as if someone had laid a hand on him from behind.

'Surveillance?'

'I'd prefer another word', the voice said. 'Surveillance doesn't cover the scope and depth of my regard for you or our connectedness to each other'.

'That does not give me a warm feeling'.

'That's a pity because we could hardly be closer. You see, your breathing is my breathing, your eyes are my eyes, and your blood is my blood. And this intimacy is not some passive observation or registering, this is way more intentional. Does that make you feel any warmer?'

'Fuck you'.

'I'm sorry you take that attitude because I have nothing more to offer by way of *bona fides* except to say that I have better things for doing with my time than playing some kind of joke. You can take it from me that you will not skip a pulse but I will know'.

'You are saying that not a sparrow falls ...'

'If you want to use those words'.

'There are other words?'

'Let's put it this way; you're a man of habit, certain things about you are predictable. That predictability is part of the reason why you are sitting where you are. Add to that five years' incarceration and let's say that it is sometimes easy to read the habits of a lifetime'.

'You're avoiding the question'.

'No, it's a question of our relative positions. I am here and you are there and that's how I know what I know'.

'I have three days'.

'Yes'.

'So there's no hurry'.

'Readiness to comply is a factor in all this. Foot dragging and obstinacy will make you no friends'.

'I'm popular enough. I do not need any more friends'.

'I strongly advise that you make a start. Anyway, we'll talk again'.

And once more the phone went dead.

Scanlon was a man with a ready guard. A life of skirting traps and hazards had honed all his senses to immediate danger. Add to that five years navigating his way through life in the toughest prison in the land and he knew that the one thing he could rely on to tell him how things stood was the hair on the back of his neck. And right now it was telling him nothing, which was another way of saying that he was in no immediate danger. Whatever confrontation was ahead – and he had no doubt but that there was one – lay some way down the road.

On the other hand he knew that he would remain stuck in the present situation if he did not make some sort of move of his own.

He sat a few moments longer weighing up his options. The day ahead now stretched out in a grey, ashen expanse. Sooner or later the urge to play the game would begin to gnaw at him – it was there and because it was a game it had to be played. It gave no other choice.

He rose from the table and went to the sink. He ran off a glass of water and headed back into the sitting room where he pulled the chair closer to the television and sat down.

He laid the glass of water down by the chair and picked up the controller …

Birthday Present

Celia de Fréine

It's been quiet in the Twangman Inn since the night of the shooting. Glasses make less of a clink as they're trundled to and from the glass-washer and when a customer pushes in the door, the sound of traffic and bustle of city life seem reluctant to cross the threshold and follow inside to the oak-panelled counter.

The Twangman's where I meet Mick every Friday and Sunday. And Wednesday, when I'm flush. It's renowned for its pints – Mick maintains they're the best in Dublin. As do the locals from the Flats over the road and the criminals who use the pub as their headquarters.

Couples having affairs make up the rest of the clientèle – not that Mick and I fall into that category. He isn't married and the only man I'm into is him. I'd marry him in the morning if he asked, though I know we'd be at each other's throats inside a week. It suits us to meet in the Twangman because we never meet anyone we know there. Mick's pupils or his mother. My students or colleagues. And the criminals tend to keep to themselves, though Mick exchanges a few words with them now and again.

'How's it goin'? What happened your man in the wheelchair? Fell off a roof? On a job, yeah, right!'

And they say things to Mick like.

'Nice bird. Always fancied redheads meself'.

I never thought of it as a dangerous place. The criminals bring their families on Sunday. Wives who sip Bacardi and chain-smoke, and kids who frolic in frothy dresses, patent leather shoes and white frilly socks. Friday is different. That's when the men huddle together and bundles of cash change hands. Couriers in leather jackets and motorbike helmets – most of them young and good-looking in a dangerous sort of way – come and go all evening. 'Gurriers is what they are, Miranda', Mick always says, enjoying the pun. Though he's an artist he takes an interest in wordplay and crosswords. He once told me it was he who coined the phrase 'the whore in the sewer' to describe the Anna Livia statue in O'Connell Street, but with Mick you never know.

On the night of the shooting one of the gurriers walked right up to the man in the wheelchair and pumped three bullets into his head. Blood spurted out in every direction. Up the flock-wallpaper and down the dralon upholstery. Your man slumped forward onto the table, and more blood gushed out, this time into Mick's drink, his chaser. Mick always has a chaser with his pint. Needless to say I was terrified. I got down on the floor, but had enough wit not to start screaming. The week's teaching had left me too hoarse in any case.

'For fuck's sake', Mick growled, not moving one way or the other. 'There's blood in me Paddy. Mari had better give me another on the house'.

Mari is the owner's daughter. The best puller of the best pints in the city. She adores Mick, but he makes out her arse is too big and her ankles too thick, though he likes her Botticelli eyes and corkscrew curls. She keeps a speak-easy in the back and we go there at Christmas and on Bank Holiday weekends. Or when Mick gets in money from his students, or when he sells a picture. He's an all right kind of painter, but lazy. His speciality is bowls of fruit and vases of flowers, and little old ladies are never long about snapping them up.

I doubt Mari was screaming the night of the shooting, and from her vantage behind the counter, there's no telling what she saw. I stayed on the floor until after the gurrier had left. After his boots, with the glob of battleship grey paint on the left toecap, had belted out of the pub and onto the back of a waiting motorbike.

Mari gave us all drinks on the house. Large ones. And Lizzie, the woman who cleans the toilets, rang for an ambulance. Everyone began to calm down, apart from the bereaved – the dead man's two sons and his brother. The brother kept yelling at the paramedics, who arrived twenty minutes later, to do something. Mari refilled our glasses when the coppers arrived and stopped anyone leaving. Some were in uniform and others in plainclothes. A *Bangharda*, and a detective called Diarmuid MacSomething interviewed Mick and me. Mick wasn't long about telling them he'd noticed nothing out of the ordinary and as for the guy with the gun: 'he looked like all the other guys in leather', he said, 'just like a motorbike cop'.

I wasn't thinking straight and the large Pernod had gone to my head, but I knew there was something familiar about that battleship grey paint. I'd seen a large tin of it only recently. And I reckoned Mick had seen it as well. Though, even if I could have remembered when or where, I doubt I would have mentioned it. My mother had always warned me about coppers. 'Never trust them, Miranda', she'd say. 'Never let on you know anything or next minute they'll have you locked up and the key dumped in the nearest canal'. Everyone else's mother must have taught them the same because the entire pub said they hadn't noticed anything strange or unusual about the gunman. Nor had they seen him before. The detective gave me a card with his name and number on it and asked me to get in touch if I remembered anything, no matter how trivial. I ran my eye over his ginger hair and high forehead, past his watery eyes and down the hook of his nose, and knew there was no way I was going to drop coins into a phone-box , press Button A, and ask to speak to him.

Mick is seated at the counter on the left, halfway through his first pint, when I push in the door. It's my birthday, the first Friday in April, a couple of weeks after the shooting. The place is deserted apart from himself and a few locals. I look at his reflection in the mirror advertising Jameson, the 's' curled around his left jaw like a giant scar and wonder how I could ever manage without him.

'What kept you, dear?' he grins, casting his eyes over me as I unbutton my velvet reefer jacket.

Underneath I'm wearing his favourite ensemble – black stretch jeans and a peach ribbed top. He's wearing the denim shirt I bought him for Christmas. He usually wears it on Friday and Saturday, and the plaid one his mother gave him on Sunday.

'The usual, is it?' Mari asks.

I nod.

'And the same again for Mick'.

Mick follows me to a seat in the corner under the gas heater, bringing with him his copy of the *Evening Herald*. He has the crossword almost finished. I glance over the last few clues.

'*Submit to the harvest* – this one is easy', I say. 'I do it all the time. Every Friday and Sunday. *Yield*'.

Mick puckers his eyebrows, annoyed at me getting the better of him. He licks his pencil and fills in the missing letters. I lean over and stick my tongue in his ear – something he likes. I never worry that he'll have wax in it because he always scrubs himself before we meet. And the hairs in there are silky smooth, not like the hair on his head. I suppose that's because he doesn't bother to dye them.

Since I met Mick I've stopped dyeing my hair – not that it was going grey like his. It used to be bright red when I was a kid and the butt of everyone's jokes, but is more of a chestnut now. Until a couple of years ago I used to keep it cropped and dyed burgundy, but the roots kept forcing their way out faster than I could afford to touch them up. And I've stopped wearing tinted glasses and got used to having hazel eyes. Another reason I hated my colouring was because all the dolls I had as a kid – not that I ever had that many – had blue eyes and blonde hair. And I wanted to look like them. I wanted to look normal. Now I've let my hair grow halfway down my back. Mick tells me that's why he loves me – my chestnut hair and the other chestnut clump. He says that has a special flavour.

He shoves his hand under my camisole and runs it up and down the small of my back. I can't wait to get back to his flat. The thought of his finger or his tongue or his dick inside me, poking and prodding, is almost more than I can bear, but it's the first Friday of the month and I've just been paid by the nuns. Money is plentiful and there are three rounds to go. Three Pernods and whites for me, and three more pints, and three more Paddys for him. I know well what it is that won't be stirring inside me later on. But we've the whole weekend ahead of us. A long-promised visit to the Hugh Lane Gallery and a meal in the new Chinese restaurant in Fairview.

Mari brings over the first round and plonks the glasses down on the table.

'Howaya, Miranda?' she asks.

'Fine', I say. Like I always say.

Mick throws a couple of notes onto her tray and smiles.

'Keep the change'.

Mari would go to bed with him in a flash. She's always giving him the once over, groping him at every opportunity. Even now, as she leans down, her Botticelli eyes popping out of her head, she squeezes his shoulder in thanks for the tip as if it sealed the two of them in some secret bond.

Where Mick is concerned the one thing that keeps me sane is knowing that no matter how much he flirts with her, or with anyone else, and no matter how much he hurts me, he still wants me. I know he was infatuated with an artist's model when he was in college. And there was that blonde actress he'd been screwing for years before we met. But I believe him when he says he never cared for either of them.

What I like best about our relationship, apart from going to bed, is the way we're so tuned into each other we can almost read each other's mind. Without a word we know when it's time to knock back the dregs in our glasses. Help each other on with our coats. Nod to Mari and what's left of her band of criminals and paramours. And head.

When Mick pulls the door behind us a blast of sleet lashes my face and an icy wind cuts through me to the roots of my teeth. Typical weather for the start of April. Mick's hand is still warm and he slips it down my jeans. I move in close to him and we scurry around the corner and down the backstreets towards his flat.

I've got so used to Mick I can tell when he's going to come even before he knows it himself. And I know when he isn't. He says he gets his pleasure from giving me pleasure. Anything extra is an added bonus. He's still spry for his age, though I don't know what that is exactly. Somewhere in his mid-forties and at least fifteen years older than me but, apart from his dyed hair, you'd never guess, until you get him into bed. He likes when I comb his curls with my fingers, especially if my hand is cold. And he likes me going down his back, vertebra by vertebra, rubbing each one like it's a big blue and white marble.

I never drank it.

'It is full of nourishment', Mick sometimes says. 'Jackie Collins and these wans write about it in their books. High in protein. Low in polyunsaturates. Good for the heart'.

I'm afraid I'll puke if I try swallowing it. I've often read on the paper of some young fella getting drunk and choking on his own vomit. And I can just see myself gasping for breath with a glob of come trapped in my craw.

'You'll do it in your own good time', he says. 'And when you do, I'll know you love me'.

It's always there – the final hurdle in my whoring skills. The Beecher's Brook I've baulked at more times than I can remember.

Mick rents the ground floor of a Georgian gaff a few streets from the Twangman. In it there are two inter-connecting rooms. The front one is used for his classes. And the back room is his sitting-room cum-bedroom cum-dining room cum-anything-else room. On the landing he shares a grotty kitchen and bathroom with Danny, a sort of caretaker, who lives upstairs in the two pair back. It's Danny's job to keep the hall, stairs and landings clean and tidy. And put out the bins. He has a nephew, Bill, who helps with the odd maintenance job. Between them they give the place a lick of paint from time to time.

Instead of going into the backroom, as usual, Mick brings me into his classroom.

'I've something special in mind tonight', he whispers.

Mick likes to keep this room separate. It's tidy enough, with bare boards that Danny scrubs once a week. The stools and easels are stacked on one side, near the doors that open into the backroom. And over by the window there's a worktop with brushes, and jars, and tins of paint, and palettes caked with years of mixtures, alongside a Belfast sink with a spluttering tap. There are several mirrors on the wall, and a table in front of the fireplace where he sets up his bowls of fruit and vases of flowers.

Mick has spread a tapestry on the table. It's made of felt, in all the colours of the rainbow, with every shape you can imagine tacked onto it. Circles, ellipses, triangles, rectangles, octagons, hexagons. He often uses it as a backdrop, or as an example of how to design patterns.

'I've been thinking about this all day', he says.

'Your tapestry?'

'I've been thinking about fucking you on this table', he says. 'To celebrate your birthday'.

'You want me to die of pneumonia?'

Mick hauls a rickety Super Ser out of the alcove to the right of the fireplace and sticks a match in it. I used to be afraid he'd blow the place up, what with all the paint and white spirits. But I've got used to the sense of danger. I like doing irresponsible things with Mick.

He pushes me back onto the table and pulls down the zip of my jeans.

'Everyday from now on', he says, 'when this room is crammed with five or six or seven old biddies, who don't know their arse from their elbow, trying to reproduce a bowl of oranges, I'll imagine you lying here. Your legs spread'.

His tongue is in my mouth now, and mine in his, pummelling back and forth. His hands are on my ribs pushing up the peach top and the camisole. And my arms are around his neck. I feel safe and helpless.

I don't notice the cold, or the smell of gas, or paint. I run my fingers through his hair and up and down his spine. My legs are around his, pushing down his jeans. He takes his tongue out of my mouth and zig-zags it down over my stomach until it's inside me. He moves it in and out, exploring all the nooks and crannies, then backs off.

'I want tonight to be special', he says. 'I want to see how far you can go. How far I can push you'.

I close my eyes and feel his tongue back inside me. I don't know much about transcendental meditation, but I remember at the school retreat a nun telling us about saints who used to starve themselves. Then they'd have visions and start levitating. There was one in particular, St Joseph of Cupertino, who used to take off and float up over his mates.

I feel a bit like that now. Like my soul is rising out of my body. I see Mick beneath me – his head of dark-dyed curls, his broad back inside his denim shirt, and his strong hands with their chipped nails. A lovely warm feeling comes over me and I start to moan.

'Let's not disturb the neighbours', he says. 'There've been complaints'.

'You been fucking other noisy women?' I ask, releasing the week's tension onto the rough felt of the tapestry.

We wake around twelve the next day in Mick's bed in the backroom. There are two dirty mugs and a full ashtray on the bedside locker, and it's cold. My face is the only part of me outside the blankets, and my nose is freezing. Mick is lying behind me, one hand over my left breast, the other between my legs. I can feel him stirring.

'Sleep well, my dear?' he asks.

'Fine, and yourself?'

'Not as good as you. You kept me awake with your snoring'.

'Fuck off', I say, turning towards him.

His tongue is in my mouth again, and he's on top of me.

'I'm not past it yet', he whispers.

'You'll never be past it', I answer. 'Not if you give up the jar'.

'Guess what I found yesterday?' he asks.

'What?'

'The first grey hair on my bollocks'.

'And?'

'I plucked it out straight away'.

'Eejit', I whisper. 'Even the dogs on the street know if you pluck one out, seven will grow in its place'.

Our bodies move in a steady rhythm of bedspring creaks and squeaks until a loud knocking stops us in our tracks.

'For fuck's sake', says Mick. 'Who the fuck is that?'

He pulls on his jeans and shirt, and rushes to the door. It's Danny.

'Phone call', Danny says, 'didn't you hear it ringin'? 'Twas enough to waken the dead'.

Danny peers into the room as Mick pushes past. I dive under the blankets, but feel his eyes bore through them.

'Don't think I don't know you're in there, Missy', he shouts. 'I know all about you, and what youse two do be up to'.

'And I know all about you', I shout back, wondering what there is to know about this wheezing gap-toothed old man.

After a few minutes I hear Mick walk back down the hall.

'Thanks, Danny', he grunts, slamming the door. 'You can come out now', he says to me. 'What is it you're hiding from anyway? And what the fuck are you doing opening your big mouth?'

'How do you mean?' I ask.

'*I know all about you*, for fuck's sake!'

He buttons his shirt and pulls on his socks.

'Gotta go', he says, leaning over and planting a kiss on my forehead.

'Go where?'

'Home. To the Ma. Her sister's due back from Lourdes on Tuesday. She needs the kitchen painted'.

Mick doesn't realise I know where his mother lives. One day I got the bus out as far as Drimnagh. I'd seen her address on an ESB bill – which her devoted son was obviously paying while I was subbing the pint and the chaser. It's in one of those huge estates built in the fifties – rows upon rows of houses that look the same. Except for hers, of course, which is covered in cladding and has a porch, occupied by a huge statue of the BVM, stuck onto the front. There are two windows, one above the other. Both painted pink like the porch door and the inside door. Two by two – a woman who likes doing things in pairs. Too bad she doesn't have another son to attend her many needs. I often laugh at the thought of Mick turning his key in the lock every Monday, Thursday, and Saturday. Nodding to the neighbours. Sidling in past the statue. God knows what it's like inside. The bowls of plastic roses at the foot of the statue and the frilly curtains are a good way of judging.

'What colour paint?' I ask.

'Primrose. I'll give you a ring during the week'.

'What about our trip to the gallery?'

'You can go on your own'.

'You know I hate going to things on my own. We were supposed to spend the weekend together'.

'Gotta go', he says.

Then he leans over, pulls back the blankets and forces open my legs. Next thing he's inside me, and the creaking has begun again. But I feel nothing. He gives a kind of groan when he comes – it's just a small squirt, really. There's not much left at his age.

After he's gone I lie in bed for some time. So much for thinking I'm the only one he cares about, when it's his mother who has him by the short and curlies. After a while I get up and stand at the window, pressing my breasts against the cold wet glass. Danny is pottering around, sweeping the back yard and arranging the bins in a neat row. The back-wall has just been whitewashed by his nephew, Bill, who also painted the back door. I see it now, glistening under its new coat of paint – battleship grey. Danny looks up, but I don't try to cover myself – at this stage I don't care how many caretakers are looking at me, or how many murdering nephews they have. I push my way into the front room and run some water into the sink.

ANGEL OF HOSPITALITY

Ken Bruen

The R Hotel.

Simple, right?

The R for refuge.

At a hefty price.

Ok.

Run by a legendary second-generation Irish woman. Name of Nora. Her surname, she wasn't giving that out, least not anytime soon. The stories, you got a babe, and fook, she was all of that, with a mouth like a fishwife, there were going to be stories. The current being she'd gotten her set-up money off a bent cop who she then gut shot. The guy lived and was still looking for her. No one had sold her out, yet.

If the story was true. Certainly no one was going to rat her out to the cops.

There are rules, flexible and very few but they exist.

1 ...Tell the cops fook all.

2 … see above.

She came in at about 110lbs, all of it lethal. Unusual for a broad of Irish descent, she was blonde, with a rack to die for, terrific legs, and a face that missed being pretty due to a scar above her right eye.

Guys, with one boiler maker past caution, said it looked like a small angel. The booze talking. All I know is, it was livid and when she was pissed, which was often, it seemed to have a life of its own. But it was the eyes, dammit, eyes that haunted you. And no, that was without a few brews in me. A deep blue, almost transparent. They shimmered, caught the light in odd ways, so when you were talking to her, the eyes seemed to dance in her head.

Horse shit?

You may be right.

I have no stake in selling her assets.

Did I have a jones for her?

Fooksake.

I gave up that fools game when my wife fooked off with a guy from the UK.

A Brit.

Jesus wept.

A lesbian I could maybe stomach, even a regular guy, but a Brit.

So, I want the urge dealt with, I phone up my hooker No 1, for five hundred I get round the world in one night and to have my bed to myself in the morning.

Guys say … well guys say a lot of stuff, most of it bollix. But their favourite …

'I never pay for sex'.

Don't make me freaking laugh.

Fook on a bike.

Every guy pays, one way or another.

And a lot and incessantly.

… But how I got there?

I was first generation Irish, had left the States in a Romantic and Jameson haze to help the Cause.

The Irish sure saw us coming.

Them laughing … 'Yah want to be a boyo, help the struggle, sure, here's an Armelite, get your arse out there, show us your stuff'.

Put us on the front line.

Iraq would have been safer.

The three other Yanks, even though we thought we were real Irish, were always regarded as real stupid to the Boyos.

Those three were gunned down within a month.

I learned … quick.

Kept my head down, my mouth shut and my rifle on ready.

Took out a top guy in The Paratroopers. A dude they'd been after for months.

From the roof of a building in Derry, a shot they said couldn't be made. The distance was too far. I'd had my rifle modified, without shouting about it. Made the shot and earned their respect, if 'Holy Fuck!' is a good response.

I was in.

Then after a bloody fiasco, I had to leave fast, went back to the States, where I was supposed to raise funds.

I did, a lot, nigh on a quarter of a million.

Good huh?

And ran with it.

Crazy?

Oh yeah.

But I was tired.

Wanted out.

You don't get to retire.

I figured, I was born in the USA, I'd know more about hiding out than the Boyos.

So, I was running, fast.

And heard of The R Hotel.

Situated just off Herald Square, but a shopper from Macy's.

It was a shit hole, the Square that is, decrepit, seedy and the only light being a lone Starbucks.

When you see Starbucks as some sort of light, you know how desperate it is to find something to say about an area that is fooked and gone.

A cautious hundred yards from there, is the hotel. You need to have been given the address or bought it.

I bought it.

I could see how you'd easily miss it. It was a Brownstone, rare in that part of the city. But you could tell immediately, this was no run-down flop house. This was carefully renovated, freshly painted and more exits than Clinton's career.

Sure sign of a safe house, exits.

I expected the front door to be locked, no. Went into a small foyer. Saw the biggest man I ever, swear to fook, ever saw. Not black or spic or even mulatto. Just mega and hostility oozing out of his pores.

Nora was behind the reception. I recognized her from all the stories I'd heard.

I had a beat up Gladstone bag, carried my worldly possessions. The money was strapped to my body and the gun, used to be your regular handgun but I like to modify them.

Now it had a slide, eighteen shots in the clip that slammed into the handle and a slide, made the velocity as accurate as you were going to get outside of The Texas Rangers.

She looked up, no expression, asked 'Help you?'

Her intonation suggesting that help was the very last item on her dance card.

My holdall was heavy and I went to put it down, she asked 'You doing?'

'Am putting my bag on the floor'.

She fired a glance at the big guy, I fingered the customised in my waistband, she said 'If you were staying, you could put the bag down but who confirmed that?'

Ah fookit.

A ball buster.

I'd been married, I knew the drill.

Asked 'Please Miss, may I stay in your fine establishment?'

She debated for a moment on whether to unleash the dog of war. I could sense he was good to go.

She did what she was to do, in the all too brief time I knew her, she surprised the hell out of me.

Went the opposite of what I was primed for, said 'Pretty arrogant for an ugly fucker, yeah?'

God knows, I'm no gift, I know, my mother told me often enough. Used to holler 'Sweet Jesus, what an ugly child!'

Yeah, like that.

My ex wife, an old movies' buff, used to say, a lot, 'You look like Victor Mature, after the plastic surgery went down the toilet'.

I said 'It isn't arrogance when you can back it up'.

She liked that.

Asked 'Is that a quote?'

'Cassius Clay'.

She looked at me, then 'Interesting that you use his pre-Muslim name'.

I shrugged.

Then 'How long can we expect to have the pleasure of your company?'

Who the fook knew.

I said 'It's flexible, can we do per week?'

We could and she named a figure.

Holy shit.

She was actually smiling, an invite, to what? Asked 'So, can you back it up ... Cassius?'

I laid out the freight on the counter.

She took a key from the rack, said 'Top floor, nice view and lots of space'.

I nodded.

I was heading for where I hoped some elevators might be when she threw 'What you had in your waistband, Plato would have been faster'.

Plato?

Jesus.

Welcome to the madhouse.

The elevator zinged and about to climb aboard when 'Hey'.

I turned.

She tapped a heavy book on the counter, said 'Registration'.

I gave a theatrical sigh, learned from the best, my ex, snapped 'That necessary?'

A tiny smile, not of warmth, Jesus, maybe glee, sprinkled with malice. She said 'Only if you want to stay here ... or ...'

Glanced at Plato.

Plato? ... fooksakes.

He was grinning, gunning to go. I stomped back, my boot heels echoing on the mock Terrazzo floor. She turned the book to me. Christ, Thank God, I'd a pen.

To ask her?

No freaking way.

Plus, I was getting more than a little tired of her mouth, gorgeous as its shape was.

I signed 'Ralph Finnerty. Home … Ohio'.

She looked at it, asked 'How is Ohio?'

'You ever been?'

'No'.

'Then, it's lovely'.

She glanced at my Claddagh Wedding band. Heart … the heart turned out. Meant you were on the hunt and Sweet Jesus, the heart is a lonely hunter. The days of predator as dust in the Ohio wind.

I said 'Not no more'.

Her eyes, that deepest blue, reeling and a rocking in her head, asked 'Couldn't hack it, huh?'

I let that hover, seep its viciousness, said 'Couldn't hack her smart mouth'.

Did Plato smile?

The room was large by Manhattan standards. Meaning it was larger than a closet, just.

Joy though, a glass-door window opened to the roof. Stepped out there, stood, calculated.

Perfect.

I was invisible to prying eyes, unless they had a helicopter. An old disused air conditioning vent was attached to the side of the building.

Looking good.

Prised a board back, oh sweet Lord, nearly perfect.

For storage.

I'd need to put all weather wrapping, maybe a large briefcase. Got my face in tune, headed out and neither then, or on my return, did I see Miss Congeniality.

Had grabbed a Starbucks double grande latte and slice of danish. Snacked on those as I went shopping.

By late afternoon, I'd stashed the money, how safe it was?

I'd find out.

That evening I'd to meet a guy. Wore my battered leather bomber, 501s, converse, nicely scuffed and a T ... with the logo ... Lizzie rock.

The guy, not a friend but we had a history, purely financial.

Sheil's.

A scumbag who made scumbags look bad. He'd sell me to the Boyos in jig time.

I was counting on it.

I met him in a bar on the Lower East Side, as soon as I entered, I thought 'Fook, cops'.

He was in the back, sucking on a Corona. Looking like a rat who'd been turned inside out and then drowned.

He said 'Finn, looking good bro'.

I asked 'You meet me at a fooking cop hangout?'

'Chill buddy, take a load off, cop bar, safest joint in the Five Boroughs'.

A waitress came, pretty wee thing. I ordered a Jameson, Bud back. Sheil's said 'Get me one of those babe, he's paying'.

Oh, his winning fooking ways. I asked 'You get it?'

A new passport, driving licence, library card, the works. Primarily a new name.

He looked round, furtive then, passed over a slim package. I took out a fat envelope from my jacket, pushed it across the table. Now, crunch time, I said 'Wee bonus for your trouble'.

He peeked inside, said 'Ah, you're a grand man'.

Displaying once were teeth, once were off white. Tipped his forelock.

I drained my boilermaker, stood, then as if a thought suddenly hit me, said 'Next few days, you need to touch base, I'm at The Chelsea Hotel, then I'm in the wind'.

I swear to God, he sang, yeah, and very badly, like this '... writing sad eyed lady of the lowlands for you'.

Ruined it by adding 'Dylan'.

No freaking clue.

I was moving, said 'I'm more your Rory Gallagher kind of guy, check out the track Philly'.

The only truth I told.

I figured I'd bought meself about two weeks grace.

Then Mexico or bust.

It was arranged I'd join a batch of German tourists in Houston, to make the coach trip into Mexico.

Had my flight to Houston, my ticket for the coach.

Until then, all I had to do, was stay alive.

Four nights in, I got back late, had caught a late movie and a late dinner, both forgettable. I'd had a few brews, was feeling a nice buzz. The hotel lobby was quiet, bathed in a warm amber light, muted.

Nice.

In the corner of the lobby, were two leather chairs, coffee table. Hadn't noticed the figure until I heard 'Mr Finnerty'.

She was dressed in a short black dress, tight black t-shirt, killer heels kicked to the side of the chair. Her long blonde hair, cascading down to her shoulders, catching the amber light. A vision.

I asked, trying to catch the gulp in my throat 'Late hours?'

'Lame, right?'

A bottle of Black Bush on the table. Dented but still three quarters full. She said 'A relative died and the Irish, they take a drink, yeah?'

Same old tired fooking clichés, I added my bit, said 'Or, the relative recovers, a drink'.

Laugh, if brief.

She bent over, seeking a second glass, allowing me a full jail term appraisal. She asked 'Join me?'

'Sure'.

... and so Dear Reader, I married her.

Kidding.

Jesus.

We were at it like rabbits within two drinks, howling at some dark moon.

And thus, fookit, I lost focus.

For the next week.

I was mesmerised, was I in love, Jesus, I don't know, I was on torrid heat.

Then, time to skip time.

My flight to Houston was that day, at noon. I got out on the roof, retrieved the stash. I'd left my gun on the pillow, would have to take it apart, flush it. Homeland Security were top of their game.

I was thinking 'Going to miss her'.

Got back inside.

She was sitting on the bed, my gun held loosely in her right hand, like an afterthought.

Dressed in white jeans, faded denim shirt, bare feet.

She asked 'Running out on me lover?'

Jesus wept, she looked irresistible.

I smiled, went 'You jerking my chain sweetheart? Come on, we have a great thing going, I'll be back in a week and what do you say, we grab some days in the Caymans? Sound like a plan?'

She gave the briefest smile, said 'I have a plan'.

Shot me in the gut. Oh Christ, they're right, it hurts like a son-of-a-bitch. She leaned over me, the tattoo over her eye looming clear.

Whispered 'You arrived in the very nick of time, the hotel is fucked, debts like a cheap Enron'.

Ball breaker huh?

She stood in front of the mirror, ran her lovely hand through that glorious hair, asked 'A cut maybe, you think?'

Then hefted my case of cash, stopped, asked 'Ohio, this time of year, nice?'

And was gone.

I'd wrapped my hands around my stomach, trying to hold my entails in, blood seeping then gushing through my fingers.

All I could see was the mark above her eyes, muttered 'Definitely

          … sure

       … an

         … angel.

You think?

HELLKITE

Geraldine Mills

Slither of dark under the base of the door sucked out any remnant of light around Doyle's fingers that he stretched out in front of him. He knelt there in the cubbyhole, his knees roaring pain, his heels digging into his arse, his back curved and scourged as if a cat-o-nine-tails was being flailed across it. He lifted up one knee, to give it some ease, cradled it in his palm, until the other one caved in from the strain. So he swopped knees, cradled that one too. How many hours now, his watch sitting on the bathroom window of his flat where he had placed it that morning while he had shaved before meeting her?

He envied it, the night, its ability to come and go as it pleased. Nothing to stop it, no one to tell it where it could or couldn't go as the rain continued to mallet down outside. He could hear it on the windowsill, somewhere on the landing just above his head, that is, if he had his bearings right.

He tried again to shift his body, even the tiniest bit, to get some little ease from the cramps searing down his legs. His feet were bent back against the floor, like the beak of a flamingo grazing algae from the lakeshore. He concentrated on his toes, from the big to the little, mindful of each one as he tried to wiggle them. That set up a chain of pins and needles which finally came to an orgasm of relief. Such gratitude. No sooner had they waned but they started up again. He wouldn't give up, he just wouldn't.

He needed to piss.

It didn't take long for the dark to fill the tiny space he was locked into. He lifted himself from his hunkers and stretched out his hands, inching them forward for the Braille of the fuse box in front of him. He could play a little memory game with himself. How many switches? What was written on them? Get them in the right order: Lights: Upstairs. Downstairs. Cooker. Sockets. All turned down to the ON position, as if electricity was flowing into rooms beyond his reach, lighting them up, occasional lamps illuminating occasional tables at the arms of cosy chairs, a pan searing meat on a halogen ring, the American fridge humming a sinful tune to itself about all the food it held in the cave of its shelves. He flicked all the switches up again into the OFF position. Once more again to ON. It's what she asked him to do, wasn't it? To make sure that the power was coming through when she had known bloody well that there was nothing there to come through.

He shouted out her name, 'Cora, Cora'. But no sound came travelling back. The bitch. Put the 'b' of that in the belly of her name and it was what she was, a snake swaying to its own pernicious music. Stupidly, Doyle had become so distracted by it that it gave her the moment to strike. She had the key turned before he could say, 'Fuck you, Cora'.

No elbow room, cats and swinging no joke, flies an afterthought of dust, rat droppings. He could hear her car pull away, changing gear before she drove out into silence. Whatever way he tried to manoeuvre his limbs, there wasn't enough leverage to get a swing at the door. Even if he could he had heard her pushing something against it. An off-cut of scaffolding, left behind when the builders scarpered, now wedged it tight. A door that he could smash into tinder wood if he was in the right space had left him as helpless as a pigmy shrew when it came down to it.

He tried to stretch, but it only made things worse, pain jumping behind his scull, bringing tears. It reminded him of the time he was in hospital as a child, he was seven, in isolation with the whites of his eyes all yellow and getting sick on the syrupy cherry medicine they forced him to take. There was another boy in a cubicle in the far corner, the curtains permanently curled around his bed. The doctors would come and do something and the boy would cry out. Doyle had imagined them pushing the boy into a corner and forcing his neck down to his knees. He had no idea why he should think that but that's how he felt it must have been. Nothing else would have made his cry carry such agony like that. He cried out himself now for he didn't know which muscle ached more, the one that he could move or the one that he couldn't.

He called again. 'Is there anyone there?' His voice louder and louder in the dark. He stretched out his elbow to connect with the door. Pound it, someone might hear. He tried but there was only a wimp of a thud that fled through the keyhole rusting in the damp.

How long was she going to leave him like this, before her fit of pique shrivelled away? How long was a piece of string? He laughed, a sounding madness in the enclosed space. It was alien to him, hearing his own laughter tumble back against his chest with no one to hear it. Was it any better that he couldn't see the moon keeping itself to itself, flutter of leaves blown in through the broken glass of the windows? Somewhere outside a piece of metal sheeting had come loose and flapped; back and over, back and over as hailstones smashed against it. Thumping him with its frolics. Laughing in the dark, the black humour of that.

'Cora!'

For their children's sake, they had been civil to one another at the parent teachers' meeting, the Wednesday before. They even managed a united smile to hear that Beth was a high achiever whereas Aaron preferred to sit back and watch everyone else work.

While they were waiting to pay over their yearly contribution, Cora had asked him if he would take the children for the weekend; she had the chance to fly to New York with Richard. Doyle didn't want to argue with her so he said nothing for a few minutes, searching around for the words. In all the three years since he became a failed husband how many times would he have been ecstatic to have had his son and daughter for an extra weekend? Having long since accepted that it was never going to happen he had made plans for the coming one. If there was any way to change it he would, but he couldn't, so he explained about someone new in his life now, flights booked, yes, to see Prague. Ellen, her name was Ellen. Maybe another time?

He was relieved how Cora took it. Said she understood; it was short notice after all. Sure she'd get him again.

As they walked across the schoolyard, she had told him about the batch of houses that Richard had bought, dirt cheap, auctioned off because of the state of them. She might have some work for him if he played his cards right. Hanging doors, skirting boards, that sort of thing. Odd jobs. The way she said it, said it all. He would love to have told her to stuff it where raspberries don't grow but beggars and choosers and all that.

Anyway, it was better to keep on her good side, especially after turning her down on the New York business. Last time he tried to stand up to her she decided he could only have one of his children for the designated weekend. She juggled the names in front of him as if it were a choice of beef or salmon, red or white. Aaron or Beth. Beth or Aaron. Oh, she knew what she was doing, all right. There was no way he could do that, pick one over the other. He had always sworn to them that he loved them equally. So he took the only way out he could. He told them he was busy that weekend. They held it against him and cried that his word was not his bond as he had taught them. It was weeks before he got back on an even footing with them again.

'Fine', he had said as she stepped into her car. 'No harm in having a look'. They agreed a time. She said she would pick him up.

They had driven out through the city, onto the motorway. Traffic rumbling to and fro, cars driving to early shifts or leaving behind the late ones, lights on, a claxon of lorries hitting manhole covers on the side of the road. A crow, almost beautiful in its blackness on a bare tree, stretched its corvine wings. It had more colour than the dingy grey all around them, windscreen wipers battling with the rain.

They had turned off at Lucan. She had stopped at a garage for coffee, skinny lattés which she knew he hated, that she slipped into the holders on the dashboard. Letting them cool down, letting the milky scent fill in all around him. Barely taking her foot of the accelerator, she veered onto a secondary road, all pit and potholed. His teeth rattled as she drove right into a crater and gave her tyres an almighty wallop. What did she expect driving like that?

They had pulled into the estate. Richard's new venture. They were well suited: ex-wife and dickhead, his bluster to her breeze. All spit and no polish. Big-bling-things. The bigger the better. The estate was a cliché of all that was bad about the bust. Roads hadn't been surfaced, there were no foot paths. Lakes of water languished in gardens and between paths. For every standing house there were ten that were in ruins, joists and beams curved by the rain into currach ribs. Ghosts leaned out of broken windowpanes of any window unlucky enough to have been glazed. The house she wanted to show him had its porch facing away from the road, its driveway sloping towards the door. Rivulets ran down and lodged in a puddle before the step.

'First job needs doing is that drain, there', he said, just to show he was on the ball. 'Could cause you trouble down the line if the climate keeps changing as it's supposed to?'

'Climate change, bollocks'.

He had looked at her then, the cruel lines etched each side of her mouth. How did he ever marry her? If it wasn't for his children, he would never darken her life again. She had taken so much as it was. He had woken up one morning to discover that he had walked up the aisle that fateful day with his own house, said 'I do' and by the time he turned to walk back down again he had given half of it away.

That stung as much as the ball of fire-pain now stoking his spine from the permanent curve of his neck. He could no longer tell where his legs were on the ground, he could no longer feel them. Phantom legs as if they had been amputated from the knees down but still left with the memory of where they were. He tried to move them side to side to keep the blood flowing but there was no room at all to sweeten even one nano-second of relief.

The mahogany veneer on the front door had peeled away, exposing the white PVC underneath. Opening it they had met a flurry of panic. Tails disappeared into holes in the plasterboard. A dank harvest of fungi, striped and gilled, dropped spores onto bare cement, exposed wires hung from the ceiling. The coffee was beginning to repeat on him.

Once Cora got over her fit of pique, came back, laughing at her little prank and let him out of the cubbyhole, he was going straight to the gym. It would mean a bit more work, more weights but he would practise. He would build up muscles until there were thick and gnarled as tree trunks. Then he would swim the Amazon, powerful in the rush of it, each splash of his arm drawing attention to himself as the killers all around him smelled meat. Dodging the bull sharks, piranhas, malicious logs of crocodiles floating on the surface, while he plundered through the water, evading the giant catfish that could swallow a child whole and come back for his brother. What he wouldn't give for a catfish now, gladly hand her over to it, given half the chance.

Another wave of anger hit but there was nowhere for it to go. Sounds. He shouted out: 'I'm in here'. He listened but there was no response to his call. Only a shuffling like an old man across the floor somewhere outside the cubbyhole, Badger? The house was probably built on the animal's path through fields that they had traversed all their lives, making this their own corridor to wherever they wanted to go until it was swiped from them by the diggers. Well they had the last laugh, didn't they? Repossessing what was truly theirs.

Then a skitter, something scraping at the bottom of the door. It started to gnaw at the wood, tiny incisors eating into it. Not a rat, no, not a rat. A rat would have been able to squeeze in through the tiniest of spaces under the door.

The creature scratched away for a while, trying its best to get at him. He could smell it, the vulpine stench of it, reek of damp pelt and viscera. It must have been hungry. It stretched in a paw and tried to dig its claws into the indigo of his jeans. Doyle put his hand down and grasped it. The animal gave out a squeal as it was clenched in the trap of Doyle's grip. It was a vicious little bastard and pushed the other paw which it hooked into the skin of his hand. Doyle screeched back at it. 'Ahhh', and the animal finally scampered.

He needed more than ever to piss.

Cora had never wanted him. In all their seven years of marriage she was only biding her time. She was the one who had walked out after all. Gone off with dickhead in his big vulgar jeep and bull bars. What Doyle failed to understand was that even though she had it all, she just couldn't bear to see him find a little bit of happiness. The way she flattened her neck when she moved her head back was like the poisonous serpent. It wasn't enough that she squirted her venom in his eyes pretending to be charmed, she had to have everything.

Cora.

Bitch.

Cobra.

How she got him into the small cubbyhole under the stairs was worse than the act itself, the shame of falling for it. All she wanted him to do, she had said, was to trip the switch on the meter box in the tiny space so she could check the lights on each floor. Asking him to crawl in to check it, citing her tight skirt and fear of spiders. Him hunkered there, on his knees like a penitent, shouting out to ask which lever it was. She, slamming the door shut. Reinforcing it.

And what would Ellen think when the voice announced the last boarding over the whole fucking airport and he hadn't shown? People bundling themselves into clothes to keep their luggage limit intact while she stood there, her faithful-as-a-small-dog wheelie case to heel as she scanned above chatting heads to see if she could spot him hurrying towards her. Relief brightening her face. He would never ask for another thing, if he could see that relief on her face.

These were pits of houses, ghosts roaming around, going nowhere but in under the stairs. What did Richard think he could do with them? Pigs in pokes. The rain falling down. Why he bought this heap of junk was anybody's guess. A late developer, dickhead described himself to Doyle, with a laugh, when Cora introduced them, saying his name all rolling and simpering. Doyle wouldn't have taken Richard for an eejit. Late developer or no he wouldn't have invested in this heap of shit. And if that was the case then … She wouldn't have? Would she? Lured him there with the promise of the extra few bob just because she could?

His head nodded and his body gave an exhausted jerk. He could only have dropped off for a few minutes. He woke frantically. His trousers were soaked. He had pissed in his pants. But if he had, he was up to his knees in it. He could feel it soaking through the denim, his runners, in his socks. He lifted his feet as much as he could manage. He slapped his toes onto the ground. A splash. He did it again. Then he remembered what she had said. Flood plain. The blocked drain outside the door, swollen river and rain promised for days to come.

De Noir Au Noiret

Des Kenny

The bar of the Sacre Coeur Hotel was heaving. Galway had just beaten Mayo in the Connaught Semi Final up in the newly revamped Pearse Stadium and, after last year's bitter defeat in the Final, the Galway supporters were celebrating with a vengeance.

'We beat the shite out of them!'

'Donnellan skinned them alive!'

'We're on the way to Croker!'

With the hoarse yells came the orders for drink.

'Four pints of Stout, a glass of Lager, two gins and tonic, one vodka and white, a hot whiskey without the cloves and a Coke for the young one'.

The two barmen, PJ and Eoin were going like the hammers behind the counter, the sweat pouring out of them. As PJ started to fill the last order, he spotted Don in his usual corner, grinned openly and shouted: 'just like the good old days'.

In the middle of all this organised mayhem, Big Jim, the Dublin Truckie, stood tall. He was soaking up every minute of it. Yesterday a Treble had come good and Arsenal had beaten Man U 3–2 in Old Trafford. And then today Dublin had beaten arch rivals Meath and were now in the Leinster Final. To cap it all, the Queen was sitting beside him, majestic, beautiful and smiling. Man! If this was Heaven, he might become a Holy Joe!

From his imperial position, Big Jim's eyes swivelled the bar and fell on Don. As always there was a book on the counter in front of him. A sound guy, even if his head was always stuck in a book. Jaysus, he even got Big Jim to read one once. The Queen couldn't believe he'd actually finished it. What's more he'd enjoyed it. All about Dublin! The second one he gave him was much tougher. Couldn't handle it!

Don't know the guy he is with though. Never seen him before! That doesn't stop our Don. Talk for Ireland he would! Look at the hands going all over the place. Must be talking French!

On his way out to the toilet and for a smoke, Big Jim caught Don's eye who responded with an enthusiastic wave. As he began to go towards the Gents, he spotted Pete the chef in the kitchen, a huge side of beef on the table in front of him, a massive carving knife in his hands. Mighty, he thought, he's making the sandwiches to be handed around later on. Just what the doctor ordered after the feed of porter! There's no doubt about it, you never left the Sac either thirsty or hungry.

Big Jim had guessed right. Don was speaking French. He had met his companion at the match and, having fallen into conversation with him, had suggested they continue the conversation over a drink. He was thoroughly enjoying himself. After a three-year stint as a student in Paris, he relished every opportunity to speak the lingo.

As he watched Big Jim leave the room, Don realised yet again just how lucky and privileged he had been. Born and reared in Salthill to wonderful parents, a house full of love and laughter, a wonderful upbringing and education, finishing up with a three-year scholarship to the Sorbonne. Now fluent in French, he delighted in the sense of power he got anytime he had the opportunity to use it in Galway, especially when there were friends about him that didn't understand a word he was saying.

Not that the path to this fluency had been all a bed of roses. It hadn't! Especially at the beginning, learning it *as Gaeilge* with that big bollix of a French teacher and that smaller bollix Jean Noiret, the main character and personal daily nightmare in that Irish language French text book, *Nua*fucking*chúrsa Fraincíse Cuid a h-Aon agus Cuid a Dó: Jean Noiret Dans La Foret, Jean Noiret et Le Tour De France,* lessons not properly learnt, or more likely forgotten through fear, the slow movement of the black soutane, the swish of the black leather viciously brought down on the quivering hand, black pain, black tears, black humiliation.

Day after day, night after night for three years, always number four on the list, always the same three before Don, always six slogs each, twelve if the hangover was bad, until one day, one glorious day, the other three having being dealt with in the usual way, Don stood before the teacher and missed two of the first three questions. Just one more, he said, but Don got thick or maybe it was out of fear it was and answered question after question after fucking question and he got madder and madder and madder until the bell went and he left the room in a white fury forgetting to give any homework. The class cheered and Don sat down mentally and physically exhausted but with a warm wave of triumph growing inside him. 'I got him, I got the bollix', and from then on he never asked Don another question. Don got over it, conquered the language, but had never forgotten the pain or the tears or the dark black humiliation.

Don smiled, pain, tears, humiliation, yerra what am I talking about! 'Twas nothing to what hundreds of thousands went through! Look at Big Jim. The horror stories he had told Don. An alcoholic violent father that beat the crap out of his mother and when he was finished with her laid into the kids. More often than not, no food on the table, no heat in the house! School was another nightmare. No leather there, but fists, sticks, or boots instead, anything the psycho teachers could lay their hands on. It was extraordinary how Big Jim pulled himself out of it. He was a good guy to know, even if a little volatile. Decent with it too! That time he was trucking to France he brought back several crates of wine at the right price which were much appreciated. But when he started to describe his life as a kid you could see the shutters coming down and the pain darken his eyes.

Don shivered involuntarily and, trying to shake of these dark thoughts, renewed with vigour the conversation with his Gallic companion.

The early euphoria of the crowd in the bar had dissipated somewhat. Conscious of the breathalyser those with cars had left for home. A small drunken group in the corner were loudly murdering 'The West's Awake', while the more serious fans were debating the chances of Galway going all the way and bringing Sam over the Shannon in September.

Still in high spirits, Big Jim came back into the bar. At the door, he stopped, suddenly sensing something uneasy in the air, a scent, a strange, sweet, smothering smell that put him on edge. He stood still for a moment trying to identify it, but then dismissed the sensation as bullshit; he joined the Queen full and ready to continue the party. Hearing the serious fans discussing Galway's chances of winning the All Ireland, he told them they didn't have a hope in hell the way the Dubs were playing and soon found himself in the middle of an energetic but friendly slagging match.

Turning to order another drink, he was surprised to find Don at his shoulder.

'Was it just outside Amiens it happened?'

Big Jim froze, the nightmare of his last trip to France coming vividly back to him. Three cops suddenly surrounding him, just as he was leaving a café. They bundled him into a van, never knew why. Took him to a field and beat the crap out of him. Back into the van again and into the barracks! Thrown into a cell and stripped arse naked. Practically raped him! He never knew such pain in all his life. They threw him out the following morning, not a mark on him.

The hand they had stood on started to throb with pain at the memory. He flexed it and the anger boiled, enveloping him like a wet blanket.

'I think the guy I am talking to is one of them', Don continued. 'He told me that he and two of his mates had done over an Irish guy outside Amiens, that you looked like him and that maybe now he'd get a chance to finish the job'.

The smell, the smell he got coming at the door, the stinking shit the French call aftershave, that was it. He remembered one of them leaning over him breathing down his neck. Big Jim started to shake, his face alive with a boiling anger.

'I'll kill him! I'll fucking kill the bastard!'

'Listen', says Don, 'You've had a skinful and he hasn't. He's as fit as a fiddle and knows how to handle himself. He'd make mince meat of ye. The best thing you could do right now is to leave quietly'.

Big Jim looked around. PJ the barman already had the Queen on the move. Smiling sweetly, she took his arm and quietly, neatly, without looking left or right they left the bar.

The following morning the early jogger recoiled in horror as he came to the end of the Golf Links. On the rocks there was a naked corpse, a massive carving knife pinning a placard to his chest with the legend 'The name is Noiret, Jean Fucking Noiret'.

A TELL-TALE, HOT MILK AND OTHER RELEVANT THINGS

Aoife Casby

Keith lives alone.

Never hung posters on the wall himself, though he would stare at the blankness and could imagine things squared up there but only ever things he has seen in other people's gaffs, not like something that he could have made up himself like that picture with those creamy-blurred stars or that silhouetted figure with the beret. Easy. One long Thursday he bought Blu-Tack, enjoyed the sinewy feel of it when he rolled it between his thumb and middle finger; then put a few lumps balanced on the wall where pictures could be. He was satisfied with that.

Lives with no-one. Quite remote from any people, like when he was a small boy and those ghost see-through parents of his just floating invisible enough for him to be alone. There is a little flaw in his solitude. When he is alone with his thoughts he makes a madness with all sorts of people, even strangers, and this makes him want to do bad things in a way he can't explain, like break into houses or take that woman's bag or scratch those expensive-looking cars in the upstairs car park on Merchants Road where any fucker could just go walking in if he looked like he had a purpose. Keith could do that. He's good at it.

Keith's work means that he spends a lot of time walking the grey carpet of the open plan office appearing to be busy. He watches the others; leans against dreary cabinets feeling the stretched muscles high up his thigh; watches these people, listens to their pathetic language, laughs at what they called happiness: nice dinners, school plays and two weeks in the sun.

He observes them behind their half-partitions, sipping coffee like half-people and the way they whisper and make foolish half-expressions with their foreheads and eyebrows about how one of the directors had his car vandalized in the hotel carpark on Station Road and *isn't it just awful this random vandal thing*. He smiles and says the fucker probably deserved it, who knows what goes on behind closed doors and who was behind the closed door in the hotel then and they laugh and say *you know you're probably right*. Keith pities them. Easy to fool people with a bit of intelligence and saying out loud what they're thinking themselves.

Keith met Jasmine in the kitchen of the staff room that smelled of smoke from the ignorant bastards who tried to blow their stinking fumes out the window. Keith shut it against the cold, the black hairs on his arm visible when he stretched. She murmured approval. He asked her if she'd like a cup of tea and she had four sugars she stirred in so much they had a dizziness attached.

Time passed.

They had their first kiss. (On Quay Street)

They had their first dinner. (Near Spanish Arch)

They had the first time they made love. (Somewhere in Corrib Park)

He liked the way she didn't care and the way that a smile didn't suit her.

There were other things too. He liked that she wasn't able to name his faults. That she couldn't see his danger. And she smelled of a woman that didn't remind him of old ladies and warm piss. Even better, doing it with her was easy. She never complained and wasn't like one of them leggy bitches with the bottle tan. He just did what he wanted. Sometimes he was real attentive but it kind of disgusted him to see her smile so he didn't do it too often. Keith had no hobbies. He liked to think that he didn't have to distract himself from himself by some expensive diversion.

He could tell her things that he didn't mean. She believed in fate. She didn't care if he meant the things he said or not. He never asked himself if there was anything he didn't know about her. He thought he could see it all.

More time passed.

'Why do things always happen at night-time?' she says half-watching Sky News and eating a salad out of one of those plastic containers. She looks real innocent there on the couch making chewy noises and curled under herself.

'What things?' he says.

'Like assaults and murders and robberies and that sort of thing'.

'Safety in the dark'.

'Safety?'

'Yeah'.

'Safety for who?'

'You know'. And he starts thinking about it. No reason why but he felt that she might be scared of the dark when she was on her own, and this led to another thought, and he got to thinking, and one thing led to another and well … Keith thought that you knew somebody by the little incidents that you visualise have happened to them. That little story they tell you and it had no real signs of being anything until you take it and make it something in your head, like, to know a layer of the person, and in your head this, this … thing, the incident, is a defining moment for the other person and you are, oh, so absolutely sure that you understand the meaning, the cause of how the person is how they are. It was easy. Keith thought that Jasmine was afraid of the dark … because when she was a teenager Jasmine scalded her arm. She was left alone in the house because she had refused to go in the car with her family somewhere in Mayo. Boiling milk for hot chocolate, she tripped against the handle and didn't know what to do and the pain made trouble, trouble, trouble and the heat stuck to her and she fainted and when she woke up it was dark and she had a bruise and blisters and pain, pain, pain and it was dark and she was on the floor and it was dark and … burned by milk and her mother said *this is what happens when you try to do things on your own and don't ask for help*. Keith remembered that she said it was dark. This wasn't important to Jasmine.

The first time that Jasmine had come to Keith's flat she had felt herself being subjected to its clean, feeling like the walls were examining her and had big loud voices. It was a while before she understood that the space was barren and by then she wanted to fill it with her and him. He told her once that her abhorring emptiness was the same as someone being afraid of darkness or at least that's what she heard. Jasmine thought that she would do something nice for him so she went out and got two posters. While he was in the bath she put them up using the pieces of Blu-Tack he had carefully stuck to the wall. She stood back and admired them and admired the way that they changed the voices in the walls and rehearsed what she would say to Keith when he came out dripping. He didn't say anything. He simply stood and stared at the blown up black and white photo and the bright Kandinsky blocks and she knew she had to take them down.

Keith had never hurt a person. It really hadn't occurred to him. He liked to look at Jasmine across a room or over a table in a pub and see her with other people and try to imagine the girl she was when she made her first holy communion. He always saw her outside the cathedral, near the canal. All dressed up in white and nervous and trying to remember the order of walking and praying and that first small feeling of being a woman with the white gloves and the pearly-white bag. He liked to see her like that.

'Have you ever been so mad that you wanted to hurt someone?'

She thought about it. 'How do you mean?'

'You know – if you had a gun and you were so mad that you'd like to blast a hole in someone'.

He could see her trying to invoke the image, fighting with it, trawling through movies she had seen to get the picture.

'I don't think so. Not that mad'. It didn't matter to her one way or the other. Life is there and then it is gone and you get used to it. Like when she saw the man on the train … well a man throw himself in front of a train. People vomited. The man's last living movement was a flash in the side of her eye where you know what is happening the instant it happens but you deny it and look to others for confirmation of the denial. She thinks about this often and about how she never saw the man's face, as if by seeing his eyes she'd have gleaned something, seen what despair looks like. She decided *how fragile we are*. It was deep in her. It didn't matter. So she lived from day to day … went to churches to look at other people to see if she could understand what they were trying to believe in.

'Aren't you interested in how it might feel to do that kind of easy damage to someone?' and he had this tone in his voice that made it sound like a reasonable thing to be talking about. She looked at him and her look advised that she knew more than she expressed. He didn't see it.

On days when she was quiet the thought that she had a shadow intrigued her. Or sometimes it would make her laugh, the idea that she had this darkness following her around, always there, ready to spring out. The shadow was alive in the dark, but she didn't know where it went.

Jasmine has grey eyes, her ears have gold rings hanging like excuses, her hair is dark brown when wet, her nails are neat. Her lower lip thrusts forward gently and is always moist and of a pink colour that has blue in front of it and red behind it – pushy pink, pale cherry and slightly purple. Even with such interesting lips her smile is not nice. Her jaw from ear to chin is shapely and graceful. Makes subtle shadows in her cheeks and neck. She covers these shadows with a scarf and blusher. Up close her cheeks are feather veined. Thin skin broken. From a friendly, but not too close, distance of a few feet, she glows.

The seventeenth time that Jasmine stayed over with Keith was an unsettled stormy night. She liked the patterns on his bed-clothes. There was a power cut. They lay in darkness in the bed.

'Darkness is just shade. An absence of light. Everything is the same', Keith said.

'No it isn't. It isn't like that at all. It makes everything different'.

'What does that mean?'

And Jasmine is thinking, he doesn't know, he doesn't know that the darkness could be filled with horror and terror and blots on purity or that the darkness could be devoted to destruction and shadow or that the darkness could be so so warm and safe.

Keith started to leave the bed.

'Oh stay here', she said and touched his arm with a little pressure so he could imagine the red marks that her sure fingers left. He didn't respond to her intimate stroking, didn't need to share fundamentals with her.

'We could open the curtains and let the storm light in', she said.

'No. It will let out the heat'.

Keith felt that he saw a fear bloom in her. This excited him. He thought she was scared. Fucking women he thought. They need men like me. He left the warm bed to go get a torch or a candle. She heard him out there in the roaring silence and knew that he thought he was scaring her. The trying scrape of the duvet cover between her teeth stopped her laugh.

She lay silent. Thinking. Eyes waiting for light.

It was like the darkness had a morality.

He fancied he heard the wind whimper (a low complaining noise) and call his name (Kee-e-eeth) and that the sound of a voice in that silence was unsafe and he waited – feeling the cold and hearing the wind and imagining it was her whimpering, until the cold on his nose was too much and he went back into the bedroom. She was lying there singing softly. He felt her smile in the dark.

Once she and Keith talked about guilt and where it came from and how you'd know it. Guilt, that sudden jolt of emotion for the person you are wronging. A kind of sad loneliness for their lack of knowledge, the feeling that they are benumbed like the cold has got into their brains and anaesthetized the part that would let them see through you, see your guilt because you think that it is very clear. He knew. But it really was only still an idea with him that he get her to do something bad.

He talked to her about death. And hurt.

'Why are you talking about these things?'

'Because things like that are interesting. It's something we read about, see, talk about every day but we never *talk* about it, why so you think that is?'

Jasmine asked could she move in. Again.

Thursday night. They went for a drink on Shop Street. She asked could she move in over a pint. Waited to see what he'd say. It made him see things differently. They had dead conversation after that, then stopped for chips. Going home, back to his. Late. Beery. The gang of drunken lads. Silly taunts about what they'd do to Jasmine. If he was a real man this is what he should do to her.

'Which one of us would you like', they slurred.

Menacing. Keith and Jasmine stopped at Wolfe Tone Bridge, Fr Griffin Road. To let the boys pass and to stay in brightness.

'Assholes'.

'Keith. They'll hear you'.

'Assholes'.

'Fuck you', she said to him.

The boys were shouting on the far side of the water now. Keith didn't want to go home to the place that she thought would be hers soon. To the place she had tried to defile with posters.

'Are you scared?' he asked.

'Well it's not my idea of a good time but they're more drunk than scary'.

'Not nice'.

'No'.

'In fact, something should be done about them'.

'You think?'

'Yeah'.

'Like what?'

'I dunno. Kick the fuckers to death. I dunno. Something'.

He watched a young man teeter totter along the edge of the water by the Spanish Arch. He looked at Jasmine sideways, the thought just creeping up on him.

'Come on', and he grabbed her gloved hand.

'Where?'

They re-crossed the bridge. The young man weaved and tacked along the water's edge.

'Down by the water', Keith said.

'He's one of them', he whispered.

'One of who?'

'One of the gang that were harassing us'.

'I'd hardly call it harassing'.

'Sssssshhhhh'.

'Keith, he's not one of them. Are you looking for trouble?'

'No. No. Come on'.

She followed him. They got closer to the oblivious boy.

'Push him in', Keith whispered.

'You're crazy!'

'I mean it. Push him in'.

No I won't', she said wearily and he whispers to her, she tries to walk away, he tells her he loves her and his hot breath old and warm on her neck and the waft of whiskey breath, and how can you get caught, sure look around, everyone tucked up in bed or drunk, see them all over drunk, and he'll go home and be sick and drown in his vomit, oh Keith shut up, I'm serious he will or he'll beat someone or do something to hurt someone and he'll be better off and many other people too if we do this now.

'You don't know him' but I know his type, you've seen them, we read about them and it really doesn't matter does it, no-one can do anything, there is nothing to be ashamed of and he's bad or else he wouldn't be there, look staggering insensible, and there was disgust, real disgust, and he held her tight, and she said I want to go home to your place. And she was exasperated at his desperation and she looked at the young man and she didn't feel anything for him or for who might be at home waiting, and he said but it's dark and we'll go soon, let's just talk and they leaned over the bridge and watched the man stagger and fall and pick himself up, and she could imagine him licking snot from his face. Do you really think it would be bad? he said. Who has the right to tell us it's bad, yeah, who, and his voice was insistent and Jasmine heard his words and knew he didn't understand, she knew he didn't see, and he said we always have the right to decide and held her hand tight in his pocket warm and close, and all about the darkness glowed, and he tugged her gently, and they walked towards the man, and Keith didn't talk anymore, and she sang a little and the man didn't see her or see him because he was busy, and Keith looked at her, and she could feel his hand, and he said I love you because he couldn't think of anything else to say, and breathing rough, easy, easy, easy, and there was bile in his throat and a tremble in his bladder, and Keith was like he was scalded from his ideas, but suddenly quicker than his thoughts, faster than his fear, she moved hot and invisible, wasn't it, wasn't it, and he doesn't know if she tripped or did it herself, but the man fell, he fell real quiet into the river and there was no extra sound of water, he fell in while he was peeing into the darkness and no extra plop or shout and he never reappeared, never came into sight above the roar again, and Keith's hand was wet in hers and she's thinking about all that darkness, and about his shadow, and if it fell in before or after him, and Keith ran to get the buoy, the ring, and he threw it, and he said oh jesus, oh jesus, oh jesus, what the fuck, oh jesus, oh jesus, and Jasmine said, 'well it is a burial of sorts isn't it'.

Keith said nothing.

Jasmine said 'what do you think happens to shadows in the dark?'

Keith said nothing.

STAND BY

Alan Caden

On Saturday night, I am thinking about 2002 when the bed starts to shake. I am thinking maybe it is an earthquake. I have never heard of earthquakes here. Then I realise it is Hassan in the bottom bunk, masturbating. Again. I hit the frame of the bed.

'Hey, Saddam! Use the showers like everyone else!'

He doesn't skip a beat, just extends his free hand and raises his middle finger.

'Fuck you, black bastard'. That is all he ever says to me. At the beginning it made me angry, but now I just laugh. He turns up the music on his headphones and keeps going.

Most Saturday nights I used to rent Bolo's taxi. But now his brother-in-law is here and Bolo only gives me Mondays or Tuesdays. It's not really worth it, they won't let me back into the hostel until 8am. So I have to sit at the taxi rank in Eyre Square or Bridge Street, long after everyone else is gone home. Sometimes one of the 'Guaranteed Irish' cabs is there. They are always talking the shit to me. They say I skip the queue, I steal the fare. But they never say I don't look like the photo. Even Bolo doesn't look like the photo.

I can't go back to sleep so I try to steady the frame. I think about Hassan and his country, where his family is and what he did over there. I think it is all sand. Sand, and people who explode themselves when they get angry. Hassan is an asshole, but there are different degrees of asshole.

It is a long time before the shaking stops. Maybe Hassan is practising in case he meets a woman. This can be a problem, you know, if it has been a long time. We all do it. Afterwards he starts snoring and I play games on my phone until the morning. In my dorm I have the highest score at Snake.

Breakfast on Sundays is always fried egg, fried bacon which is called rashers, and fried sausages. If pigs could lay eggs, Irish people would be happy. The Moslems complain but Breda just shrugs her shoulders and gives them an extra egg.

'Sunny side up?' she asks.

Breda calls this 'messing'.

I sit with some of the Africans at the table beside the window that is salty from the sea and the rain and the wind. Always rain and wind. Bolo is eating Mohammed's fry.

'Chelsea will win', he munches. 'Not because of the money. Or the Russian. Look at the players. Drogba, Essien, Kalou, Malouda. Strong Africans'.

'Malouda is French', I say.

'Yeah', he laughs. 'Same like you are Irish'.

Bolo is from Zaire, like me, or Congo, or Congo-Brazzaville, or Democratic Republic of Congo. We're not sure. It has been a long time.

'So where were you born?' the refugee woman asked me again last week.

'In a hospital', she smiled. 'In Kalima'. There are two Kalimas, close to each other.

'In ...?'

'Zaire. I mean, Congo. DRC'.

'Which will I put down? I mean, which was it when you were born?'

'I don't know. Any'. I started to get angry.

'Ok', she paused. Irish people always pause before they speak. Like they have a big secret they don't want to tell. Like they know something you don't. 'And then you moved during the civil war, is that right?'

'Which one?' I asked.

'In 2002 to 2003'.

'This was not really a war'.

'Well, then, during the troubles'. She has started to use this word.

The Irish girl who works in the shop beside the hostel where I buy my cigarettes when Andrei doesn't have any, she told me what this word 'the Troubles' means. Very bad. Three thousand people dead in thirty years.

'You were very lucky there was not Africans in the IRA or the British Army', I said to her. 'We can do three thousand a day, no problems! We don't even need guns!'

This was 'messing'. She didn't laugh. Now when I come in to the shop, she always pretends to be talking on the phone to someone.

At breakfast, Ivan, a ten-year-old Moldovan boy, is trying to sell us magazines. They are the ones from the top shelf, with the prostitutes, so I don't know how he stole them because he is only as tall as a six-year-old. Here, no-one is the age they look. Or say they are. That boy always has money, always has something to sell. Always has a smile. I wish I could be like him.

'Go on, go on. Big tits. Everything! Cheap'.

'Go ask Saddam', I tell him.

Sunday afternoons when it's not raining, which is almost never, we play football on the pitch beside the sea. It's called the Swamp. It's fun, but the Romanians only pass to the Romanians, and never to the Roma – these are not the same; the West Africans never pass, only dribble; the East Africans can run all day but don't know what to do with the ball when they get it; the Eastern Europeans tackle too hard and sweat vodka, and the Arabs smoke cigarettes and shout at girls and old women while they play. We are all stereotypes, you see. Sometimes Irish guys join in, they like to pass but not to shoot, and it's good, but they never hang around to talk afterwards. It is so windy when you cross the ball it comes back to you. I get out of breath from the cigarettes and I tell myself 'you have to exercise more, you have to smoke less'. I never do.

Sunday nights if I have played football it's the only night I sleep good. Most nights I am happy with a few hours. There are some kids in the room crying, but it's not this.

'Your eyes are like two pissholes in the snow', says Breda. This is a good one.

While I stay awake I try to remember the names of shops in Kalima, or the bodies of girls that I was with. I try to put the different body parts together to make the perfect girl. Other times, it's jobs I did, or relatives in other countries. I try not to think about 2002. The camp. The jungle. The people.

On Mondays debts are paid. Most people get their Direct Provision Payment that day, but they usually owe it. Nineteen euro and fifty cents. You're fucked if you smoke. Once I tried to give them fifty cent so I could get a twenty euro note. The man could not understand why I would want this.

Some nights I add up all the things I could buy for that money in Congo/DRC, like forty-five beers, two prostitutes, thirty-two kilos of rice, six machetes … Maybe prices have changed. Maybe things are better now, but I can never go back.

Wednesday morning I get up at 6am, but when I get to the showers, Oli is washing her boys under the hot shower.

'How are you, Oli?' I say. She doesn't respond. Shortly after I came here first, we made love in her room while her kids were at school. She was crazy for it, I couldn't imagine she was a mother. It was good. Then the next week she asked me for a loan for school-lunches. No problem. Then the next week there was a school tour. In the end I got angry.

'Look, Oli, just tell me the price! At least then I will know what this is'. It was the wrong thing to say, but I couldn't help myself. That was the last time I was with an African woman.

One night, I think it was Wednesday because it was student night, I went out with Bolo and his friends.

He lent me fifteen euros. 'One drink for you, one drink for a girl and then a taxi to their place. You can get the nightclub free with a stamp. Simple'.

In the club, one Irish girl talked to me.

'Tell me about your country', she said. She was pretty, with straight hair like all Irish girls. She had a stud in her nose and a skirt to her knees. She was from a place called 'Ah-loan'.

'It is very hot', I said.

'Doh! I'm in Second Soc and Pol'. I nodded and concentrated on what she was saying. This is what you do with women. 'Ok. So what country in Africa?'

I tried to think of a peaceful country in Africa. 'South Africa'.

'Oh. Cool. My brother was in Johannesburg on his honeymoon. The car he was renting was stolen. Car-jacked, you know? He said it was very dangerous'.

I nodded.

She asked me to dance and we danced to some techno music. Well, I danced, she threw herself around into other people. She laughed at my dancing.

'Wow, you've got some rhythms. What kind of music do you have in South Africa?'

After a while I went to the bathroom. I watched from the balcony and waited until she got bored and went back to her friends.

On the street after we met a group of girls. They were crazy, really drunk. I said I thought they looked young but Bolo said no, they're students, they must be 18. He talked to them and they invited us back to a party in Newcastle. Late in the night, I was sitting with one of them on a couch. She was drunk and was worried about an argument she had with her best friend. We were drinking sweet wine. Bolo was smoking weed, teaching two other girls to do African dancing. The girl on the couch put her hand on my crotch and whispered.

'I'm knackered. Dja wanta go upstairs and listen to music?'

We went to a room and she took off my clothes. She was giggling and falling over. When I was naked, she seemed a little disappointed.

'What is it?' I asked.

'Nothing'.

She took out a condom and waved it in front of me.

'C'mere. This is a condom. Con-dom. You're not riding me if you don't use it. You put it on your thing there. Get yourself started'.

I laughed.

She turned around to let me put it on. Then she pulled down her knickers and pulled up her miniskirt. She lost her balance and fell back on the bed laughing, her two legs up in the air. The inside of her legs, high up, was really white. It made me think of 2002, this woman, or girl, lying on the ground in the clearing, after. Her legs were like this. Same position, but black. She was not moving.

'Come on so. Put it in'.

I couldn't get an erection.

'Can't you touch it?' I asked, embarrassed.

She touched it but nothing happened.

She walked to the other side of the room. I followed her and then she went crazy.

'Come on', I said. 'We can try again'.

'Leave me alone!' she started screaming, 'Get out, get out, you bastard! Don't touch me!'

Then she slapped and pushed me out of the room and locked the door. I knocked to get my clothes back, and after a while she threw me out my jeans. I kept knocking on the door, 'Please. My clothes. My shoes. Please'.

But she was crying and screaming. 'Fuck off, fuck off. Leave me alone!'

An Irish guy who was in another room came out. He had a phone in his hand. I stood in the hallway, holding my jeans to cover myself.

'This is fucking bullshit! Give me my fucking shoes!' I said, and started to kick the door.

'Look man', said the Irish guy, 'get out of here now. I'm calling the police'. He was really scared. It wasn't his problem.

I stole a coat from downstairs. I got lost and walked around barefoot for hours. When I got back to the hostel the next day I had a cold. Bolo was at the breakfast table, telling the story to all the other Africans. After that, every now and then at night one of them knocks at the door and whisper.

'Please, please, my shoes'. And then laugh. Oh, they are very funny in my hostel.

When Oli is gone I start to masturbate in the shower. Nothing happens. It doesn't feel right. I sit down and start to cry. After a few minutes I straighten up and take a shower. Then the water goes cold.

Hassan is outside.

'Fuck you, black bastard', he says, just like 'good morning'. It makes me laugh.

I put on clean, ironed clothes, aftershave and deodorant. Some of the others say it's better to wear old clothes because if you look too good they won't have sympathy on you. But the others are all still in the hostel too. No refugee status. No residency. I go to Immigration.

'How are you today, Mr Chanagansa?'

'Not-so-bad, Róisín. How's yourself?'

She laughs. 'Your Irish accent is getting better'.

Months ago I told her she could call me Georges, because she asked me to call her Róisín. It means 'Little Rose'. I like the Irish names, even though they are difficult to say. But they find our names difficult too.

'The application, has it come back, Róisín?' I ask, unable to wait any longer. She puts on the smile-that-is-not-a-smile.

'Well, yes, Mr Chanagansa, it has, but that's what I'd like to talk to you about, you see. The Appeals Review Board still has a few reservations about the application, in particular the sections ...'

I did not hear the rest as she produced my file, my life, cut through by green highlighter pen. Asylum Application Commission. Review Board. Appeals Review Committee. Reservations. Clarifications. Four fucking years I am here. And three in England before that.

'What they really want to know is exactly where you were from ... ah, let me see ... March 2002 to December 2003. During the, em, incidents'. Each time she calls them something different. War, killings, genocide. It was what it was. 'Everything else is accounted for'.

'In fairness I have told you this before, Róisín', I said, using the smile-that-is-not-a-smile. 'I was in the UN Refugee Camp'.

'Yes, I know that's what you've told us. It's just that there's no record of you there. Now I understand the UNHCR doesn't have comprehensive records for this time period, but it's just ... the Appeals Review Board is concerned about discrepancies. For example, on the 19th January of this year, Mr Chanagansa, you told me that you stayed with a cousin of yours in Kisingani between ... let me see ... August and November 2002'.

I took a deep breath. 'Can I ask you a question, Róisín? Where were you in November 2002? June 1998? Last Thursday at a quarter past eight?'

'Look, George, I can understand your frustration, but that's not the issue here'.

She avoided my eyes and tidied the pages. She began to ask me the same questions as before. When? Exactly what dates? Do you have documentary proof? Think, Mr Chanagansa, think. I wanted to hit her. I wanted to take her computer and smash it on her head. She didn't want to know what happened when I was Georges-Francois Sangana.

I got up and walked out.

I went down beside the river and tried to think where I was at that time. 2002. So long ago now. I don't remember. I have to connect the dots, imagine. I tried to imagine myself as another person to see if that might help. This other 'Georges', yes, he was definitely in the Refugee Camp, but then everyone left the camp. Then everyone came back. Where did he go? He went to the jungle, yes. In the jungle where it happened. How long? What happened?

My head hurts. Maybe it is because I am hungry. I go back to the hostel. Everyone is in the dinner hall. Breda gives me the plate. Dry hamburger and soggy chips.

'Can I supersize this, Breda?' I laugh.

'Come on, Mister'. We have had fifty conversations but she never says my name. Maybe she confuses me with someone else. 'Other people waiting'.

'Can I ask you something, Breda? Do you know what cassava is? Plantain? Dumplings? This is what we eat'.

'Well now, Mister, I'm very sorry, but this isn't a fancy restaurant, you know'.

'I know'. Then it happens again. 'We all fucking know, Breda! It's a de luxe prison, Breda! With food for pigs!' I say.

I throw my plate across the room. They said later I hit one of the Afghani boys in the head. I reach over and grab the metal tray with the burgers and empty them on the floor, that's where the burns on my hand come from. People start clapping and cheering. It is like an American movie. Except for the Afghanis who start to throw their shoes at me. Breda is crying. Some oil or hot water has spilt on her.

'Sorry, Breda. I'm really sorry'. I say. I stand there and it just seems like there's no point anymore. There's not enough of me to create two people.

In the office, Jimmy Murphy listens to the radio, and then tells me that they are 'seriously considering moving me on to alternative accommodation'.

'Jesus, George, in all fairness, it's not the first time, is it?'

Jimmy is always very nice, but he has no idea what is happening in the hostel.

'To be honest, we understand, you know, how difficult it is for you, Jesus, we do, but we don't make the rules, do we? But sure we all have to obey them, do you see where I'm coming from?'

He goes on and on. Jimmy always asks questions, but never listens to answers. He is a nervous man.

Bolo tells me later that everyone, except the Afghanis, are on my side. They will walk out if I am told to leave. I didn't know that anybody here liked me. I thought I had no personality any more. They're probably just sick of the food.

They put one day a week where a different nationality can pick the food and on Friday they move me to another hostel. Nobody walks out. On Tuesday I go to see Róisín again. She tells me my application has been rejected.

I go down beside the river. The African kids are on lunch from the school and are shouting at each other, some with Irish accents and some with African accents. Something about this makes me feel a little better. I watch the river and the way it's moving, without moving, so fast. It makes me dizzy. I close my eyes and listen to the river and the kids.

Then I can't help it. I start to hear 2002. The women and children are all running into the jungle, screaming or trying to stay quiet. We are behind them, shouting or trying to stay quiet. They are tripping and falling and crying. They reach the clearing and that is where it happens. I don't know what I did. I don't know.

When I can walk, I go to the SPARK volunteer group and they say that it is not over yet, they will help me fight it. I am on the internet in the SPARK café, checking Facebook to see if any of my relatives are still in the UK, when a woman on the other computer speaks to me. In French.

'Can you tell me how I can sign in, please? What is the password?'

Her name is Sophie. It happens that she is from Congo/Zaire/DRC but after we find this out, we do not ask what part we are from, or what tribe, or where we were in 2002. She has only been here for three weeks. She is staying in the hostel I have just moved to. Her eyes are refugees, running away whenever I try to hold their gaze, but I understand this. It makes her more beautiful. She has a scar on her chin. I want to touch it, ask her if she knows whether it is possible to delete one year of your life, one day. Just one. I invite her for a coffee in a real café across the road, but when I have to pay I do not have enough money. I smile at Sophie, who is sitting down, nervous. I lean across the counter.

'Please, I swear to you I will give you the money on Monday, you can have my watch, whatever ...'

The Irish guy behind the counter is young. He has blond streaks in his spiked hair and spots on his face. His eyes are red. He looks at Sophie, then taps the cash register and deletes the two items.

'Don't worry about it, man. Happens to the best of us. No problems'.

FLOUNDERING

Siobhan Shine

Once they had gone to New York. Connor and Marie. Marie and Connor. She often did that. Rolled their names off together while she was doing some mundane task around the house. He had to go there on business, he said. Would she like to accompany him? No elaborate persuasion on his part, or sly hesitation on hers. Yes.

From the beginning of the affair she was amazed at how easily she could lie. The ease of treachery, to her husband, her children. 'Just a couple of days ... back before you know it'. Then she would think, or even say aloud to herself, 'I am tempting fate, that's what I'm doing'. What if some disaster were to happen, an accident, and someone was to die, or be left in a coma, some awful collision of the fates? But she knew even as she thought this, that if she had such foreknowledge, she would still go. She would flee them, her obligations. Anyway they would wait for her. A body did not go off so fast. And she would have been with him, with Connor. After all the trials endured,

New York could not be undone. When she looked at her husband Gerry, she thought, 'you poor man, poor fool. Can't you read me? If you knew me better you could'. But they had been imposters for such a long time. Twenty years of formalities and politeness and an engulfing lack of intimacy.

Yet, she was a good wife. Or at least she was good at wifely things. She fulfilled her marital obligations willingly. She wore little things to entice, to keep her end up. But there was no urgency in it. No sense of depraved longing, or even hope. For years she had prided herself on her loyalty and sacrifice and dedication, whilst inside she burned. Did Gerry care or notice? She didn't know. It wasn't the sort of thing they could discuss. Nor did she want to, not now. She no longer wanted whatever it was that was wrong with them to be fixed. She kept the house nice, cooked and baked. It seemed to be enough for him. The outward show. She shaved her legs, even in winter. She abhorred women who let themselves go, little fringes of hair over ankle socks, tracksuit bottoms, tufts of hair sticking out of moles, bad teeth. She put on makeup while she did the housework. She made men regret their wives.

They met at an art exhibition in Kenny's of Middle Street. He had drawn her away from the crowd and said, 'You look like the sort of woman who has never been properly …' He whispered the obscenity into her ear. She felt her cheeks flush. He was short and stocky and pompous with a Bob Hoskins' face, thinning dark hair. She admired Bob Hoskins, his acting consummate, the way he courted Maggie Smith in *The Lonely Passion of Judith Hearne* was thrilling, but he had the kind of physicality that repulsed her. Bestial. And yet here she was fascinated by a man that exuded that same energy.

'Why … what gives you the right?' she started to say this even as she realised she was never going to, or ever could, resist him. For days she tiger-paced her house waiting for his call. 'Yes', she said, 'yes', when he did phone, her voice breathless, though she had rehearsed restraint. Their love making in the hotel that afternoon was so savage that she felt them to be like two feral beasts.

'I am in danger', she thought. 'Terrible danger and yet, I am in love. That is what this is, this feeling. I am in love and all of this is going to end and when it does it will be even more terrible'.

He was a successful businessman, married like her, living in Dublin, but with business interests in Galway. They saw each other often. He was at ease with himself, his body, his nakedness. Men were. Yet it was the hardest thing she had ever undertaken. And because she was no longer so young there was such work involved in it, such preparation before their meetings, depilation and exfoliation, endless creams that had to be applied to give an illusion of a fresh-faced dewiness. Frothy lacy creamy things to enhance a dulling complexion, to camouflage stretch marks, lumpiness, thread veins, inevitable deteriorations. Sometimes she pleaded with him to let her leave something on, but he said he liked the feel of her naked flesh against his. What was so awful to her was that once she was perfect, and she had walked around casually with it, her loose-limbed youth, wasting it on things that were of no importance, washing, cleaning, cooking, minding children, and now that she needed it to hold him to her, it was waning.

'What will you do over there … in New York?' Gerry said.

'O you know … shop, sight-see, drink it all in … the atmosphere'.

'Ah … is that all … nothing else?' His voice was casual, flat. Not really questioning. No subtext there. Still … you never know.

'What do you mean … what else is there to do but … see things?'

'Anyway … remember we're not millionaires'.

Winter. New York was cold and very light. It was a different world. She thought it smelt of snow, and even though it didn't snow, it seemed to her to be always on the verge. This disappointed her. Snow. How romantic it would have been if it had snowed. To watch the pure white flakes float down. Open her mouth and hope to catch one, a single flake, like one tries to do as a child, when everything was new, untainted, clean. No trace of her future wickedness, her unlawful desires. It felt strange to her not to be watchful every time they went out. Not to be scared of recognition. Anything that would put them in jeopardy, hasten their end. They could go places, to a show, and walk in Central Park hand in hand, shop, and not be watchful. They could go back to their hotel during the day. A couple. No one cared. No odd looks. She was hungry for him all the time. It was a hunger that had grown, not abated, all through the months of their affair.

This amazed her. She hadn't known that about herself. Sometimes, as they lay there, in their mingled sweat, she could feel him withdraw, his mind filling with business, itching to turn on his phone, become slightly bored with her lying there on him, spent, her fingers twirling his chest hair. She tried always at these times to be gay, interesting, to reclaim his attention.

She told him, on one of these afternoons, her theory on golden people.

It was this.

There were people walking around the world who just exuded. People who attracted others no matter what. They were born that way. Probably because they were on a last life, or something (if you believed in that whole Buddhist stuff) and had earned it. Usually rich, beautiful. They had a Midas touch, a film star quality. They did not form attachments. Attachments were what caused suffering, even to their own children, anyone really. This was what made them so alluring, set them apart, gave them their power. They were fatal, of course. She told him how she had not recognized him to be one of them in the beginning but that now she knew he was.

'One what?'

'One of them ... the golden people ... like I was just saying!'

'I worry about you ... I hope this is not going to get out of hand'. He was already up, coldly putting on his trousers, distancing himself.

'Where are you going?' She tried not to sound alarmed.

'Didn't I say ... I have a meeting in an hour'.

'O ...'

'Well I have ...'

Then he said.

'Do you want me to tell you what it was?'

'What?'

'What attracted me to you?... It was that you were so stiff ... everything about you was ... so ... controlled ... the way you crossed your legs, your hair, your clothes. So perfectly stiff and so clean. I wanted to ... unstiffen you'.

She felt the tears sting her eyes. She was so happy and miserable all at once, all the time they were in New York. That's what she remembered most when she looked back on it. Her fear and pleasure, both of them inexorably linked. Someday, someday, this is going to end. And when it does it will be terrible.

They went to Chinatown for a meal that evening. Connor said you couldn't go to New York and not go to Chinatown. It was as important as seeing the Statue of Liberty or visiting Ellis Island, or walking over Brooklyn Bridge. He told her how the best Chinese restaurants were the ones where the Chinese themselves went to eat. 'Forget about fancy restaurants just for this once', he said. 'Trust me on this'. Someone, one of his business associates, told him where to go, and to order ahead. He kissed the palm of her hand and her hair in the taxi on the way to the restaurant.

Even dimly lit it was a shabby place. It was very full, and sure enough most of the patrons were Chinese, except for one other couple, elderly, Americans she guessed, who raised their glasses to them when they were seated. The other thing she had noticed when she came in, apart from the shabbiness, the plastic tablecloths, and slightly soiled glassware, was a huge, lit fish tank, very high up, just about a foot and a half short of the ceiling, with a ladder leading up to it.

As they waited for their order to be filled, she watched as every so often someone, a kitchen hand or cook perhaps, came, climbed up the ladder, performed some manoeuvre and removed one of the fish. This was always accompanied by splashing and thrashing which was largely ignored by the other patrons. It disturbed her. There was this one fish, an enormous creature with a very flattened body which held her attention. It had a fierce strange look to it, a small jaw. It thrashed and bolted every time another fish was excavated from the tank. Her eyes kept straying to it. After she and Connor had had their soup and some sweet tasting Chinese tea, a different man came from the kitchen. He had a grander air, superior, the proprietor she guessed. He came over to their table which surprised her, stood in front of them, smiled, gestured towards the tank and said something in Chinese which Connor seemed to understand.

He bowed to them, then proceeded to climb the ladder. While he was talking and smiling at them, she was aware of him holding something in his left hand. Now she could see what it was. A sort of slash hook.

And then she just knew. Everything happened very quickly after that. There was a great thud and splash and the huge fish was there, on the ground in front of them, flapping and writhing, the man with the slash hook cursing. It looked even stranger close up, its two eyes on one side of its head, as if squashed together. She was up on her feet screaming. 'No, no ... no, don't kill the fish ... please don't kill the fish ...'

'Sit bloody down'.

'Can't you order something else ... Connor ... please ... oh please. Put it back? Let the fish live!'

Everyone looking at her. And Connor ... his face a sort of disturbing contempt. Disgust.

And as she watched him eat both fillets, his face a warning, she imagined how afterwards he might use the trite worn out excuses of why it had to end. How someday on a street she would see him, his golden edges all gone blurry, and she, just another woman, past caring, brutally aged, hair stringy from the rain, a plastic carrier bag in each hand.

SHADOWS

Conor Montague

It was one of those bright fragrant Saturdays sent to test schoolboys in the run-up to exams. Tom Flaherty ambled up Cappagh Road; slumped shoulders masking the recent growth spurts that left a faded black *AC/DC – Highway to Hell* t-shirt stranded an inch above the belt. His acne-speckled face was discoloured on the left side, puffed and swollen around the eye. He swung a length of ash that clipped heads off juvenile dandelions as he climbed the small hill at Gannon's white two-story farmhouse. Seed fairies stowed away on the gentle breeze to float over the small granite-strewn fields that lined the narrow road. Two red-setters threw themselves at Gannon's gate as Tom passed. He kicked a stone in their direction. It pinged off the metal to inspire a chorus of howls. Mrs Gannon exited carrying a basin of dishwater to throw onto the street. She swung it towards the dogs. It splashed across their backs to send them yelping around the side of the house. She laughed as she turned to go back inside, waving at the youth.

'Howya Tommy?'

'Howya, Mrs Gannon?'

'Lovely day'.

''Tis'.

Hawthorns bloomed white on either side of the narrow road, hunched over stone walls like farmers shooting the breeze, an occasional blush tinting the flowers. A splatter of teal-green dung stained the route Conneely's cattle took earlier. Its sweet perfume hung heavy in the air as Tom negotiated his way through, back-handing filthy brown flies and lashing fresh tips off the briars that peeped out from dense ferns on the verge. Up ahead, a lone magpie pecked at a flattened frog. It peeled it off the gravel and took flight as Tom put the stick to his shoulder and aimed. The bird veered to the right and swooped into a hollow, splayed legs dangling from its beak.

Sheba barked a welcome from a side-shed as Tommy walked through Moran's gate. Mick Moran appeared from around the gable, lean and stocky with a rolling gait. Teenage bristles blackened his chin and upper lip. Dark curly hair dropped to where silver studs sparkled on the shoulders of a sleeveless denim jacket. Phil Lynott's iconic image straddled his chest, a precious relic of the Renegade tour.

'Ah the bould Tom Flah, you're just in time'.

'Howya, Mick. Time for what?'

'Have to get rid of the pups; the auld fella's goin' mad'.

Yaps sounded from the shed, accompanied by the deeper woof of the thoroughbred Golden Labrador purchased by Mick with a view to breeding and 'making a few handy quid'.

'Who'll take them?'

Mick looked sideways at him. He registered the bruising on Tom's face before bending to pick up a hurl left on the grass. He threw a stone into the air and hit it with a dry crack that sent it thirty yards into the thistle-plagued field across the road.

'Take them? Who in the name of Jesus wants those mongrels? And the village full of them. Down to Lally's I should throw the lot of the little fuckers'.

'Snipe again?'

'Who else, that dog is fuckin' deadly. I mean a Jack Russell, how is it even possible?'

'Unbelievable'.

'Little fucker has pups with every bitch in the village'.

'You have to admire him, in fairness'.

Mick belted another stone into the air, dropped the hurl and walked back to the porch. He reached in to grab a cloth potato sack from a window ledge. Tom followed him into the shed. Sheba watched Mick place her six offspring into the darkness one by one, all whimpering at the mystery. There was no mistaking the genetic history of the litter. Every pup had the black hair and brown eyebrows of their father.

'Take a fair salesman to sell them as Golden Labradors alright'.

'Don't talk to me, and she locked in the fuckin' shed, I swear to God I thought I was seein' things when I opened the door to Snipe lookin' up at me, and he proud as a fuckin' turkey cock'.

'A wonder ya didn't give it to him?'

'Jesus I tell ya, t'was the shock that saved him; still can't figure it out'.

The two scanned the shed for a non-existent opening, like so many had done since this shape-shifting ghost dog joined the village. Mick grabbed a length of baling twine off the boiler and patted a bewildered Sheba on the head. He closed the door and turned to Tom.

'What happened the eye?'

'Nothin'. Walked into the door of the press, you know the high one in our kitchen, over the sink, corner caught me right under the eye'.

Mick rooted through a small pile of rubble by the wall. He picked up half a concrete block, banged it off the ground twice, and handed it to his friend. He stooped and selected a slightly larger piece for himself.

'Looks a sore dose'.

''Tis grand, had worse than this'.

Mick led the way through the lush tunnel of Willhamín's *bóthairín*. Grasshopper spit sprinkled the brambles and ferns on either side, like a giant had sneezed during the night, and evaporating dew harboured the scent of the wild garlic that grew along the verges. They walked to the crest of a small hill, then cut across the heather through a gap in a stone wall and followed a rabbit-run between the clumps. The beige sack yelped and gyrated in Mick's right hand. He carried half a concrete block under his left arm. Tom followed. He watched his friend's black Doc Martens squelch along the soft ground, stick in his left hand and half a block under his right arm. They paused at a promising bog-hole. Tom tested depth with the ash.

'Hardly enough'.

'Nah'.

'A child can drown in four inches of water you know'.

Mick looked at his friend.

'Well, next time we're drowning children we'll use this one so'.

Their laughter unfurled along the springy heather, lightening the load in Mick's right hand. He spoke back over his shoulder as progress resumed.

'I tell ya one thing, Sheila Joyce might avail of the service. Up the fuckin' stick again, can ya believe it?'

Tommy shook his head in a gesture of disapproval a Catholic bishop would be proud of. Mick paused to look back the way they had come. There was a black smudge on his brow, turf dust from the floor of the shed.

'I tell ya, Flah, I wouldn't mind availing of her services'. He looked skywards to lose himself in the vision before turning to Tom. 'Who's the stallion this time? Hardly Three-Piece again is it?'

'Sure Three-Piece is in London for the past year, doing well too they reckon. Putting down cable he is'.

'Still pullin' his wire all day so. I tell ya. When that fucker can get a ride, there's hope for the rest of us'.

Tom tapped Mick on the left shoulder with the ash.

'I think I know who the father is'.

'Who?'

'Sure isn't it obvious. I can't believe we didn't cop it before'.

Mick put down the sack, took the block out from under his arm, dropped it to the ground, spread turf dust across his forehead with the back of his hand and waited, hands on hips, for the revelation. Tom spread his arms wide.

'It's Snipe, sure who else? The little fucker's done it again'.

A blast of laughter shot shockwaves back down along the *bóthairín* and onto the road. Blackbirds abandoned cover in fright, and cattle three fields away paused their grazing to look around. Even Tommy Feeney's Jack Ass, known for his ill temper, hee-hawed approval from where he stood spanceled on the far side of the Cappagh Road.

Mick imitated Snipe going at it doggy style, his little paws clutched onto Sheila as he hammered away.

'Oh, Snipe, you're so big, give it to me, please, more, more'.

Two yelps and a prolonged howl signified climax. The two fell to their knees clutching midriffs, struggling for breath. Two pups waddled yapping from the sack. Mick made a clumsy grab for the nearest one.

'Quick, Sheila's sprogs are getting away'.

They rolled over onto their backs. Mick held the escapee to his chest. It piddled down onto Phil Lynott, causing him to fling the pup onto the heather. It was too much for Tom, who curled into a foetal position. A blue-green world swirled through salty tears. Snot and phlegm choked him as he struggled to control his bladder. It was some time before they quietened down, each attempt at speech reigniting the furnace until eventually it burned itself out.

Mick reloaded the sack, grabbed it by the neck and swung it over his shoulder. He bent at the knees, picked up the block, and tucked it under his arm. They weaved their way through gorse and heather towards Boleybeg, pausing occasionally to consider potential bog-holes. Mick spoke back to Tom without turning his head.

'You weren't in yesterday'.

'Nah'.

'How come?'

'Couldn't be arsed'.

'Ya missed fuck all, revision this and revision that, and me sat there thinking I didn't see any of this shit first time round. All a load of bollocks if you ask me. Sure there's no work anyway. What the fuck would ya want to be studying for?'

'Suppose. English on Wednesday. Shouldn't be too bad'.

Mick stopped and swung around, eyebrows arched into black smudge.

'Not too bad? I tell ya one thing, Flah, I'll ram that exam so far up my arse, I'll be chewing on it for a week. I mean for fuck's sake, sonnets? What in the fuck good are sonnets to anyone, ha? "I wandered lonely as a cloud", Shakespeare my fucking arse'.

He turned and continued across the bog, shaking his head. A cock robin joined the pilgrimage, hopping frantically from stalk to stalk at a safe distance.

'That's Wordsworth'.

Mick stopped, stiffening slightly. He put the bag down to readjust the block then looked over his left shoulder at his companion.

'What?'

'"I wandered lonely as a cloud", that's Wordsworth'.

Tom watched Mick turn around, enjoying the indignant expression, the stained forehead, the dramatic pause as he dropped his block to pick up the gauntlet.

'Is that a fact, Wordsworth no less, and did he not write sonnets?'

'I don't know, Shakespeare wrote them anyway, cause that's what we're supposed to read'.

'Are we now, and have you been busy reading the bould Shakespeare in your spare time?'

Tom laughed, dropped his block, and bent forward to pluck a green reed from a clump at his feet. He pulled the end off with a twist of his wrist and placed it into his mouth. He looked over the tip at Mick before answering.

'I have in my arse, I just know "The Daffodils" that's all'.

'"The Daffodils"?'

'Yeah, the Wordsworth poem, that's the only one I know'.

Mick spread his legs and leant back slightly. He glanced at the squirming bag at his left foot before returning his attention to Tom. A bee circled his head like an enemy bomber. He backhanded it on the third lap to send it careening over the heather.

'What? Ya just love daffodils, is it?'

Tom looked down at the bag at Mick's feet, took the reed from his mouth with his right hand, turned and spat to his left. He wiped his lips with the back of his hand, placed the reed in his mouth once more then looked south to where Galway Bay sparkled in the distance. He immersed himself in the view for a moment before turning back to Mick.

'The mother loved daffodils. She used to go on about that poem. Sure I'd have to know it, wouldn't I?'

Tom didn't wait for an answer. He led the way over the bog, picking his way carefully through a hoof-churned wet patch as Mick followed, using the same tufts as his friend. Once back on solid ground, they paused to survey their surroundings. Black Jack walked a distant field to the south, his bright red *geansaí Nollag* a beacon in the greenery. Mick shook his head at the sight.

'Jesus he loves that jumper'.

'Wouldn't do to walk in front of Lydon's bull wearing that'.

'That's for fuckin' sure … What time's the mass tomorrow?'

'Twelve'.

Tom started across a wide green patch, Mick by his side.

'Jesus, ya don't feel a year goin''.

A half-hearted nod was Tom's only retort as he looked towards the sun to consider its trajectory, like he was calculating the feel of a year. A grey heron rose twenty yards ahead, awkward and graceful. It tucked its head back into its shoulders and let out a single sharp squawk as it traced a gentle grey arc south along the blue canvas. It landed near the tall pines behind Gannon's house. Tom watched its progress.

'Down there his nest is'.

'Bet ya there's a good hole up there'. Mick pointed to where the bird had risen and walked ahead. A brace of snipe rose ten metres ahead. They skimmed rushes then zigzagged sharply to alight at the far side of a slight mound. Tom traced their brief flight with his stick.

'Have to get them before they turn, the auld fella'd have them shot from the hip, *bang, bang*'.

'You any smokes?'

'A nipper'.

Tom dug into his left-hand pocket and produced half a Major, badly disfigured, and a box of matches. He sparked up the cigarette. The smell of sulphur mingled with tobacco smoke in the still air. He inhaled deeply, enjoying the head rush of adulthood, then exhaled a rapid succession of rings through pursed lips, repeating the ritual twice before handing the fag to Mick. He looked up at a jet streaming towards the North Atlantic. Flotsam trailed in its wake, slowly dissipating into nothingness.

'Another bunch gone, lucky fuckers'.

Mick blew smoke into the midges that swarmed around.

'Would ya go?'

'That's for sure, be gone tomorrow if I could, out of this shithole'.

Mick sucked the dregs and flicked the butt into the mud. He watched it smother then turned to his companion.

'Nice head on ya for New York alright, your neck'd be fucked from lookin' up at the buildin's'.

Tom lurched towards his friend to grab him in a headlock but slipped on the soggy ground. Mick swivelled to the left and sent him over his right hip onto the heather. He knelt with one knee on Tom's chest and slapped him across the face, careful not to hit the swollen eye.

'You'd want to be faster than that over there, boy, no second chances in New York City'.

Tom grabbed denim shoulders and swung his friend to the right and onto the bag of puppies. Mick sprung from the ground like a kid goat, twisting in mid-air to land with a foot each side of the squealing bundle. As Tom climbed to his feet, Mick twisted the neck of the sack to prevent escape. They walked to where they had seen the heron rise. Sure enough, there was a decent-sized pond, about four foot in diameter and a couple of foot deep in the middle, half-way up Tom's staff. Green rushes encircled the brown water and a smattering of bog-cotton sprinkled its way northwards towards McComisky's house. Mick twirled the package anticlockwise, left it down, opened the sack and dropped his block into the litter. Tom flinched at the frightened yelps.

'Jesus will ya mind, you'll hurt the poor fuckers'.

'Do ya really think it matters at this stage?'

'No point making it worse'.

Tom placed his block gently in among the squashed little faces. Eyes squinted towards the bright light and whimpers intensified. He closed the sack and turned to his friend, who pulled a length of yellow baling twine from his back pocket.

'Is there no one who'll take them?'

'What's on ya, if ya can't stomach it just wait down there'.

Mick gestured towards the road. Manhood rested easy on his young shoulders, its weight expanding his barrel chest. Tom heaved the bundle to Mick's feet.

'Course I can stomach it, just a pity that's all'.

Tom stepped closer to the bog-hole. A water boatman skimmed across his shadow. Two dragonflies chased one another in circles, swooping to touch the surface sporadically, emerald and scarlet beneath blurred wings. Mick's shadow merged from behind to hoist the sack into the middle of the pool. It landed with a dull gulp. Skimming insects surfed splash-waves towards the edges, where they were absorbed by the peat. Tadpoles embraced the green slime cloak by the far side of the pond. Countless manic tails glistened as they pierced the skin of the surface.

The bag floated momentarily. Trapped air fought dead weight as the soft water gently seeped through the cloth. Panicked squeals sounded as the litter sank slowly, fighting inevitable silence as best they could; threads of tiny bubbles in their wake. The sack came to rest on the mud bed. Visibility was regained as the disturbed sediment slowly settled. The last of the air loosened the baling twine as it left the bag. One tiny black snout poked through the slight opening. It wriggled desperately into wet embrace. Mick shook his head and exhaled loudly.

'For fuck's sake, will ya look at this fucker'.

'Ya didn't tie it properly'.

Mick turned to Tom with a snarl. 'Course I fuckin' tied it properly'.

He calmed at the sight of Tom's smirk.

'There's always gonna be a bit of give. It'll be grand'.

He turned to face the pond as the pup's head broke the surface, black eyes hysterical under brown eyebrows. He swam dazed in a circle like a dwarf sea-lion. Mick grabbed the stick from Tom's hand.

'For fuck's sake'.

He placed the point of the staff on the pup's crown and pushed him under. As they waited for the bubbles to cease, a sibling surfaced dead with lips curled back over virgin white teeth, like it grasped the comedy in its dying breath. Mick lost concentration and his charge popped up once more to flounder towards the edge.

'Ya little fucker'.

Mick speared the pup into the side with the ash and drove him down into the murk, leaving his weight on the stick until he felt it pierce baby ribs. He looked wide-eyed at Tom before he pulled the shaft sharply from the water with a loud 'Yeah!' Tiny red bubbles shot to the surface, tingeing the brown water. A curlew sounded a keen from across the bog. It rose in wistful intensity, peaked and restarted, stabbing the silence.

The two shifted position, moving around the pond until shadows disappeared and closed the window to the death below. A tinted sky mirrored on the water, one solitary corpse floating among wine-coloured clouds. The traffic returned. Nymphs, water beetles and tadpoles invaded the murky crypt as water boatmen and pond skaters skimmed across the heavens. As they turned for home, Tommy spotted the pulsing white throat of a camouflaged frog as it watched from the edges. He said nothing.

They walked in silence back over the bog and down through the *bóthairín*. The tommy-gun staccato of a roused tractor pulsed from the direction of Barna. Mick glanced sideways at Tom.

'Hear your auld fella's back on the beer'.

'He is'.

'Since when?'

'Thursday night'.

Tom looked down across the fields to where crows rioted around the small copse of spruce beside Tom Paraicín's cottage. He swung his staff upward with his left hand and cleaved the prickly bulbous head off a thistle. It soared over a stumpy blackthorn into an adjacent field. Mick's eyes followed the missile then returned to his friend.

'You're quiet'.

'Just thinkin' that's all'.

'They're better off, Tom. Sure nobody wanted the fuckers. If nobody wanted you ...'

Mick's voice trailed off mid-sentence, leaving a silence that deepened as they walked. Tom decapitated another thistle, then another. The swish of the ash punctuated their thoughts, set the pace. They continued in this manner for five minutes, Mick stealing an occasional glance at his friend. When they reached the road, the cock robin fluttered to the top of a hawthorn and proclaimed their guilt to the village. Brendan Lally sped past in his white Renault 4, leaving the road briefly at the hump of Martín's Hill. He beeped a greeting upon landing then disappeared around the bend in a flurry of gravel. Tom watched him go then swirled to face his friend.

'Do ya know what the tragedy is, Mick?' Mick looked into Tom's face but couldn't hold his manic stare and shifted uncomfortably. Tom grabbed his shoulders, forcing eye-contact. 'Do you know what the *real* fuckin' tragedy is?' Mick shook his head.

'How many males were in that litter?'

'Four'.

Tom loosened his grip on Mick's shoulders and stood back. A grimace tightened his lips.

'Those four dogs will never get to enjoy the one god-given gift they possess'.

'How'd ya mean?'

'Don't ya get it Mick? Those poor fuckers will never get to lick their own balls. The one thing that makes them better than us and we took it from them. Fuck your *Macbeth* and all that shite. That's a real tragedy'.

Tom's guffaw infected his companion instantly. Mick, bent double by the sucker-punch, placed a hand on Tom's shoulder as he fought for breath. He took advantage of the veil to pull Tom into a brief tight hug, then pushed him away and punched hard into his right bicep.

BANDWIDTH

Celeste Augé

'Slap me again. Harder!' The hiccups will not go away. My body shakes with each delicate 'hipp'. 'C'mon Siobhan, do a right job, would ya!' I slap myself hard, once on each cheek, and hiccup again.

We're standing near the bus stop, three rows of terraced houses and one apartment block over from our own road. An old lady and a worky-looking type are in the bus shelter, reading and re-reading the large full-colour ad for Xavon Technology.

I roll my eyes at them. I don't have broadband, live on the last street in the city left unconnected. The Council blames the old gasworks the row was built on, claims the private contractors did substandard conservation work and that it would be dangerous to dig up the ground now, just to lay some fibre optic. And besides, there is free access if you register down in the Facilities Centre. That's what the council said when everyone on Dev Road complained. Like we'd rush down to the homeless shelter to connect up.

Siobhan looks over at me when I let out another hiccup. 'Sure you're up to this, culchie?' The girls call me that sometimes, just because my mother's from Galway. I don't bother to answer her. It feels as if we're trapped in an invisible bubble of restless energy that makes a gap between us and other people. Everybody thinks hormones are responsible for this, but I know different. I'm waiting.

My mother has me filled with visions: of life without the background hum of product after product, bright colours flashing past your eyes with voices that whisper 'buy us, buy us', life without the extra bandwidth that lets you keep up with the stream of a better world. A life where people turn to books and stories for comfort. A place where you can say peculiar things, and not have to experience a digital version of everything. Where things don't have to be checked out online before they're trusted. I suppose it doesn't help that my mother grew up in that dreamer-town out west. Plus I'm starting to think maybe she has been working in the basement of Trinity College library for too long. All those books, too many dead ideas. Shelving them in the stacks, cataloguing the new ones that the indie publishers could be bothered to produce – work I've watched my mother do anytime I visit her there.

I can almost feel it again: shivers as I sit in the corner of the basement, my hands tight around a bottle of Lucozade, wrapped in my mother's fleece. Trying not to think about the school trip I'm missing. Watching my mother shelve and re-shelve old books in the stacks, books few people would know about. Or care about.

Siobhan scans the length of the busy road while I watch the pair at the bus stop. The old lady pulls her raincoat closed and turns away when she catches me staring at her. She seems uncomfortable – she can probably tell that I don't have streamed media, super-culture pumped into my house, the right words or hairstyle.

'Just 'cause you're not looking at me doesn't mean I'm gone away, y'know!' I shout over to the lady. I love the mute shock of people when I don't act normal.

'I wonder what that'd be like – if Mum had ever bought into it, if she'd have had the money, y'know – if I only said what I'm supposed to, if I never messed up in front of the headmaster', I say to Siobhan.

'Wha?' Siobhan doesn't care about school or thinking about the different ways the world could be. She wants Aidan, her favourite black boots and entertainment on a Saturday afternoon. 'None of that professor shit, not now. Lookit, how long is it since your woman went up to the shop?'

'Dunno, I think –'

Louise trots up the road towards us, half-running, half-walking across the road, weaving between cars that barely slow down to avoid her. Her white hoody stands out against the dark blur of the traffic.

Our energy surges instantly; it feels as if every cell in my body is splitting at the same time.

Louise hops on the balls of her feet, her toes acting like springs in her running shoes. 'Nessa's just coming out of the shop now, she bought one of those new Xavons, y'know, the one with the uploads'. She gives us this information as if it is a gift, wrapped and ribboned.

'Remember that time Nessa broke the lock on the Rugby Club, set off the alarm, nearly got us all caught? Stupid bitch', says Siobhan. 'I never could stand the way she thought she was in charge, just 'cause she was almost an old wan –'

'And 'cause she was going to be moving to Sea Point Road –'

'Posh bitch', the three of us say in unison.

She was never one of us, Nessa. We never could tell when she would turn around and walk off rather than skip on the Dart with us to go skimming downtown. She liked pills, even though we stuck to hash for fun. And she fell for the new thing too easily. Couldn't figure out why we all liked retro music, that we liked being different and couldn't care less just to piss people off. Bad enough when you're out of touch because you chose parents on Dev Road. No reason to let other people find out that your geography bothers you.

We lean against the wall, the three of us, waiting.

A bus comes by, hissing as it pulls off with the man and old lady. Siobhan and Louise and I watch the double-decker drive away, then turn to face the opposite direction. Nothing is said; we stay calm, it's too easy to give yourself away when you talk. We've learnt this the hard way.

'Here she comes', I say, my voice low and taut.

Nessa is busy cursing the bus for leaving on time, half-running towards the bus stop as though she might miss another one. The three of us have her; she has yet to spot us. We don't say a word. We just watch her steps slow as she gets close, senses the trouble.

A nod from me, and Louise closes off the path behind the girl.

'Hiya Nessa', I say in a voice that sounds like a challenge. 'Hear you made it past transition. And there I thought you'd be out on your arse and serving me breakfast in Mickie's'.

'Angie', replies Nessa, by way of hello.

So she's trying to play it cool. We shift our weight and pitch our bodies at a stronger angle, chins out now, hands waiting in pockets.

'How's your mam holding up these days?' Nessa asks, as far as she can stretch towards ruffling me. She has all the media her parents can afford, filtering her impulses, keeping her language pitch-perfect. I bet the only confrontations this lovely girl has been programmed for are meetings with the alphas.

My brain is busy. Through a buzzy haze: the suit I have to wear to take care of my mother, her nappies double-bagged in hazardous warnings. An oxygen mask crowding out kisses. Hand squeezes and knowing exactly what I have to do, the two things that sustain me.

'Just fine', Siobhan answers for me, swinging her elbow out a bit to nudge my side. I snap to, check my wing-girls. Time for action, their eyes say, time to get their piece.

A slight nod, and Louise moves up close behind Nessa, her movements easy but barely held under control. 'Bit of a shopping trip today? What you got there, what's in the bag?'

Nessa steps forward, to get away from the low voice next to her ear. Cue Siobhan. 'Been looking for a new phone myself', she says, her voice so calm her arms are nearly twitching with the suppressed energy. 'Need an upgrade'.

I watch them; note Nessa's reaction, a mix of surprise and realisation. A hint of pleasure washes through me, and I wait for the scent of fear to hit. Waiting, not saying a word. I square up to Nessa, look into her eyes, see everything Nessa has, every single chance she will get for the next fifty years, and the huge size of it grinds into me.

'Seen enough?' Nessa asks, pushing even when she has to know this will only get worse, pushing to get to whatever is coming next.

The first blow knocks her back a step, so she falls against Louise. I shake out my hand and my blood soars with the sight of Nessa holding her chin. Louise shoves her off, the girl's balance so shaky she lunges toward Siobhan, who has a knee ready to meet her soft belly.

Warmth swells in my chest – this girl is a part of me, she could be mine. As though I could take her destiny, and everything could change. 'Possibility', I whisper into the girl's ear. She is on her knees on the concrete path, her jeans shielding her skin, and I bend over the girl, feel her sobbing as I reach across her to claim the bag. My breath deepens as the moment freezes inside me. I can't figure out how I went this far, don't care.

'Got it', I tell the other two, their limbs waiting for more. And I walk away, don't look back at the crumply clothes of the girl on the ground.

Siobhan is the first to fall in step with me. Louise has to run to catch up to us. We three friends walk down the hill, around the corner from the pier. Our faces are flushed with the buzz; our skin glows with a thin layer of sweat. We're connected, as though the space between us has become solid and joined us together. 'Jesus, did we really do –'

'Shut up Siobhan, there's nothing to say'.

'But –'

'For fucksake Siobhan, did you hear what Angie said? Just shut the fuck up', Louise says, as if we do this kind of thing everyday, as if we haven't bruised Nessa just to get her phone.

I'm worried they'll start on each other, so to shut them up I hold up the phone. 'So who wants it?'

Siobhan and Louise look at each other, a pause before either of them speaks.

'You have it', they say together, then laugh hysterically, and I join in, as if this jinx is the funniest thing I have heard today. I don't want the phone. I never wanted the phone. Truth is, I'm already thinking of where I will go next. How to get out.

'Take the phone', I say to Louise, holding the handset out to her. 'You're the one set it up'.

We head down the road, people moving out of the way of our teenage forcefield, and cross over to the market where Louise can get the phone unblocked. I only see the Guard when Siobhan grabs my arm. He is standing outside a butcher's shop, looking at the pedestrians.

'Just keep walking, say nothing', I say, faking confidence.

We slow down, as if the Guard is a speed trap, and pull closer together. We focus on the entrance to the market, aiming for the arch. Space is growing between us. We squeeze in tight, knocking each other's elbows.

I hold my breath for a moment, work it out. I laugh and ask Siobhan how the boys liked her new black dress on Thursday night. Wait through the pause, my eyes bright, willing my friends to join me in this scam. 'Well?' I say, as we near the butcher's.

Louise is easy, she joins in, gets a dig in as soon as she susses what I'm up to. 'Did you keep it on you for the night, then?'

By the time we pass the Guard, Siobhan is blushing and telling tales for the girls.

I glance up at him from beneath my fringe and flick back my hair. He checks us out, moves on. We've fooled him. Just three teenage girls out for the afternoon, trading stories and makeup tips, carefree. As we should be.

Insurance Plan

Edward Boyne

I had to burn the car to claim the insurance. No choice. I needed the money. There was no way I could sell it. It needed a new clutch, the engine mountings had worn out and there was a knocking noise under the bonnet when the engine was running. Rust was appearing on the wheel arches and the indicators didn't work.

I couldn't just set it on fire and then make a run for it. Not with my luck. I'd be sure to get caught. I had to work out how to give myself enough time to get away and be long gone before the car went ablaze or blew up. I really needed an incendiary device with a timer. Short of joining the IRA I couldn't figure it out for a long time. I fiddled with different things in the back shed. I needed something simple and cheap. In the end it came to me by accident.

I'd been smoking a cigarette while reading the paper, and had left the cigarette down in a glass ashtray on the kitchen table. I was pouring over the classifieds for job vacancies, security jobs, commission salesmen, debt collecting, that sort of thing.

Maybe the cigarette tasted stale but for some reason I let it smoulder by itself, a Silk Cut King Size, slowly burning down to its brownish paper tip. I like the idea of King Size. It means there's nothing better. Before the red glow reached the tip there was a slight flare and a crinkling sound. I saw it out of the corner of my eye. I'd been staring at a vacancy for a nightclub doorman, trying to imagine myself looking tough, turning younger guys twice my size away from the door.

The flare-up came when the tip of the cigarette touched off a live match in the ashtray, then scorched some loose cellophane. When I thought about it, I reckoned five minutes to burn down, maybe more, and not like a fuse that will snuff out for no reason. Reliable.

Out in the shed I took out another cigarette, pushed the red sulphur tips of two matches into the filter, then lit the cigarette with my lighter. I left the cigarette to smoulder in an ashtray on my workbench. I timed it; seven and a half minutes it took before the sulphur ends flared up. The next time I tried it I put a sheet of newspaper six inches above the lighted cigarette. Seven minutes later the cigarette burned down, the sulphur flared, little darts of flame shot out, the newspaper caught fire. I had the right weapon.

Went on reconnaissance one afternoon, drove to a remote spot on the beach near Bull Island bird sanctuary. I timed everything on my watch, taking notes as I went. There was a long jetty nearby, plenty of dunes around to give extra cover. It would have to be at night of course.

Back home I salvaged the spare tyre and the jack. I removed the tool kit and the warning triangle. I took the AA maps and handbook out of the glove box. There were loose Smarties mashed into the glove box's metal edges. I wanted to swap the two good tyres for two bald ones. A mechanic I know gave me two old tyres. I didn't tell him what I wanted them for, but they turned out not to fit the car. I couldn't manage to get the leather steering-wheel cover off. I remember at one time using glue to hold it in place. There was no shifting it.

On D-day, it was already half-dark when I set out with little Dominick belted into the back seat. I had two fishing rods propped up on the front seat, the long tops of them bent back nearly to the rear window. They were my alibi, along with Dominick. Who would suspect a father out with his kid, even if after dark?

I left a hammer and a glass ashtray beside me on the passenger seat. There were stacks of old newspapers in the boot. I had two boxes of matches, in case one misfired, a plastic container full of petrol, a torch with good batteries I made sure was working. I had planned for everything.

It was one of those late autumn evenings when the air is still and the gathering dark is moonless and becoming total. After I left the city I stuck to the Coast Road. When I'm nervous the certainty of the sea nearby is reassuring.

'I want to stay in. I want to watch *The Simpsons* on the telly. Please Dad let's go back. It's starting to rain', said Dominick.

He can be a dreadful whiner sometimes.

'It's not raining', I said. 'I need to go out to do some things and there's nobody to mind you. It's not often I ask. You can watch the telly later, before I put you to bed'.

'But it's dark. I should be in bed now. If I was with Mom I'd be in bed'.

'Oh come on. I can't get you to go to bed most times. You don't have any school tomorrow. Tell you what, I'll buy you a comic tomorrow before I bring you back to your Mam's, but you won't get it if you make a big fuss'.

'I don't want a comic', he said. 'I want a Manchester United shirt'.

Children are decisive. They know their own minds and they can live in several worlds at once, moving between them without noticing.

'I'll get you one when I can afford it. They're expensive. Christmas maybe. In the meantime think yourself lucky to get a comic'.

I got close to the part of the beach I had planned. The sky darkened and thickened. I lost the last street light on the Coast Road. Shortly after that I turned down a lane towards the beach. The car started to feel lumpy as we hit the first shallow sand ruts on the tarmac. At the end of the lane the beach stretched beyond the fanned-out yellow search of my headlights, to the edge of the darkness. I slowed down expecting a human figure to appear at that edge. There must be someone out here, so close to the cramped city. A black short-haired dog scurried across the lights. I jammed on the brakes, sensed Dominick stiffen, picking up on my fear. I told myself to calm down, to pretend I was doing nothing wrong. This was an evening out with my son, we're going fishing off the jetty. The darkness is good for the fishing. People have been fishing the sea in the dark since biblical times and before. A young boy has to learn, and learn from his natural father. That's all there is to it.

I drove along the beach for about a mile as planned, then took the car through a sandy gully between two tall shadowy sand dunes. Away from the sea and the city lights it became much darker. As I slowed to a halt the front tyres sank in the powdery sand. I drove further in, inch by inch, until the car cut out. It occurred to me that I'd never get the car out of there on my own, even if I'd wanted to.

'Ok, Dominick, hop out here'.

'Why are we stopping?'

'I have to meet someone'.

I gave him the torch and told him to go collect stones or shells near the shore.

'Don't go too far', I said to him.

He took off fearlessly into the dark, delighted to have the torch to play with.

A few moments later I could see the light prowling the shoreline a hundred yards or so away.

I took out the fishing rods and stuck the handles into the sand. Then I sprinkled petrol from a can over the back and front seats. I kept the car's interior light on so I could see what I was doing. When I'd finished, the seats looked weirdly the same as before, except for the rising petrol fumes. My head felt light and clear from breathing the fumes. I took up the hammer and smashed the driver's window and the windscreen as quietly as I could. When I stopped there was silence and a thin moving light out near the shore where Dominick was probably searching for shells.

'Are you ok, son?' I shouted. He didn't reply.

I had to move quickly, he'd soon get bored.

I organised the cigarette with the embedded sulphur tips, lit it carefully with my lighter away from the car, put it in the glass ashtray and placed it in the boot. I arranged a single sheet of newspaper over the ashtray. Then I let down the back seat so the flames could travel through. Seven minutes to get away. Military precision.

Dominick was still playing by the shore. I calmly imagined sea-water gushing into his footprints. I'm amazed at my own calm sometimes.

I climbed up to the top of one of the dunes nearest the car. I wanted to see if there was anybody around in case someone wandered near the car and got themselves hurt. I didn't want any civilian casualties. The city made a low glow on the horizon. The place was empty.

'Dominick', I shouted. 'We've got to go now. Dominick son!'

He stood up and suddenly the flashlight went out and he disappeared. I clambered down the other side of the dune, not able to see much.

I grabbed at the two fishing rods in the dark. Suddenly Dominick was beside me, panting. He swung out of my arm for a second, kept running and went ahead of me.

'Dominick, turn on the flashlight so I can see you'.

'I'm playing a game. The big sea-shells are fighter bombers attacking the city'.

He made a noise like a jet engine and zoomed on.

'Stay close to me', I said. 'We're not going back the way we came. Through the dunes over this way'.

'What about the car?' he said, his voice muffled.

The sand shelved away under me. I could feel the tug on the backs of my legs as I plodded on. Dominick went racing off on his own. I went down into a slight hollow which meant I couldn't see him. I tried to follow the sounds he was making.

'Boom, eeaaah, boom, boom, eeeaaah'. The fighter bombers were attacking the city. Then there was silence. I kept walking as fast as I could. Sounds, city sounds came to me on the breeze.

'Dominick', I shouted. 'Don't go too far. Stay near me'.

I still couldn't see him. It felt strange to be shouting into that void.

I looked around for the first time and saw an orange glow in the sky from the direction I'd come. Must be a car's headlights in the far distance, trick of the light. I kept walking. I knocked my toe against a sharp rock. It throbbed and I wanted to cry out, but didn't. It made me go slower. Should have brought an extra torch. Tactical mistake. Again I couldn't see Dominick or hear his voice.

'Dominick, turn on your torch'.

My eyes were getting used to the dark. I could see shapes and things up close. Scattered sods of grass appeared through the sand, the beginnings of soil. I stopped and stood still, trying to hear Dominick's fighter bombers. No sound. He must have gone off in another direction. The tall dunes made it harder to hear as well as see.

There was a loud thud and an orange flash from the direction of the car. Less than three minutes, not seven. I turned to see the scattering flash of the flames in the distance.

'Dominick, Dominick?'

I said it in a lowish voice. No telling who else was around. The explosion might attract the wrong people. The dunes loomed up like the walls of a maze. There was silence.

What if he'd gone back to the car? What about shrapnel from the explosion? He could be lying back there hurt. I cursed myself again for not bringing another torch. Where is he? Damn him.

'Dominick', my voice was low and hoarse.

I turned and started to run back, guided by the orange glow in the sky. Did he have the sense to stay clear? What if he's lying somewhere injured? How am I going to find him?

Sweat drops ran cold down my back. His body could be lying beside me in some of these dunes and I wouldn't see.

I climbed up to the top of the largest dune. I could see the car below in the distance. There were orange flames lapping out from where the petrol tank must have burst and exploded. There was no sign of movement. I scrambled over one dune, then another. I got to the top of the dune above the car.

There was sand in both my shoes. I could feel the first drops of rain on the crown of my head and the beginnings of a breeze off the sea. I shouted for him now at the top of my voice. I shouted until I was hoarse. The dunes hushed the sound like a conspiracy.

I started to think of Gillian and what she would say, what I would say to her and to Dominick's new stepdad, the bloody army Captain, who didn't think much of me anyway. I was stuck for money, on the edge, I didn't know what else to do. I couldn't sell the car, nobody wanted it. But why put little Dominick at risk? Why? I needed an excuse to be on that beach in case I was seen. No, I was fishing with my kid and vandals set fire to the car. We weren't near it at the time. I never thought I'd lose him in the dark. I'm not always the best at thinking ahead.

He can't be hurt. The only way he could be hurt would be if he got too close to the car and the explosion. The area around was all lit up by the flames. He was nowhere to be seen. I went back the way I came. The pressure in my shoes from the sand became too much. I had to stop to unlace and shake them out.

I was sitting on the edge of a dune facing the sea when I saw a familiar small shape move across the line of the shore. I shouted again at the top of my voice, forgetting all caution.

'Dad', he shouted back, 'I'm over here'.

I thought he'd come running, but he didn't. As I came up beside him at the shoreline I could see him bending down to pick up shells or crabs, then moving his hands over the surface of the sand, reading it in the dark like braille.

I threw the fishing rods down, knelt and hugged him. I cried tears into the crown of his head. His hair smelled salty.

'Where did you go, I was frantic'.

'I came back to get a shell I liked. I can't find it. Will you help me look for it?'

'What about your flashlight?'

'I lost it. It stopped working. I put it in my jacket pocket. It's not there now'.

I stayed with him in the light drizzle, croached over, fingering the sand, searching for a lost shell with no clue as to its colour or shape.

'I'll know it when I find it', he said.

I felt like I'd been throwing everything up in the air and the bits were starting to land. It's good to do that sometimes. Makes you come alive.

A car's headlights moved towards us along the beach. I let myself calm down, breathe again, feel the minutes pass.

'Did you hear a big bang?' I asked eventually, as casually as I could.

'When?'

'About twenty minutes ago'.

'How long is twenty minutes?'

'Not very long usually'.

He had his head down towards the damp sand and I could barely see his hands, nearly buried, searching.

'I want to go back to the car', he said.

Headlights flooded over us for a long moment that felt like a collision. There was a young couple in a van. They didn't look at us as they passed.

'Come on', I said, 'we'd better go'.

It took ages to get back onto the main road. I held Dominick's hand tight enjoying the heat of his little palm. I swore to myself I'd never let it go again. He kept moaning about having to walk, but I didn't mind.

On the road I waved the fishing rods at every car that moved. An old white Mercedes taxi pulled in thirty yards ahead of us. I could see the driver beckoning to us. He made no effort to reverse back. It had been a long time since I'd used a taxi but it was a special night.

'Where's our car?' Dominick said.

'Be quiet and I'll tell you later'. I knew he was tired, too tired to make too much of it.

In the confined space of the back seat I thought I could smell petrol. At first I reckoned it was from the taxi. Then I smelled my hands, the front of my coat and my shirt. Jesus, I thought, I reek of it.

I was sure the taxi driver would smell it. I slid over to the farthest side of the seat from the driver and opened the window.

As we drove through Fairview and the North Strand I tried to imagine the explosion I had heard but not fully seen. I imagined a great ball of orange flame throwing sparks and shrapnel into the air. Shrapnel.

What if someone had been hit by shrapnel from the car? What if they had been killed? A courting couple perhaps, or an old man out walking his dog. People I missed in my sweep of the beach. Would it be murder, manslaughter? What would I say to their families?

'Catch anything?' asked the taxi-driver.

'What?'

He gestured back towards me with his left hand.

'Fishing, fishing-rods'.

'Oh yeah, sorry. No, nothing. The rain came on and we gave up'.

'No rivers near here', he said in a definite tone.

'We were fishing the sea out off the jetty'.

Dominick started tugging at my sleeve. I knew what he was going to say.

'Shush', I said, and meant it.

I smiled to myself. After a while Dominick lay his head on my lap and snuggled into me. The whole complex operation had been a success, despite some initial setbacks. We were heading home with no casualties. Nobody could call it botched, it was planned and executed by a true military strategist. For the first time in ages I felt a sense of achievement, of victory.

Night Caller

Gerard Hanberry

I saw him before he saw me, slinking like a rat into the dark alcove by the closed-down boutique. A matted tangle of red hair and filthy army-surplus clobber.

I had left the office minutes before. The streets were empty. People with homes to go to were already gone. Turning the corner onto the docks I met a breeze with an edge that would slit your throat. My plan was to down a hot toddy in Burke's. It might ease the chill that had set up home in a deep corner of my heart.

'You're out, you little bollix'.

'Good behaviour'.

'They'll be keeping that cell warm'.

'Never again. Anyway, as I said at the time, I'm just an innocent victim of circumstances'.

His twisted mouth sucked on the last of a butt then he flicked. It arched to a spot six inches from my shoe.

'Kelly, you're a scumbag. Knew that the first time I set eyes on you and the army wasn't long finding you out either'.

'Well, fuck you Captain Duffy, Sir, or is that just plain Micky now seeing as how you're no longer in uniform like myself'.

I felt his tongue lick a foot of slime across each letter of my name then he drew himself into a snarl.

'I've served my time and I haven't forgotten who it was put me inside so I'd head on up that street now if I were you and mind how you go'.

A quick glance told me witnesses were scarce and I knew there was no surveillance at that spot. After all, security is my business.

'You wouldn't be threatening me now, ferret?'

As I moved closer I caught that distinctive whiff of badness and whatever booze had made him feisty. He shrunk against the dark glass but his mad eyes flashed hate.

'Leave me alone!'

I had him swivelled with his nose pinned to the window and his right arm in a lock before he knew what sprung.

'Duffy, you bastard ...!'

'Mister Duffy to you'.

I jerked his arm just a single notch higher.

'Arggg! You fuck ... Argh!

'Mister Duffy – say it, bollix'.

He began to buckle.

'Ok ... Mister Duffy – now let me go'.

'I saw the way you left that old pensioner, you heartless fuck, and his poor wife living in fear ever after. And for what? Not even the price of a good piss-up. And that young one you pounced on by the railway station. Got away with that too, you pervert. But you slipped in the end. Didn't think there was a camera, you dickhead?'

'I'll report you for assault. You're not the big man now Duffy ... arghh!'

I dropped him with one dig to the kidney then patted his head like he was a greyhound, felt the wet straw.

'Be seeing you again, ould stock. Take care now. Keep a good look out'.

I made my way up the hill by the bookshop. Crossing the street I caught a flash of blonde. A tall woman with a fur-collared coat was coming out of the new Japanese place I had yet to try.

'Susan, is that yourself?'

Why do we say such foolish things sometimes?

'I haven't set eyes on you for ages'.

'Michael Duffy, well now, long time no see is right'.

'I've been lying low. Licking my wounds, so to speak'.

'I heard about the break-up alright. I'm sorry, Mike, I know Sheila meant a lot to you'.

'I'm just heading up to Burke's. Have you time to join me for one'.

'I'm supposed to be ... ah, why not. Just the one, mind'.

'Good girl! I could do with looking at a pretty face for a change'.

I glanced down the hill. Kelly was nowhere to be seen.

I was still very raw. Fifteen years of marriage. What went wrong? So many damn things, but it takes two to tango. A Supermacs dad now and I hate that. Fucking Happy Meals on a Sunday afternoon. Marie Louise at fourteen makes the effort but Cian is struggling. First year at secondary and his home life crumbles. Maybe that's an exaggeration.

They still live in the house with their mother. I would never change that. At least there is peace.

'You look miles away Mike. A penny for those thoughts'.

We had settled in a nice corner of the bar and, to tell the truth, I was enjoying the chat and the odd envious glance from the pint-drinkers.

'That's about all my thoughts are worth these days'.

'I think we could improve on that, recession or no recession', and she flicked back her hair with one of those female shimmies I hadn't seen for a while.

Did I catch the vibe correctly, I wondered. My social skills with women were buried under years of sediment. Anyway, the last thing I needed was complication. Keep it simple Mike, stick to the routine. I caught the young barman's eye and gestured for two more drinks.

'Do you ever see Tony these days?' I thought I'd shift the conversation to the opposite pole.

'He's in Dublin, new life, new partner. Moved on, as they say'.

'No kids makes it easier'.

'It's never easy, as you know – but a sordid squabble over bricks and mortar is bad enough without little lives being hurt. I always thought you and Sheila would make it. What do you reckon happened or am I prying?'

'It's difficult to say. There were changes. I left the army. Set up the security business. No more disappearing off to Africa or the Lebanon. Maybe she thought I'd become Brigadier General of the Blue Berets instead of a glorified bouncer'.

'Let me say one thing Mike and then you can tell me to go. I knew Sheila in school, she was a spoiled snob then and she never changed. Her doting Dad had her believing that no one was good enough, not a handsome young cadet in uniform, not even a tycoon with a private jet. There now, I've said it. Cuff me, I'll go peacefully'.

I knew Susan since we first sat in lecture halls together years ago and she was always one to speak her mind. I liked that. This time she walked to the bar and ordered another round. Gin and tonic and a whisky. I watched her at the counter, shapely in trousers and pink top, a late-thirties divorcee refusing to be put down.

Two hours later we were still in the corner. All plans for the evening on hold. 'To hell with it. I'm enjoying myself here', she giggled and her cheek rested just for a moment on my shoulder. Somewhere deep inside my head I could hear music striking up, lively fiddles and banjos. I hadn't heard that for a long time.

'I think we're getting pissed'.

'So what', she replied, 'we're troubled folk, so therefore it's allowed'.

'Do you want him back?'

'No way, it's all over now, baby blue. And you, would you have Sheila back?'

'Yes and no'.

'She's been seeing someone you know. Regularly'.

I didn't know but tried not to show it. My voice, when I called for two more drinks, was loud. Too loud. Heads turned.

'You hadn't heard?'

'No. Are you sure it's not just, how should I say – harmless out?'

'I heard they met on some college course'.

'She finished that course well before we broke up'.

Silence. I could feel the world's tectonic plates moving beneath my feet, then click into place.

'I've said too much. Always was a fault'.

'You mean no harm ever and I'm glad I heard it from you. I'm blind and stupid and …'

Her hand closed over mine and it said I know it's hard but keep the faith.

'Come on', I nodded towards the door, 'let's get out of here'.

I threw a twenty on the counter and told the barman to have the last round on us, we had to go.

Outside the night had turned to drizzle.

'We can get a taxi'.

'Do we need a taxi, Mike, don't you live in town now?'

'Christ you're right. I forgot for a minute, imagine that. Whisky you're the devil, as the song says'. We leaned on each other, laughing like school-kids at the foolishness of it all.

Then my mobile rang.

'Sheila?'

'I was going to call the Guards but thought I'd call you first. Someone out of your sordid world appears to have turned up at my gate'.

Her serrated tone would gut mackerel, but I knew her well enough to detect an undercurrent of real fear.

'Sheila, what's wrong?'

'I'm looking out the window now at a man who is shouting threats and being extremely obscene. He's exposed, to put it delicately, and gesturing. Michael, he knows our names. Mine, Marie Louise's, Cian's. The door is locked and I told the kids to stay in the kitchen'.

'Has he a combat jacket and long red hair?'

'That's him. I don't like the look of him Michael. I think he's drunk or on something'.

'Put off all the lights. Get upstairs. Lock the doors. I'll be there in a few minutes'.

'I'm not sure but I think he has a knife'.

I killed the call and rang a plainclothes mate of mine. He didn't hang about.

'I'm sorry Susan. You heard the story. Here's my keys, the apartment is only down the road. I have a spare set. The address is on the tag. Make coffee, please wait. I'll be as quick as I can'.

'I'll come with you'.

But I was already running hard for the line of taxis by the river.

The squad car was already there when I arrived. Blue light flashing in the quiet cul-de-sac. She'd love that alright.

'Any sign of him, Guard?'

'No, he was gone by the time we got here. We're checking the neighbourhood'.

'He might have a weapon'.

'A weapon?'

'A knife or blade and he's well fit to use it'.

'You know him so, do you?'

'I know him from old. He was a private in the army for a while. Got tuft out. I testified against him in a case a few years ago. He's not long released'.

The drizzle was turning to rain. Cold and spiteful. It trickled down the back of my neck. Sheila was at the bedroom window. Cian on one side, Marie Louise on the other. A vixen with her cubs.

I rang the doorbell like a stranger.

'Who was that bad man Dad? Why was he saying such horrid things?'

'Don't worry, angel, he won't be coming back'.

'But he knew my name and my school. I'm scared Dad'.

She was near to tears. I hugged her close, Cian beside her trying hard to be macho.

'Don't worry my pet, he'll not be bothering you again. I promise'.

'Will we get protection?' Cian asked. 'They get twenty-four hour protection on TV'.

Sheila reappeared at the living room door and flung me a towel to dry my hair. I noted the new timber floors, the wallpaper. Someone had been busy.

'Will you be staying the night, Dad? You know, for security reasons'.

'No need, pet, he's gone and the squad will patrol'.

'Go make your Dad some coffee kids. Looks like he could do with it'.

A barbed dig? Maybe not.

'This is just more of it Michael. You're gone and you're still trouble'.

'He won't be back. I promise you that'.

'Who is he anyway? He looks dangerous'.

'He's unpleasant'.

'So what's he doing hanging around this house?'

'Revenge fantasy with drink. I helped put him away for a while'.

I didn't want to say too much, enough to alert but not alarm. It wouldn't do to tell her his true form – burglary, assault on the elderly, probable rape – he'd gut you without a thought. All they could pin on him was breaking and entering, possession of stolen property and resisting arrest. My people set up the sting.

Marie Louise came with a mug of instant. I settled into the armchair, saw my old coffee stain. 'Well Cian, any other excitement? How's school?'

Sheila's mobile rang. I caught the look.

'We're fine. I'll call you back later', she was almost whispering.

'Sheila, take the fucking call'.

The rain had eased. Drizzle swirled around the streetlamps and the tidy gardens. I knew the shortcut through the alley between the semis and the green patch. Is this it? Settled suburbia. Is this all life is about? Pay the bills, raise the kids, retire, die. He was a nice man, they might say. He was. He fucked everything up. He did, he did.

No sign of Kelly.

I crossed at the roundabout, heading back to town on foot, turned right then along by the University. Always admired those cut-stone walls, some happy days spent behind them. A lifetime away. The moon appeared over the Cathedral, racing thought the tatter of cloud.

Then I saw him. About half way across the Salmon Weir Bridge trying to light a cigarette but the wind had other ideas. Water rushed angrily through the stone arches, the river swollen and churning from the recent downpours. The sticky sound of a passing taxi on the wet road, then silence. Options? I thought of Marie Louise trembling in my arms. 'He knew my name Dad, he knew my school'. There weren't any options. I moved.

Kelly's wild head spun around but too late. A fist of hair and his nose and forehead cracked off the stone parapet. Limestone, polished smooth from all the bodies leaning over to watch the fish bend in the river below. One swift cartwheel, up and over and he was gone. Surf that, you fuck!

My apartment was in darkness although the heat was on and there was ground coffee percolating in the jug. I called her name but no answer. My keys were on the table in the kitchenette. Beside them an apple. Someone had taken a single bite.

SNAGGED

Aideen Henry

I wake up with the feeling of a warm wetness streaming out of me. Naked from the waist down. I feel cold, so cold. My hands reach to check. It must have been a dream. I'm sweating but my pyjamas are still on and I'm at home in my parents' house. On the ceiling a knot of wood is in the shape of a sharp-beaked bird, looking like he'd peck you.

Two weeks left in this place then I'm free. I can smell the rasher fat burning from here. It travels through the keyholes, under the doors and up through the floorboards. Best alarm clock ever made, according to Mammy. Once it's nine o'clock she wants all her guests up and out, fed and paid and gone from the place so she can get the rooms sorted before Mass. Well, so I can get the rooms sorted before Mass.

I remember the first summer she let me do the bedrooms, I'd just turned thirteen and got my monthlies. She showed me how everything had to be done. She had her method, you see, and you daren't stray from it.

First the ensuites, polishing the mirror with a squeaky rubbery cloth, cleaning both the sink plughole and the plug itself on both the topside and underside, with a small angled toothbrush. Using another brush on the base of the taps, especially underneath where the dirt collects, she said. Where dirt might collect if there was dirt and if it was let. The shower doors, polished inside and out. The jiff-soaked green scrub to the sink and shower enamel until the scratching sensation is gone and the cold surface is smooth to touch. Fake tan or hair dye, a divil to get off, bleach your only man. Every surface sprayed and wiped and the bathroom floor washed by hand, no other way to do it right, backing out the door on your hands and knees to finish.

Then the bed. Stripping the sheets, duvet cover and pillowslips. Making sure the crackly plastic protector is pulled well down over all the corners. There was no telling what state you'd find the bed in. Well, I lie, you could put money on it that an old couple or a settled married couple would be neat and tidy, the bed covers pulled over and pyjamas and nightie under the pillow and a book on the bedside table if they were staying a few nights. But if it was a singles' night-out in Galway, then man or woman it made no difference. There'd be clothes scattered everywhere; dresses, jeans and blouses at the door of the room, bras and socks down behind the bed, knickers and boxers stuck in the sheets or in the bed cover at the foot of the bed.

Mammy had me wear gloves.

'Never know what they get up to, love'. Her nose'd wrinkle up. 'And wouldn't want to know either'.

So at thirteen I was like a forensic investigator in my gloves, gathering all their clothes into one pile, stripping the soiled bed linen and dressing the beds again with fresh linen.

There's no kettle or coffee-making facility. 'Sure, can't they go out for that or have it before they come here'. Mammy said. 'This is no café. They're coming here to sleep, well ...' So that was another cleaning job I was spared.

Once all the surfaces in the bedroom got a squirt and a wipe, hoovering was the last job. Then I'd open the window and sit on the bed and breathe in the fresh smell of weeds from the river. The sweat from the effort of hoovering would trickle down the side of my forehead and down the top of my stomach. I'd wait there, letting my heart slow until the breeze felt cold on my face. Then I'd gather all my bits and move onto the next room. That was my summer job from then on through school and college.

'And aren't you lucky to have a job at all?' Mammy used to say.

Very lucky, I'd be thinking, even luckier if I was getting paid.

The radio's turned up. Talky voices, must be *Sunday Miscellany*.

'How can you bear it?' Frances used to say, through her mane of hennaed hair. Her red dangling earrings clicking with each word, as if agreeing with her. 'I just have to get out of this country every summer. Don't know how you stick it'.

Not much point telling her I never had a choice. Family business, give and take. Or take and give. But we're quits now. She'd get so angry, Frances would. I think she enjoyed getting angry. The righteousness of it. Reacting to every injustice, or whatever she thought was unjust, students' rights, workers' rights, a woman's right to choose. Got her involved in the Rape Crisis Centre of all things. She even did their counselling training programme. Imagine going to her if it happened you. She wouldn't be able to listen to more than half the story before she'd blow up. She'd have to leave you midway to build a political campaign about it or write a strong article to the paper or go on radio or confront someone anyway. She'd have to do something, for sure. As though doing something is the solution to everything.

I snuggle down under the duvet for one last minute. I have my own duvet cover, pillowslips and sheets. Wouldn't want the guests using mine or me using theirs. I even wash them separately in our regular machine, not the industrial one. I breathe in expecting the pinecone smell of detergent. Instead it's the smell of wet anorak. Left too long in the machine again. Out of nowhere I remember his face. Brown eyes, high cheekbones. There was something weak about him. Must have been his teeth, stained since birth. I knew at the time there was something I didn't trust. Then I persuaded myself I shouldn't judge him on his teeth, poor lad couldn't help that.

It was the night after my finals and we'd met for a drink in a quiet pub just around the corner from my flat in Dublin. He didn't say much. Kept flipping beer mats and asking me lots of questions but didn't seem overly interested in my answers. Shifty, like. I'd decided anyway to leave after the one drink. But sure, after the one drink he had me. I woke up shivering in my own bed. My knickers below my knees, my socks still on, my blouse still on but open and my bra tangled around my neck. I thought I was dreaming. I looked around. My shoes were over at the door, my jeans thrown on the chair, my jumper at the foot of the bed. I sat up and felt the warm gush coming out of me, streaming down my legs onto the bed. The starchy smell of it. Unmistakable.

I jumped out of bed and tore what was left of my clothes off me and rushed into the shower. Oh I'd heard all Frances's stories alright, all the things you shouldn't do. But no way. No way was I going dressing with his greasy touch left on my flesh, his slime inside me. No way was I going telling this story to anyone else. Bad enough that it happened without everyone hearing about it and finding out what an eejit I was to have been taken in. Bad enough that it went this far. No. It was stopping here.

I sat down in the shower and angled my hips so the water rained down inside me, washing him out of me. Cleaning me of his filth. My fingers searched all over my body wondering where he had been. I had to take it back. I rubbed my forehead and cheeks and neck, soaping and rinsing, soaping and rinsing. Then my chest and stomach and legs. Scrubbing and scrubbing. I kept thinking of other parts of me he might have reached. What about my ears? What about my mouth? I wasn't there. How could I know? Nothing for it but to presume the worst. Every part of me I scrubbed, even poking soap into my backside and crouching on the floor of the shower for the water to pour inside to rinse it out.

Once I was wrapped up in towels I found a pair of gloves I'd used for highlights and stuffed all the bed linen and all the clothes I'd worn into a black plastic disposal bag.

I put on a tracksuit and hoodie and packed up a week early. I was down in Galway before dark that night with nothing in my stomach except the morning-after-pill I'd washed down with a slug of water. That was three months ago.

'Sandra!' Mammy again, now at the foot of the stairs. 'Get up. It's nine thirty'.

I'm up like a shot, shower and dress and report for duty in the kitchen. Mammy scoops a dozen rashers off the skillet onto a dish, covers it and places it in the warming oven. She rests the greasy end of the slice on a side plate and returns the oven gloves to the hook on the wall. No point trying to have my own breakfast before the guests are done because she won't leave me in peace. So I wait. She washes her hands and dries them with a paper towel, snatching it from hand to hand as if trying to get gum off her palms. Then she squirts hand cream onto one palm and works it into her fingers, drawing each of her rings forwards to reach the skin behind them. She turns to me, stares at me and then seems to see me.

'Find out if that Murray family want three full Irish again today, would you?'

'Is Dad up?'

Her chin drops and her lips flatten out. I follow her glance out the window to the caravan. The curtains are still pulled. She crosses her freckled arms and stares at me.

'Ok, ok. The Murray family'.

When I return she is standing in front of the small mirror rearranging the combs in her hair. Dad walks in the back door.

'Morning all'. He says.

'Well?' she says, looking at me.

'Three full Irish' I say. 'Have you just the one more after?'

'Any breakfast going?' Dad says.

'Ye're great for the questions, the pair of ye. Must be your big brains, needing to suck up all that information'.

She melts a knob of butter on the skillet, spreading it with the tip of the slice. The scratch of metal on metal. I start to unload the dishwasher.

'Brenda?' he says. 'Is there any cooked breakfast going?'

I'm not getting caught in this one. It's his third time since Christmas.

'Just the one yank left', she says. 'Still asleep. If he doesn't rise soon he can forget breakfast'. She cracks three eggs onto the skillet and scoops oil over the top. I watch as the orange yolk films slowly to white.

'So when'll the conferring be?' she asks, eyeing the eggs.

'Sometime in September, I'd say'.

'Brenda?' Dad's standing next to her.

She covers the eggs with a lid, turns off the hob and pivots around to me.

'Come out to the line with me and help me bring in those duvet covers before that shower of rain catches them'.

At the line we unpeg the white sheets and duvet covers and it starts to rain so we drape them over our shoulders and hurry in, looking like two red-faced Roman senators. Dad hasn't moved.

She stands in front of him and looks at him like you'd eye an extinct animal you never liked in a glass display case.

'I did like Chris's mother's dress last night, I must say'. She says. 'That woman has style'.

Dad's about to speak when she cuts in.

'But do you know what really galls me, Sandra?'

She lifts a sheet, snaps it out and holds it by both corners. I reach for the opposite corners and bring them to her. She opens her fingers to receive them.

'What really galls me is having to put up with someone who's weak. Someone who has no word'. I bring the lower half of the sheet up to her. 'A lily-livered liar'.

She folds it again and lays it on the pile for ironing.

'What did I do?' says Dad, now seated at the table.

She presses both her hands flat on the centre of the sheet, leaning in with her weight, moving her hands from the middle to the edges, flattening the creases.

'I liked Mrs. Daly's outfit too'. I say. 'She has the height to wear it'.

'Oh, she's trailing after her husband, she is. Now that man can carry a suit, no question'. She busies herself at the hob again.

'Tell me what I –'

'Dad –'

'– Oh, don't waste your breath, Sandra. He's only looking for notice'.

She places four slices of brown bread in the toaster and hands me the tray loaded with the three cooked breakfasts.

When I return from the dining room, he's pouring milk on his cereal and she's lost in a cloud of steam over the ironing machine. He starts to suck cereal off his spoon and she jerks back the ironing cover, reaches to turn up the Irish reels on the radio then returns to her ironing.

Sometimes I wonder what it's like when I'm not here. Maybe they put this show on for my benefit and they're harmonious in my absence. As if they have to show me they need me here. Or maybe they really do need me here. Whichever way it is, it makes no odds. I'm gone. Today she's in a fit because he was drinking again last night. But there are days when he doesn't drink and she's equally raging. I bring my cereal to the table and sit down across from him.

'I was thinking, Sandra', she says. Once the focus is off him then she turns it on me. We are her two main settings. I wait her out.

'Well, I was surprised, I have to say'. She continues. 'Seemed kinda sudden'.

'Sudden?'

'Your engagement'.

'Sandra knows Chris this long time, Brenda', Dad pipes up.

The withering look she reserves for him alone is delivered and he returns his attention to his mug of tea.

After years of watching them, what's surprising isn't that she maintains this consistent level of hostility but that he expects her to be different. As though he's clutching onto his original impression of her and no hostility expressed by her will ever change that.

I finish my cereal and stand by the kettle waiting for it to boil.

She's no fool. It surprised me too, going out with Chris again, getting engaged. It's not what I expected either. We had parted ways after the Leaving cert, me off to study Social Work in Dublin, him staying on in Galway to study Science. I'd had a number of boyfriends since, most of them wild and carefree, polar opposites to Chris.

I felt very strange when I first moved back. I stayed in, did my work in the B&B and went for walks by the lake. I was jumpy, nervous, couldn't concentrate for long. I'd start laughing at something stupid, like the dog trying to hump the cushion and I'd finish up crying. I'd get upset about things that didn't matter, like when one of the kittens was born dead.

One day I was driving across town from collecting stuff at the wholesalers when I saw this old man teetering. He wasn't drunk. You could tell. He would have been seventy or eighty years old. All dressed up for his day out in Galway, his good suit and woollen coat over, wearing his best hat and he was walking along the street and he started drifting to one side and I was sitting in traffic and all the cars around me, everyone was watching him and no one was going to do anything and I couldn't bear it. I drove my car up onto the wide pavement and I parked and grabbed him just before he went down and I saved his head from hitting the ground and I sat with him and I asked him was he ok and he said he wasn't sure and I asked him where he lived and he said he'd just come out of hospital so I helped him into the back of my car and I drove him to Casualty where the nurse took him in on a wheelchair. And I looked around and wondered, does no one care? This old man and no one belonging to him with him, does no one but me care? I had to wait in the Dunnes car park for my crying to stop before I could go on home.

So I was out walking by the lake one afternoon and I heard this strange noise from a duck and I looked and out in a boat was a man and a boy. A duck seemed to have got snagged in their fishing line and they were following it to the bank. As they got closer I saw it was Chris with his younger brother. He was teaching him how to fish. The poor duck had the hook stuck in his head and the young lad was crying, thinking he'd killed it.

I caught the rope and tied their boat to the mooring and helped the young lad in. Chris managed to catch the duck and calm it and I held its wings down while he snipped one end off the hook and fed the metal through the wound to free it, without ripping any more of the its flesh.

'There now, Sandra, it's out, you can let him off, he's grand'.

I didn't want to let the duck go. I started crying. Chris took the duck from my hands, smoothened over the feathers where it had been cut, placed it on the water and it swam away. The young lad started laughing at me crying and then I started laughing. We must have looked a right pair. Chris just stared at me. This was not the Sandra he went out with at school. She had her mother's mettle, afraid of nothing. She could look after herself. He put his arm around me and hugged me and it took all my will not to cry again and I wasn't able to move out of his hug and somehow he knew that. I went back in the boat with them as far as the pier in the quiet of the evening. The quiet of no one talking and the boat creaking with each stroke and the fresh water slapping against the sides and the click and slide of the young lad's rod casting and reeling in. Each of those sounds had a comfort in them. Chris asked me would I join them again and we ended up passing the summer afternoons together out on that lake. I can't say if it was him or the boat or the lake but part of me knew that this was what I needed. Then in August the young lad went on a summer camp so it was just me and Chris and lots of quiet.

'I suppose it seems that way all right'. I say to my mother. 'Sudden, like. But it's not really. We've been together all summer'. I pour boiling water into my mug and the coffee granules melt.

I feel the cold on my leg again as if I'm naked.

'And he's a good man'.

My blouse is open and pulled to one side digging into my armpit.

'We get on great together'.

The underwire from my bra is cutting into my neck and I feel a pulsing pressure in my forehead.

'He's my best friend. I trust him'.

My hands are freezing. I can't move my arms or legs. A cold black eel slithers up my leg. I can't move away. I can't stop him. He's between my legs, he's inside me. He tunnels through me and comes out my mouth. He slides around my neck ringing it in three bands so I can't breathe and my eyes bulge and my head feels like it'll burst. He slips over my breasts first circling each, then both in a figure of eight then he burrows into the bed to come around my back looping my chest and squeezing and squeezing.

They're both standing in front of me, looking worried.

'What?' I say.

'Sit down, love. Sit down'. She says. 'You're covered in sweat'.

He pulls over a chair and I sit down.

'Are you ok?' he says.

'Yeah, course. Why wouldn't I be?'

THE LAST BLOW

Pat Mullan

Dublin

Bob McArdle was Marty Rainey's closest friend, perhaps his only friend. About the same age and similarly saddled with life's infirmities, they met about once a week to bemoan the brave New Ireland. They usually met for lunch – fish and chips for both of them – and then, if the weather was dry, they'd sit near the canal not far from Portobello Road and watch the swans.

Today they sat silently looking until Marty said.

'Bob, will you do something for me?'

Bob looked at him very strangely.

'That's a strange question. If I can do it, I'll do it. You know that. Unless it's a bank job. Can't run as fast anymore!'

And then he chuckled at his sense of humour.

'I want you to keep something for me'.

'Sure, what is it?'

Marty pulled a large envelope out of his pocket. He held it in his hand as he looked at Bob.

'There's a tape in here. It's a recording of a phone call. I want you to look after it for me. And, if anything happens to me, I want you to give this to the right person'.

'Does this have anything to do with all that Tribunal business?'

'It does. But it's even bigger than that. And there are some people who would like to get their hands on what's on the tape. That's if they knew I had it'.

'Marty, are you in any kind of trouble?'

'I'll be honest with you, I am. That's why I'm giving you this to keep for me'.

'You need protection. Are you talkin' to the gardaí?'

'They're the last people I'd be talkin' to. Can't trust anybody'.

'But you said I should give this to the right person if anything happens to you. How will I know the right person?'

'That's where I'm relyin' on you. Don't give it to the police or the Tribunal or anybody in the government'.

'That's everybody!'

'No, you have to find someone you can trust. Somebody who's not afraid to go public with this tape, get it in the papers, or on the TV. Whatever. Somebody who's not afraid of them'.

'I dunno, Marty. I just dunno. You can't let anything happen to you. Do ye hear me, do ye?'

Marty put his big arm around Bob and gave him a hug. Then he slipped the envelope into his hand, got up and walked away.

That was the last time that Bob McArdle would ever see Marty Rainey. Marty was found next day lying face-down on his kitchen floor. The door keys were still in his right hand. His throat had been cut. A professional job.

At thirty-four Sean White had buried his father and moved back into the family home to take care of his sixty-five-year-old mother in the early stages of Alzheimers.

Married at nineteen, separated at twenty-one, and divorced in 2003 when Ireland finally made divorce legal, Sean had led a hedonistic lifestyle for the past ten years. Gifted with boundless energy, his big open face acted as a magnet for many young ladies. But as soon as any relationship turned serious, Sean moved on. He feared commitment, fearing failure itself.

But his lifestyle had worn thin in the past three years and had turned into too many hung-over mornings that were beginning to affect his career. A top investigative journalist, he'd been threatened often. He hadn't made the front page in a long time. Only his talent had saved him, but he knew that wouldn't last. So, in a sense, his father's death and the need to care for his mother saved him.

It was eleven on Saturday morning and he was in the kitchen preparing tea and toast for his mother when he heard the phone ring. She answered it and he could tell from her voice and her questions that she felt uncomfortable.

Probably another damn sales call, he thought.

He walked through to the hallway and found his mother standing there with the phone in her hand, looking bewildered, 'I don't know who this is. But he says he wants to speak to you, Sean'.

Sean took the phone from his mother and said, 'hello?'

Spluttering coughs came over the line, followed by, 'Is this Sean White?'

'Yes, who's speaking?'

More coughing, then, 'I'm a friend of Marty Rainey'.

Taken aback, Sean said nothing.

The man sounded elderly and unwell as he continued, 'Marty was my closest friend. He gave me something before he died'.

Sean asked 'What's your name?'

'Never mind that. I'll tell you when we meet'.

'Why are you calling me?'

'I didn't know what to do or who to call. Marty didn't trust anybody. Not even the gardaí. He gave me an envelope. Told me if he died to give it to the right person. I asked him who. But he said he'd trust me to find the right person'.

'And why me?'

'I've seen your name on all the stories about Marty. About the documents too. Marty's documents. I know that. They killed him for them, didn't they?'

'Yes they did!'

'Well, I want you to have whatever's in this envelope Marty gave me'.

'Where do you want to meet?'

'I live near Marty's. Harold's Cross. Meet me at Peggy Kelly's. Nine tonight'.

'Ok, I'll be there. And I want to bring somebody with me'.

'Who?'

'Dave Smith. He's a trusted colleague. And it pays to be careful, doesn't it?'

The incessant coughing and spluttering had returned, finally followed by a wheezing, 'Alright'.

Bob McArdle left his house at eight and crossed the canal near the house where the Irish patriot, Robert Emmett, had been arrested. Aided by a strong blackthorn walking stick, he gritted his teeth against the pain of his sciatic nerve as it flowed through his right hip and down his thigh. But, at eighty-three, he'd learnt to live with pain. Propelling himself on his blackthorn, he intended to be at Peggy Kelly's by nine.

Sean White and Dave Smith walked through the door of Peggy Kelly's at exactly eight-thirty. A big, bustling, neighbourhood pub, it was filled with people, young and old, eating, drinking, talking, laughing, enjoying. An infectious atmosphere.

Taking a pint of Guinness and a pint of Carlsberg from the bar, they squeezed their way through and found stools at a small round table in the rear.

'If you don't know who he is, Sean, do you at least know what he looks like?'

'No. But he knows what I look like and he said he'd find me. So we'll have to depend on that'.

Dave raised his beer and clinked Sean's Guinness with a 'Sláinte!'

Taking a long, satisfying sip of his pint, Sean looked at Dave and said, 'I think this whole Tribunal business is only scratching the surface'.

'What do you mean?'

'Come on, they're getting nowhere. You know that. You could fill a library with the testimony they've taken'.

'Do you know a better way?'

'There's got to be. It's costing the taxpayer a fortune. And making more fecking millionaires out of the lawyers!'

'Look at the big picture. We have to stop the culture of corruption. End the days of the gombeen man. This is a modern democracy and the old ways have to go. You could view these tribunals as an indictment of the past and a bridge to the future'.

'I'll let the historians tell us that when they look back at this time. Maybe you'll be right. But I wouldn't bet on it. We're floating in money. And that's too much temptation'.

'I know, I know. But, dammit, we need to send a message to these people, and to the countries and businesses that invest and trade with us, that we are honest and can be trusted. Right now they're waiting to hear from us. And the tribunals are a message to them as well'.

'Ok, Ok. But I still say we're spending a ton of money on these tribunals. And for what? Have we arrested anybody? Jailed anybody?'

'No, not yet. Have faith. Look at it from another angle. We've exposed some of them. Left them with tarnished images. They'll never run for political office again. They'll never hold positions of trust in this country again. Let's face it, they're finished!'

'That's too soft a landing for some of these bastards. They should be in Mountjoy, on bread and water, for the next twenty years!'

'You're right. And if the Tribunal finds enough hard evidence they'll be happy to turn it over to the DPP'.

'I wish I could believe that'.

'Damn it, you know we're not going to depend on the Tribunal to stop them!'

'I'm sorry. I get so pessimistic at times'.

They both realized that they had got so caught up in their conversation that they'd forgotten entirely about the reason they were there.

'It's 9:15 already'.

'Shit, I almost forgot'.

'No sign of anybody yet'.

'No. But he sounded old. And sickly. So I'm not surprised he's late'.

Sean took their two empty glasses up to the bartender and said, 'Agus aris!'

A light drizzle obscured Bob McArdle's glasses. Couples scurried past him and a stray dog almost tripped him. Distracted, he didn't see the two balaclava-hooded men step out of a doorway as he hobbled along. One kicked the blackthorn stick out of his hand while the other kicked him in the ribs as he fell. He screamed in pain but the sounds died in his throat as the first assailant wielded the blackthorn like a baseball bat, cracking McArdle's cheekbone and forcing his broken dentures down his throat, blocking his windpipe. Swinging the blackthorn again, he smashed it into McArdle's back before tossing it on the ground.

Dying now, his blood merging into the rain and running in rivulets into the drain near his head, the last blow of the blackthorn was unnecessary. The few people who saw the assault fled to the other side of the street. Assuming it to be another gangland killing, they knew it didn't pay to interfere or even to be seen.

As the two assailants disappeared, another man, tall and sinister in a long Jack Murphy raincoat, stepped out from the shadows and kneeled at Bob McArdle's side. He fished an envelope out of McArdle's pocket. Then he stood and disappeared into the shadows.

At 10:30 Sean White and Dave Smith decided to call it an evening. They speculated that their appointee may have been too ill to show up. They reckoned that, if the caller had been real, they could only hope that he'd call Sean again.

The news item in the next day's paper about the brutal bludgeoning death of a frail old man did not make page one. Neither of them saw it.

FULL-SIZED LIFE

Susan Millar DuMars

Luke swallowed the bird on a cold, clear December night –
trees of bone, the river in a silver-black sulk. He'd waved
off a taxi, needing the air after all those back-slapping
pints. Crossing the bridge toward the cathedral, he
thought how the dome at night was a great green helmet;
the windows, unreadable eyes. He remembered funerals,
several, in the past year. Muttering responses to prayers,
following the coffin out slow and stiff-legged. Luke
crossed himself without knowing he did it. As his hand fell
it brushed the old stone banister of the bridge and he
thought for a moment of the river beneath him, God and
Death in front of him. Himself suspended in a comfortable
middle age. How lucky. How very lucky.

Though even as he plumped and pinked with a sense of
good fortune, another voice inside him contradicted.
'Earned! Surely, earned'. He lifted his other arm and gazed
at what he clutched. The book. His book. *Bringer of Light:
The Life and Poems of Malachy Flynn*. Launched into the

world this evening in a modest, yet satisfying, ceremony. The applause had been warm and lasting. Loyola had beamed. Afterward, in the pub, many pints of Erdinger were bought for him. Loyola had drunk half an orange juice and had driven herself home to prepare a late supper. He'd promised to be home before the meat turned tough.

Luke crossed the deserted street, thinking he might try to write a sonnet about that later. That moment of looking up at the cathedral, considering his life. He had a file full of sonnets on his laptop. Poetry writing being a sort of occupational hazard for literature professors. His had never been read by anyone. Maybe someday, when he was retired. When he was old.

He walked, and the still night suddenly swelled with a sound. The purest and sweetest of sounds. Crisp as a bell; soulful as the sobs of a lost child. A sound which made colours behind his eyes. He stumbled, looking wildly from side to side for the source of this rising, swooping melody.

It was a bird. The smallest bird he'd ever seen, perched on the mechanical arm that guarded the cathedral car park's entrance. A velvety black that was nearly purple. Its breast bloomed white. Its head was tilted quizzically to one side, and from the tiny triangle of beak gushed this music, strangely loud, winding around Luke like silk, insistent. Luke felt rapture tinged with shame. How crude were the lines of verse he'd just been assembling in his head. How … inadequate. Nothing he would ever write or say would shimmer with the eloquence of this little bird's song. This he thought without thinking, without language. It was a sudden knowing in the pulsing, primitive part of his mind he lazily referred to as his soul. A warm tear slid down the side of Luke's nose. He knelt on the cold footpath.

'Oh, little man', he whispered to the bird. 'Beautiful little man'. At this, the bird stopped singing and stared at Luke with its pellet eyes. 'Hello?' said Luke. The bird looked.

'You ok there?' asked Luke. 'Hello-o-o?' The bird observed the round cavity of Luke's mouth, warm breath escaping it in clouds. It leapt straight up and, with a flurry of fluttering, flew straight at Luke's mouth and in.

Luke felt a warm ball pop into his mouth. He inhaled with the shock and felt to his horror the bird get sucked down into his windpipe. A beak or claw scratched the back of his throat. He couldn't breathe, couldn't cry out. His gullet stretched painfully around the little body. He fell backward onto his bottom, both hands clutching at his neck. The little bird was scrabbling against the sides of his oesophagus. Blood began to seep into his mouth.

The last thing Luke heard before blacking out was a vague human cry and the sound of running footsteps. He saw only sky, coursing dark like the river.

A flying bed. Cold metal rail keeping him on board as it soared down a corridor. Not his bed. Faces. Light. Not his bed. Loyola. Why –

And all the time pain. Oh pain. Something had cut him inside. Why wasn't anyone –

This was not his bed.

The room was dark. And still. Street-lamped trees threw graceful shapes on drawn curtains. This and the tidy, clean smelling bedclothes made him feel snug, despite the pinch in the back of one hand. He moved the hand and a thin translucent tube waggled at the edge of his vision. The pain was less. He could breathe, he could think. He could not really lift his head but he could live without a lifted head if that meant the pain was kept at bay.

The ceiling looked strange – blotchy, stained. He squinted. The stains were all of the same hue and shape. He heard a door open and a trickly beam of light entered his room. He closed his eyes against it. The beam busied itself with the equipment on either side of his bed, then slid up over his face. Apparently satisfied, it clicked off and the door closed. *They're watching over me*, Luke thought, and though he didn't know for certain who *they* were, he felt reassured. As he drifted back to sleep, he realised the dark shapes on the ceiling were not random stains but the painted silhouettes of birds. Large birds. Gulls, maybe. Each with its big wings outstretched.

A new pain woke him. It was morning and a weak light glimmered behind the curtains. The painted seagulls wheeled, spun. The pain was like a needle jabbing, repeatedly, just beneath his ribs. He clutched at his midriff but there was nothing there. A young woman pushing a squeaking cart laden with breakfast trays appeared, opened the curtains, and worked a remote control so that Luke's bed raised him to a sitting position.

'Cornflakes!' she said cheerfully.

'Fetch a doctor', Luke moaned. The girl obediently turned and sprinted from the room. Alone with his pain, Luke clutched the bed rail and focussed on the wall opposite. For the first time he saw the framed print that hung there. A fat cartoon bird smiled toothily at him, one wing raised in a sort of salute. *The Bluebird of Happiness* it said underneath.

A tall woman with long blonde hair in a white coat entered. Behind her was a nervous looking young man in scrubs pushing a different cart; and a swollen-eyed Loyola.

'Oh Luke!' cried Loyola, and rushed to his side, taking his hand in hers. Luke noticed with concern that she looked older, more frail than she had the night before. Although most women would look fragile next to the Amazonian figure who was now pulling back his bedclothes and rucking up his gown.

'Bring it here', she said to the nervous young man, who pushed the cart in next to her. 'Good morning, Mr Riley!

I'm Ms O'Connor, your consultant. Lie still, please. Won't be a tic'. She busied herself with gloves and a cold blue gel which she smeared across his quivering belly.

Luke tried to form a question, a protest. 'HEYohstop-whaddarya-I-oh!'

The Amazon ignored him. 'Is it on?' she asked the nervous man, who nodded and handed her a thing that looked like a white plastic wand, connected by coiled cord to something atop his cart. The doctor pressed the wand, hard, into different quadrants of Luke's torso.

'Be quite still now and listen', she ordered Luke, without lifting her eyes from his stomach.

A sound filled the room; steady, rhythmic. Like an old fashioned train, chugging, but smaller … wetter. The doctor beamed at the nervous cart man, who beamed back.

Loyola let go of Luke's hand, pressed her palm to her chest. 'Is that? It's … a heartbeat'.

'Yes', said the doctor.

Luke glanced down at his naked torso. The wand was atop his belly. 'Not *my* heartbeat', he said, confirming.

'Of course not *your* heartbeat', scoffed the doctor. 'It's your bird'.

'*My* bird?' The implications danced in Luke's head.

'Quite. We don't know exactly what type of bird yet, though we have some specialists – ornithologists – working on that angle. We retrieved a feather from your mouth, they're working with that'.

'Isn't it exciting!' the cart man burbled.

'It is … well … it's beautiful', said Loyola of the sound.

'Quite', said the doctor, nodding at Loyola.

'But you're saying … you're saying it's alive, inside me?'

'It's managed to lodge in a sort of air pocket within your digestive system. The pain you've been feeling is no doubt its beak'.

Luke swallowed hard. 'Beak?'

The doctor lifted the wand and the hypnotic beating stopped. 'Beak', she repeated. 'He's pecking. Peck, peck'.

'It must be very confusing for him', sighed cart man.

'It's not exactly crystal clear to *me*', cried Luke, in a voice an octave higher than normal. 'How are you – what are you doing to get him out?'

The consultant gave the wand back to the cart man, and left her palm open. Cart man quickly handed her a sheaf of white tissues. She used the tissues to wipe excess gel from Luke's abundant flesh. Her arm worked in vigorous circles like the arm of a window cleaner.

'Mr Riley', said the doctor as she worked. 'I understand your distress. But we won't be removing the bird. Not just yet, anyway. If we attempted to do so, either through surgery or some type of, well, laxative – you must see, in either instance we couldn't assure the well-being of the bird. His placement is precarious. He'd likely not survive either procedure'.

Loyola gasped, a small, involuntary gasp. Luke swivelled his head to see her. Against the bright window her features were obscured. Despite the crowdedness of the room Luke felt alone. 'What the devil are you talking about?'

'Now Mr Riley, there's no reason to raise your voice'.

'But he's pecking me! Cutting me inside – I mean I –'

'Surely, Doctor', managed Loyola. 'Surely there's something you can do to help both my husband and the poor little bird?'

'What? Loyola, for heaven sake –'

'Well darling, it just seems to me that medical science, with all its advancements … surely, surely, they can look after both of you?'

'Loyola, I'm wounded! I could even be dying. And you're worried about a *bird*?'

'Mr Riley. Here at St Francis of Assisi Regional Hospital, we care equally for all our patients – whether five foot nine and covered in skin, or three inches high and covered in feathers'. At the word *feathers* her faced curved upwards into a love-struck grin.

'Feathers. Bless him', whispered the cart man.

Luke felt dizzy. 'I'm five ten!' he said, though he knew that was beside the point.

The consultant peeled off her gloves and tossed them onto the cart. 'For now we shall simply have to wait and see'.

'But –' A sudden jab from inside stopped Luke from finishing his sentence. His face crumpled. His wife retook his hand.

For three days, they waited. And saw. The bird remained alive, somewhere within the red tunnels of Luke's gut. With each passing hour its fear grew, and its scrabbling increased. Anxiety caused it to become diuretic, and its droppings mixed with the blood that leaked from Luke's compromised intestinal walls.

Periodically, the white wand was wielded and the bird's heartbeat would sound. It soothed all who listened, much like the sound of the tide, and Luke grew to hate the simpering faces that smiled, that *oohed*. 'It's not a magic trick. My heart beats too!' he shouted after them once.

Luke's pain changed from individual jabs to a blur of nausea, fever and cramp. When alone, he'd repeat to himself Malachy Flynn's poem 'Eagle', a poem from the point of view of the bird sent by Zeus to devour Prometheus' liver.

His flesh I rend, I tear; care not
That he is bringer of light.

He recalled the words of his publisher to the audience at the launch. 'Only a true scholar could do what Luke Riley has done, and only a truly generous scholar would try'. Loyola had squeezed his hand at that, and he'd smiled and lowered his head, embarrassed and delighted. 'Between these covers' – here Patrick had rat-a-tatted on the book with his manicured nails – 'you will find the most careful examination of the poems, and life, of Malachy Flynn that has ever been attempted. It cannot fail to bring Flynn's work the acclaim it so richly deserves'.

Patrick had gone on quite a bit about Flynn after that, sketching in rich colours episodes from the great writer's life. Childhood on a midlands farm. Adventures as a volunteer in the Spanish Civil War. Doomed affairs, arguments with editors. Whiskey the final gold curtain between Flynn and disillusionment; disillusionment winning one wet September evening in a B&B in Balbriggan. Only a small brass plaque there now …

Luke's smile had thinned as Patrick continued, his voice gone slippery with sentiment. Not for the first time, he'd wondered if Patrick had a sad sort of crush on the very dead Malachy. If he would next be seen lighting a votive in the bone yard by Malachy's grave. Some of us just get on with it, he'd thought. Some, for example, spend eight years writing a book and hope to be more than a footnote in their publisher's speech! We can't all live like characters in films.

On Day Four, Luke began to fall away from the hospital room scenes. A chill white space opened up between him and everyone else. When Loyola told him their daughter Claire was flying in from Melbourne, he told her, 'By the time she gets here, I think I'll be gone'. Loyola put her hand across her mouth. She didn't answer him, but her small face looked scalded. Luke didn't know what else he could've said.

They gathered at just before five that same day, arriving in clumps of two and three just as the dusk drew in on itself. It was cold, but dry, and the grass was short and sharp under their shuffling feet. They lit candles, one off another off another, dripping white wax and shielding baby flames with gloved hands. Someone thought to put a candle at the base of the plaster statue of St Francis. The flickering light seemed to animate his mild face, his dark eyes that gazed at the robin perched permanently on his outstretched arm. Someone, possibly cart man, propped a placard against the statue's stone base. *Life Is Precious!* This written in purple letters plump as clouds – and after the exclamation mark, a painstakingly rendered bird, musical notes ascending in a string from its mouth.

At exactly five, the group bowed their heads in silent meditation. They were perfectly still; only their candle flames moved, dipping and dancing in the wind.

Behind them, cars entered and left the hospital carpark. Some had turned their headlights on. A nurse, arms crossed against the cold, jogged past the group without stopping, on her way to the Tesco Express across the road. On the footpath, a man used his phone to photograph the gathering.

Loyola stood on the far side of the driveway. Watching. One hand, bare, was curled tight around the hospital's railing. She distantly felt the cold of the iron against her fingers. She felt very calm, but very old. Every thought took forever to pass across her mind.

No vigil for Luke, then.

Do they ever hold vigils for full-sized lives?

'Claire?' His voice sounded strange to him, too soft. Not much more than an exhalation.

But she had heard him. 'No Mr Riley', she said, smiling. 'It's me, Elaine. I'm a student nurse. Remember?'

He tried to take her in – her freckles, her kind eyes, messy reddish ponytail. On the badge beside her name was a sketch of a sparrow nestled among leaves.

'It's alright', she said steadily, 'you've met a lot of people here. I'm just checking your vitals, didn't mean to disturb you'.

'You look like my daughter'.

'Do I? I'll take that as a compliment, so!' Her hand, small and unexpectedly strong. Replacing his arm by his side. Skin to skin. 'Your wife will be right back, she's just gone for some air. It's *roasting* in here!' Yet she pulled the blanket up over him. 'Go back to sleep now, good man'.

It seemed impossible to him; the simple act of walking to the door as she was now doing. Unimaginable, feet lifting and falling, carrying you forward from this room. He could feel her attention peeling easily away from him. He was, he realised, a thing on a list. 'Bye, Mr Riley'.

She had smelled like pancakes.

Malachy Flynn's was an epic life.

Care not, that he is bringer of light. Himself, of course. Intellectus: the light of the mind. Malachy was casting himself as Prometheus.

The little bollocks.

Luke was suspended, now, not between river and God but between Flynn, who was bigger than life, born to be remembered; and the little bird, sweet with pure promise. Luke was the middle – he saw it now – the undistinguished middle who paid taxes, kept their marriage vows, muddled through. It was not what he expected. He had expected, any day, to be revealed as someone great. A bringer of light.

Overhead, the painted gulls circled. Drawing him toward them, drawing him up.

And what, in all the years, what had he brought? What would he leave behind? His book. Articles.

Claire.

Lovely, clever Claire.

Students, hundreds of them. How many would remember?

Only middling, but a life. His life.

Poetry.

His heart beat too.

At the funeral, Patrick would tell the congregation in well-greased tones that Luke had passed away peacefully. In fact, his sweat-soaked body curled in a sudden spasm and his eyes and mouth opened wide but saw nothing, said nothing. A final breath hissed past his lips. Elaine was helping a woman to the toilet. Loyola was waiting for the lift. Outside, candles were being blown out and the placard rolled up and carried away under an arm. Traffic swelled on the road outside the hospital. All the cars had their lights on now.

The bird died minutes before Luke did. Luke knew, because the pecking finally stopped; inside, he felt nothing. In that final silence he found that he was weeping, not for himself and not for the bird either; but for the bird's song. Those trembling, soaring notes. Perfect.

Despite everything, he was glad that he had heard it.

LITTLE VOICE

Alan McMonagle

He has blonde hair, blue eyes and buttocks as firm as spanking new basketballs. I wish. He is a saggy dumpling of a man with noisy nostrils, scalloped lips and a couple of chins. Throw in the grouty teeth and dodgy bowels and it is not a good picture. Still. It is my picture and, though my little voice often tells me his head needs opening, I make the most of what's in front of me.

Of course I am no bird of paradise myself. My nose seldom stops running. My feet don't point in the direction they should. Weevils have mistaken my hair for a place they can call home. I am not going to say anything about my own buttocks except to mention that neither one seems to take kindly to being in the other's company. They hold positions that are opposing and contradictory. Lopsided I suppose is the word I am looking for. Together then on the street Henry and me make a beautiful couple. It is just as well we don't have children. The world is harsh enough without our little contribution.

I am mulling this over in McCambridges, massaging the trigger of the nail gun I have stolen from Woodies, when the man with the thick neck and boiled head sits into the empty chair opposite me.

'Don't sit there', I tell him.

'Why not?' he growls.

'Because I need personal space in confined places'.

'This is a café, you nitwit, not a prison cell'.

'Don't call me a nitwit', I tell him. 'Now please find yourself another place to sit'.

'How about you find yourself another place. On the other side of the country, perhaps. Better still, why don't you flake off back to the planet you sailed in from'.

The man makes himself comfortable in the chair. He raises an arm to attract some service. I decide on another approach.

'I have a gun', I tell him. 'And I am a crack shot'.

'So shoot me', he says, no longer looking at me. My heart is now beating fast. I want to pull the nail gun, give him the full force of my ardour, but my hand is trembling. Inside I curse. I close my eyes and take deep breaths. Then I hear a familiar voice.

'I think you're in my chair'.

I open my eyes and Henry is standing over the table, looking from the thick man to me. He clasps his stubby hands together and cracks his fingers. At once, the thick man stands out of the chair. He looks my way as if to say, rather you than me, and moves to another part of the café. Henry sits into the empty chair.

'I love the way he moves when you make noise with a finger. I threatened him with my gun and he suggested I take a trip to the moon', I say.

'I am a Brueghel painting. I am straight out of a David Lynch movie'.

'What is that little speech supposed to tell me?'

'I ooze menace and dread'.

'What do I ooze?'

Henry chooses not to address that question. Instead he grabs the menu and starts to examine it with the intensity of someone who is eating in a restaurant for the first time.

On top of our sensational looks Henry and I do not have a bean between us. Henry has never worked on account of his principles. I haven't because I haven't found anything I'd like to do. At different times I've thought about being a flight attendant, a projectionist in a cinema, a cook and a lifeguard. Once upon a time I thought I wanted to be a jockey – I had the right dimensions. But the idea of belonging to a posse of midgets galloping around a field whipping horses didn't hold much appeal.

We are in McCambridges because we have come into possession of a meal-for-two voucher. It was in the breast pocket of the rich woman we dug up two nights ago. We were hoping to come away with a little more – a pearl necklace, ruby pendants, something made out of gold. Alas on this occasion it was not to be. Beggars should not be choosers, Henry is always fast to tell me. We take what we can get.

It was Henry's idea to start digging up rich women. Given half a chance I'd say he'd bury them too – preferably before they are dead. I join in because it's fun. Nor am I fussy. Rich man, poor man, rich woman, poor woman. It's all the same to me. Load me up with a shovel and pick, point me in the direction of the cemetery and I am a happy girl. Henry's philosophy is more mercenary. During these hard-hearted times he is always on the lookout for a way to get by. Women wealthy and dead are the way to go, he says. When they cash their chips they like to take the jewels with them. My attitude is this: when you've got nothing you've got nothing to lose. Let's chew up the entire cemetery.

Henry has put down the menu and is looking at me.

'Have you ordered?' he asks.

'I'm not hungry'.

'I'm going to have a sandwich'.

'Which one?'

'I'm not sure. There's some strange stuff on the menu. What's focaccia?'

'Don't know'.

'What's tabouli?'

'Never heard of it. Sounds like a disease'.

'I think I'll have some ice-cream'.

'There's a wine cave beyond the stairs. I might have something from there'.

'If you so much as glance in that direction I will stab you in the spleen with this fork'.

Henry doesn't allow me have wine. He is right not to but any time I see wine my happy hormones lick their lips and say guzzle, guzzle. I have an addictive personality. Among other things this is what some genius discovered about me a long time ago. One glass is too many, one hundred is not enough. In for a penny, in for a pound. My attitude to all of this is: you may as well be hung for a sheep as a lamb. By the look in his eye Henry will gladly volunteer a sturdy noose. I should remind him I have a nail gun in my bag. Maybe I will start using some of the pet names I have invented for him.

'Does the name Elisabeth Mulherne mean anything to you?' he is asking me.

'No'. I say.

'She was married to Patrick Mulherne'.

'Never heard of him, lovepie'.

'Well, shame on you for that'.

'Who are these people, muffin?'

'I've a good mind not to tell you. Let you revel in your ignorance'.

'A little knowledge is a dangerous thing, angelcake'.

'And ignorance is bliss'.

'Then I must be the happiest woman alive'.

'Patrick Mulherne is the richest man in Galway. He is a regular fixture in the Rich List given out with the Sunday paper. His wife – Elisabeth – has been unwell. At the weekend she died. She was buried yesterday. Tonight, after closing time, you and me are going to dig her up'.

'Anything in particular we should be on the lookout for, pumpkin?'

'Yes, there is. She has been buried with a Michelangelo Medal. Would you like to know what a Michelangelo Medal is? You would! A Michelangelo Medal is a medal awarded by the Vatican Bank to individuals generous enough to make a sweet donation to the catholic coffers. There are different levels of donations. And the level you come in at determines the category of medal awarded by the filthy rich in Rome. The Michelangelo is awarded to the highest donors. It is made out of solid gold. I've heard it's the size of Frisbee'.

'Wow!' I say, casting a sly glance at the wine cave.

'Is that all you have to say?'

'It must be worth its weight in gold', I reply to that.

'Of course it's worth its weight in gold. It's made out of gold, you nitwit!'

'You are the second person to call me nitwit today. I should warn you I have a gun. And I am a crack shot'.

'So shoot me', he says.

'Keep calling me names and you'll see what will happen'.

'Promises, promises', Henry says and gives me his leery smile.

Henry loves goading me. Every chance he gets he's at it. I suppose it is part of his charm over me, his devil appeal. We first bumped into each other along the river, beneath the gaze of an awestruck moon. He looked at me and said, My, my, what have we here? You're one to talk, I said right back and with both hands he clutched his heart as if he had just been shot. After that I saw him often on the street and slipped in behind. Follow a lion before you follow a man I remember my mother telling me when I was little. With Henry I get bits of both. Though when all is said and done he is probably more cockroach than anything. Indestructible.

Now his bowels are at him and he has left to try out McCambridge's facilities. At the far end of the room I see the thick neck man make a move for the wine cave and my trigger finger gets itchy again.

I've got all these parts to me. Easy-to-see parts and long forgotten parts and parts I yearn for in my problematic dreams. I have shadow parts. They do not wish me well. When I least expect it they tiptoe inside my skin, whisper awful things, needle my flimsy blood. Life is a series of ladders you have to climb, that same genius had to say when I was pouring it all out. Me? I don't go up ladders. I slide down snakes.

I reach for my bag and log on to Facebook using the iPad we found inside the coffin of a solicitor named Phibbs. That's right. Facebook. It's something I do. I go by the name HACKSAW. I was going to use CANNIBAL HAMSTER but it was already taken – they are a rock band from somewhere up in North Leitrim. Then I was going to use DRILLERKILLER, but it was also already taken – she is a dental nurse from Eureka, Oregon. Instead I use it as my password.

Rufus is my Facebook friend. I have no idea where he lives. What he does for a living. Is he rich? Is he poor? Is he a demented lunatic, like God? Moments after I had set up my account he sent me a friend request. I was so chuffed I immediately accepted. Then I received the confirmation message: HACKSAW IS NOW FRIENDS WITH RUFUS. Then he put up his mugshot. His blue eyes. His blonde curls. I just know he has wonderful buttocks and legs and all the rest. I think I am a little bit in love with him. Ssssssh! Henry is back.

Before he can see I close down the iPad. It goes back in my bag, safe beside the nail gun.

'Were you on Facebook?' he casually asks, giving my bag his suspicious eye.

'No, I was not, sugar buns'.

'If I catch you ...'

'Yes, yes, I know. Your fork, my spleen. You won't catch me, honey pickle. Hey! I almost forgot. The nail gun I took comes with a high-velocity driver'.

'Glad to hear it. The last thing you had wouldn't puncture cardboard. I don't know how we got the lid back on the other night'.

'And all for a meal voucher. What are we going to do with the Michelangelo Medal?'

'We're going to sell it to Considine'.

'Considine!'

'That's right'.

'I don't know about that'.

'You don't know lots of things. Anyway, once you have done your bit – that is, the digging – you needn't concern yourself with Considine'.

'Why not?'

'Because he no longer wants to be in the same room as you'.

'He said that?'

'Yes. He said the less he sees of you the more bearable his life will be'.

'He said that?'

'Yes'.

'Did he tell you to go ahead and say it to my face?'

'No'.

'Well, then. Why say it?'

'Because maybe I've been thinking he has a point'.

I don't know where this talk is suddenly sprouting from. Last time I checked we were a couple. Henry the ideas man, little me doting and dutiful. Together through sludge and muck. On the other hand, if he wants me out of his way all he has to do is say the word. At once I can pack a lunch and be gone. I will manage. I have the right attitude. Worship all that you can see and more will appear. That's what I had written over my bed when I was little.

Henry's ice-cream arrives. At once, he starts stabbing the vanilla scoops with his spoon. It is a slow process but I like the soothing effect ice-cream has upon him. It will disappear these doubting words he is throwing my way, make him sweet again. Now that I think about it I should have been a songwriter.

He has finished with the spoon and with elaborate sweeps of his tongue is now licking the held-up bowl.

'Have you looked at yourself in a mirror lately?' he manages to ask me as he licks.

'Is that a serious question?'

'A new hairdo might be the thing'.

'Are you sure you want to talk about hair?'

'And you need some new clothes'.

'I thought we were going to the graveyard!'

'Get something black'.

The dead are buried with amazing things. In addition to what is most useful to us – diamond rings, gold bracelets, strings of pearls – we have come away from the cemetery with bottles of Estée Lauder perfume, selections of pipes and tinned tobacco, cases of Middleton Rare, Ferrero Rocher chocolates, boxes of Barry's Tea, Viscount biscuits, hats, coats, recliner chairs and lacy underwear. When she died the third richest woman in town wanted to be buried with her Alsatian. Henry thought it wise not to take that. My own grandmother (she was ninety-nine, we thought she'd never croak it) insisted on being buried with her collection of Waterford crystal. That came in very handy when we got around to it. Stealing from the dead has its advantages. There is the sense of anticipation as you prise open the lid of the pinewood box. 'Stop thief', are words you will not hear from the tight lips of your victim. And, of course, providing you tidy up afterwards, it is unlikely you will get caught.

And so we come out at night.

We make our silent way across Taylor's Hill, home to pretty much all the rich women in our town. They hide their wealth behind high cut-stone walls and electronic gates. There are trees on Taylor's Hill. By day birds whistle. But it can be hard to hear them on account of noisy cars and cumbersome jeeps weaving along the narrow road. Before we took up grave robbing, Henry and me used to wander up the hill in the quiet hours before sun-up and paint slogans on the high gates. POOR PEOPLE WITH MONEY LIVE HERE. LOOK UNDER YOUR JAGUAR BEFORE YOU GO TO WORK. UP YOUR

BUM. Then we'd hold hands and race down the hill, screaming for all we were worth. I miss those times.

We're through the cemetery gates, the moon is hovering high and full, and I smile at the memory it conjures in my mind's eye. Henry is shining his torch on some of the older slabstones. Grey chunks of stone that sprout from the ground at peculiar angles. I loiter among the newer marbles and granites, where the scutchgrass and bindweed has been cleared away. Henry finds Elisabeth Mulherne's plot and I get busy with shovel and pick, whistling as I go.

'Hey! What's that tune you're whistling?' Henry asks me after a little while.

'It's from Butch Cassidy and the Sundance Kid', I tell him. 'Remember we snuck in to see it during the Film Fleadh'.

'That's not the tune from Butch Cassidy and the Sundance Kid'.

'I think it is, honey pickle'.

'No, it isn't. Keep digging'.

Soon the shovel scrapes against timber. I clear away the last of the earth. The screws come out easily. Henry is hovering, shining his torch. I'm already patting down rich Elisabeth Mulherne.

'Well? Can you see it? Can you see the medal?'

'She's not wearing it around her neck'.

'Check her pockets'.

'I thought you said it was the size of a Frisbee?'

'I was trying to make a point. Anything?'

'Nothing. This is a nice dress she's wearing. Hey! You know what we should do?'

'Look for the medal'.

'I wouldn't mind a dress like this'.

'Be quiet and look for the medal'.

'You said yourself I need some clothes. Hold on. I can feel something'.

But it's only a button, large and yellow, and when I hold it up for Henry, he throws up his arms and roars obscenities at the moon.

He pulls me out of there, shovel, pickaxe and all, and jumps in himself. He frisks Elisabeth Mulherne head to toe, turns her on her side, to the left, to the right, his hands disappear in places even the worms take heed to avoid. Then I hear him gasp with satisfaction and he raises his arms triumphantly.

'You useless bat!' he howls, holding aloft the shiny disc, not even bothering to look my way. 'It was around her neck all along'.

I can no longer listen. Henry's words are too much for this girl's delicate ears. Besides, my little voice is talking. Reach in your bag, it's telling me. Feel for the nail gun. Hunker down over the lip of the open grave. Press the hi-speed driver against the back of his head. Try with all your tiny might not to let your trigger finger tremble so.

Dog

Hugo Kelly

The young man was working on the inking machine when the supervisor approached. Automatically he stopped what he was doing and looked at the supervisor.

'Just keep working', the man ordered.

The young man picked up a folded carton and passed it in front of the thin nozzle of the machine. The best before date and batch number were automatically sprayed on in a fine jet of navy ink. The supervisor grunted and then leaned forward picking up a couple of the cartons from the finished pile. Some of the dates were clearly sloped on the pale cardboard.

The supervisor studied them for a few seconds, holding them up to the shining white light as if looking for a watermark or some other hidden quality. He shook his head.

'These are unusable', he said. 'Have they been passed on to kits?'

The young man nodded. That's the way it worked. The packaging was delivered to the kits team who filled them with the tubes of antibiotic solution. From there they went to every second hospital in the world. That's what the brochure said at least.

It was clear that the supervisor was not happy. His bloodshot eyes appeared bruised and worn. He had been working nights for ten years and had taken on the pallid appearance and mannerisms of a nocturnal creature himself. He called out to the other supervisor who was standing at another line.

'Tom, we've a problem'.

The two men walked over to the far wall and began to converse. They then walked through the double doors into the storeroom. There was the sound of boxes being ripped open.

The other workers around the kits conveyor belt looked back at the young man. He felt their eyes on him and his skin began to burn.

The supervisor returned after a few minutes.

'The dates aren't good enough. All the units will have to be unpacked and reboxed. Half the shift's been wasted'.

His eyes fluttered shut as if he was in pain.

'I'm sorry', the young man said.

'That helps a lot'.

The supervisor walked off again and the young man went back to work. Behind him the boxes were brought back in again and unpacked. All the plastic phials were stacked in pyramids. The kits workers passively waited for the new packaging. The young man concentrated hard, passing the cartons in front of the nozzle, making sure each date was clear and legible. The supervisor came back after half an hour and checked every one.

'That's better. But we can't afford that kind of sloppiness', the supervisor said.

The young man nodded, understanding that he was on his last chance. He had been lucky to get this temporary job. Any chance of it being renewed hung in the balance or perhaps was gone.

The supervisor left again, continuing his rounds. The young man raised his head and stared at the clock that hung on the grey wall like a circular decoration. The muscles in his back and neck were tense. Fingers of tiredness pressed his temples. In his house he had cut a special piece of chipboard that blocked out all light. It worked pretty well, except that he was woken by salesmen selling month-long memberships to gyms or burglar alarms. He had disconnected the doorbell. But they still knocked.

Around him he could hear his co-workers grumbling.

He ate his meal by himself in the canteen. Afterwards he took a breath of air in the chilly darkness. The smokers were silent as they puffed heavily. The factory was based on the edge of the city in a large industrial estate. In front of him the gleaming road lights knitted and looped together like the white limbs of a skeleton. He went back in. Three more hours and he could go.

Back at his line he worked carefully, knowing that he was moving too slow. Tomorrow there would be more difficulties because of this. But he was afraid to go faster. The supervisor appeared again and silently stood on front of him like a warning. The young man's mind began to heat with a pointless rage. On it grew in vigour until he thought he might scream or simply cry.

It was then that he began to think about the dog.

The dog was a large alsatian. It guarded a builders' providers' yard that he passed on his way home. Every night the alsatian heard him as he approached, erupting into a spasm of barking as it charged at the wire fence. The young man liked to stand and admire the animal. Its frame was full of simmering purpose and hate. He imagined that the dog sensed the odour of the sterile factory from him. Sensed also that his joints were tight and that his arms and legs were weak. Often he had thought about challenging the animal. And now as he stood by the machine enduring the sense of resentment from his fellow workers, he decided that he would do so. For the first time in hours he felt calm.

Minute by minute the remaining hours edged away until the shift came to an end. The huddled groups who had long since gone quiet now left the conveyor belts. The young man followed them into the locker room. There he took off his white coat and put it in the cleaning box in the locker room. When he left nobody looked up or said goodbye.

Outside the night was cold and he shivered after the warmth of the factory. Soon the raw light of morning would come, but for now the city's lights smouldered underneath the grey darkness. The smoky dawn clouds looked pungent, carriers of bad news. He walked down the driveway, turning onto the main road. After about half a mile he skipped through the broken fence taking his usual shortcut back to his house. This was a muddy path that led past the humming transformer plant and two parked caravans. As he passed them he could hear the sound of the generator whirring. A door opened and a woman emptied a teapot. She saw him and stared. He kept walking. He looked at his watch. It was 6am.

The path soon led him down the side of the builders' yard. He waited for the normal tremor of barking and the furious pacing of the dog as it threw itself against the wire. But, for once, there was no sound. He placed his hand on the diamond mesh and let his forehead rest against it, enjoying the coolness. Standing upright again he saw there was a small hole in the fence a couple of feet from the ground. He forced his foot into it, gripped the mesh and pulled himself upwards. The concrete uprights breathed a soft jangled sigh. He pulled strongly again and managed to hoist himself to the top of the wire. The dog began to bark. Stray wires jabbed into his thighs and chest. He lifted one leg over and then rolled his body forward, placing all his weight on his straining hands. He let himself drop, landing with an uncomfortable pain in his ankle.

He got to his feet and studied the yard. To his left there was a large building with metal doors. Pallets were stacked high at various points in front of it. A forklift truck was parked by the entrance. Close by was a skip filled with rubble. He walked over to it and pulled out a thick piece of wood and held it In front of him like a club. The dog was out there somewhere. He readied himself.

Suddenly he could hear the familiar soft padding of the dog increasing in pitch so that it merged with the rhythm of his own heart. The alsatian came into view, moving in a wide arc from behind a stack of pallets. It paused, staring at him. The ears were cocked and its slender face was sharpened in a grimace. On its left leg there was a bare patch of skin. Its rich coat was a mixture of scuffed browns and black. It growled in slow waves. The dark eyes did not leave him. It broke into a run, barking fiercely.

The young man crouched waiting for the impact of the attack. The alsatian leapt, crashing into his chest before he could even begin to swing the piece of wood. He was knocked to the ground landing fully on his back so that for a fraction he could make out the stars above him. His weapon was no longer in his hand and the animal was on him before he could react further. Hot saliva spat across his face. The breath stank of rotting meat and there was a whiff of oil from the animal's underbelly. He pushed the pointed face aside but the animal bit into his shoulder. The pain was vicious. The animal was standing on his chest and the weight made it difficult to breathe. He seized the animal's neck and wrenched it to the side. The dog stumbled, slipping momentarily before freeing itself easily from his grip. Again the dog was on him, this time snapping closer to his face. It caught his chin and tried to burrow down for his throat. The young man punched at the dog. In response the animal bit harshly, puncturing the soft skin of his hand. He scraped his fingers along the bony ridge of nose. The animal's growls vibrated through his hands and its eyes shone like dull glass. The animal bit again and the shock of pain cut through the mist of adrenalin. The pain brought anger, the luxurious sensation of hatred. He pushed his fingers into the dog's eyes.

The dog reared back, twisting in agony. The young man pulled himself up. The alsatian attacked again sinking its teeth into his thigh as he turned to get to his feet. He threw his arms behind him but he could not reach the dog. He tried to pull away but the animal now went for the wrist of his right arm, biting fiercely. He took a step, pulling the dog with him. And then another step. And so it seemed to go on. They moved in a stuttering waltz. The animal was happy to bite and grip. The young man could not break free.

He slipped on the frosty ground and fell. The impact jarred him but still the dog did not release his arm. He was losing blood and his vision was beginning to blur. The pain was melting away to weakness. His free hand swept desperately across the rough ground and he touched sharp edges. It was the neck of a broken bottle. The animal growled and grunted. The young man took the bottle in his grasp and swung back at the animal but he was unable to reach. As if in reaction, the dog bit harder but in the process it slid its mouth up the young man's wrist. The young man tried one final time. He swung in a wide arc and this time was able to reach the dog, pressing the broken bottle into its side, just below its ribs. The animal jolted at the first impact but the grip did not lessen. The young man stabbed again and again until the dog came away from him.

The young man looked at his mangled wrist, his torn sleeve hanging from his punctured skin. The dog stood there, shaking, whining sadly to itself. Blood darkened its coat. Its two front paws collapsed and it tilted forward. Its eye stayed on him, occasionally blinking.

The young man staggered to his feet. He looked at the dog but he could barely see it now. His body was releasing some strange calm that oozed throughout his limbs and mind. He walked to the wire but then realised that he had no interest in climbing out. He heard the dog sigh and fall to its side. He stumbled back towards it, becoming aware of the early morning sounds of the city. Somewhere close by he could hear the sound of laughter. There was the clashing sound of a metal shutter being rolled up. The slow boom of traffic was as always in the background.

The factory was a long way in the distance, lost in the ongoing gloom that was embracing him with cool hands. Everything was becoming faint and for that he was glad. He knelt down and his head fell forward as he passed out. He did not know that torchlight beams were waving furiously in the air only a short distance away. Or that the gate was opened and that one man was running in his direction while another man was speaking loudly on his mobile phone. Or that not far away, an ambulance was racing out of a hospital driveway in his direction. The young man heard none of this. He had fought the dog and he had won.

MAYA AND ME

Sarah Clancy

Spring, summer and autumn I work here. In the winter I don't work because there are no customers, but Maya lets me stay anyway. She says it's no harm to have a man about the place. A man after a fashion, she means, but doesn't say. She doesn't need to say it; I already know.

Sometimes it gets me down, when I go swimming, for example. When I swim I can feel my limbs' memories of going strong and deep, of propelling me out into the bay without effort, the way they did the year I moved to this coast here.

Back then I was taken on to do a bit of tidying-up about the place for a few weeks. Marshal was finishing writing that book then and hadn't time to do it and Maya, well I don't know about her. I didn't have that much to do with her until after he drowned. I stayed on though when she went to the city to arrange everything with his publishers and with all that happened afterwards I never really got to leave. I was twenty then and though it seems ridiculous to me the way time warps and distends with no apparent logic, I will only be twenty five years old next week. Happy Birthday to me, the oldest quarter century boy you've ever met.

Guns are easy to get in these parts and for a while there in the middle of winter the year I became sick, I consoled myself by measuring the weight of my old Rossi pistol in one hand and then the other. I'd sit on the porch there with rain teeming on the overhang with the empty hammock hanging beside me like a withered balloon, and pretend I was a man with the guts to put the gun in my mouth and end it. I didn't, though, couldn't, and I knew I had something lacking in me. Honestly I have always known that; I have a misfire in my make-up and sickness or none, it's always been there.

Back when I was a kid I was given a pony, Roscoe I called him, Roscoe. I tried to train him but he had something wrong with him. I'd spend hours teaching him some simple thing like how to stand tied to a hitch and the next day he'd have it forgotten. All over again he'd panic and pull and pull till he broke the rope, or worse got one of his front legs over it and tangled himself till he went down kicking on the ground. In the end my dad had to shoot him. I knew he had to do it, but still I didn't like it; 'Horse like that', he told me; 'he could kill someone what with his size and whatever's gone lo-la in that brain of his'. That was my Dad though. He made my brother watch while he shot him, but I got sent to town for a comic. A bit too close for comfort, Dad said.

That's what I'm telling you. Guts and guns and manliness, yea, I've launched right into the heavy stuff haven't I? And we haven't even been properly introduced. Meet your caretaker. That's me; boy Friday, boy Monday, Tuesday, Wednesday, Thursday, Saturday and Sunday, for all those days I am the boy. The quarter-century boy.

I'll take care of everything, with my arms and my legs and this poor wasted torso you're looking so closely at. I'll make big jobs of small ones so you can't hardly bear to watch me. I'll sidle round here and there, and I will go crabwise to the mailbox for mail. I can even hoist myself into the pickup and drive to the village where they like me well enough, and I can bring back supplies, whatever you need comrade. You won't mention my physique will you? No, no, too polite, you won't mention my smoking either, even though you'll hear the wheeze, the rattle, as I turn my insides the same wasted shape as my outer. I hope you don't think I sound bitter, or angry, or twisted, because it would be unfair of you, wouldn't it, to confuse my appearance with my nature, which is different.

Of course you'll say, 'of course', and I'll smile at you. 'Why thank you, you'll say', or 'Beautiful place you have here sir', but enough of that now, go on, you can take Cabin No. 7 down to the left there on the riverbank. Oh, that's typical, off you go, don't you, with no thought of payment? That's better, thank you for the envelope, I can feel the notes inside it. I've seen them before too, other tight hands, other men and women thinking that payment is a license to write something, to make something of themselves; a permission. A begging your pardon to the gods of talent as if they are here in this outpost waiting. Thank you, though, I'll give it to Maya. You'll find all you need in there, and if not there's an old brass bell outside the door on the porch, and if you ring that, ring it a good few times mind, and either Maya or me will come and look after you. One part of that story is me and one part is Maya, but in these parts you get what you pay for, well, what you pay for and what you can see your way to take.

I can see you wondering how I get down there, down those clumsy red-earth steps and the twisted path that veers and narrows right on the edge of the river bank. What you don't know is that I built those steps. I dug them out one by one like Maya had shown me, but slower. I pegged their edges with cut logs, bark facing outwards and then I packed in all the extra clay by shoveling, then stamping it down. Maya brought me bean stew and sausage, the oddest choice for such a hot day, but something in the pepperiness of it warmed me and I ate it with my guts caught into a smile. Those steps? This walkway? They are something to smile about. Yes, some small real thing to smile for.

I can see you wondering too if all's well upstairs with me, and it's not, but it's better than it was, and at least in the clearing away from the undergrowth, when I am free of this tangle of words and thinking, then I know what matters and that is that you'll come in here and see Maya. You'll come thinking you are someone of consequence, here to finish your novel, to work on your poems as if you could scoop up some of his talent like a cupped handful of river water and drink it. As if. You'll see Maya, in sunlight in her vest top and her shorts and you'll want her. That's what happens in this hot weather; warm air and longing. You'll want her and you'll get no work done, because you'll watch her as you think she is. Alone here. I know it, you'll see no other contenders, a man like you won't see the caretaker-cripple, who may or may not be the full shilling. For one reason or another you won't see that I am the one she has with her.

When I wake up at night time and come to in the warm air and river sounds, I know enough to lean over and kiss her, for all else I might be missing.

THE SILVER LADY

Kevin Higgins

I look up from my pint, glancing into the floor to ceiling mirror. I see Azdine the Algerian coming over towards me. Azdine is one of the characters who take advantage of the late night drinking at The Silver Lady. I could do without him right now. I just need a little silence. A nice quiet drink and then home for a quick wank before bedtime on my much used and abused copy of *Readers' Wives*. I really do urgently need some new pornography.

– *Fields of Athenry, my friend.*

However many times I object, this is what he insists on calling me.

– *You look down in your dumps. It is no good for you to be sitting on your own like this.*

Azdine speaks in the slow motion voice that usually means he's spent most of the day on the big cigarette.

– *I'm fine. Just out for a quiet one. You know the way.*

Azdine settles himself down at my table without responding.

– *I had a fucking terrible disturbance this afternoon*, he says, speeding up the voice for dramatic effect. – *Fucking terrible I'll tell you, Fields.*

– *What happened?* I am only vaguely interested.

– *Fields, this afternoon I was woken up by this screaming and shouting from downstairs. Bloody commotion it was, I can tell you. I thought it must be that guy in the ground-floor flat breaking his girlfriend's jaw again. What a fucking time of the day to be doing it and all! Anyway, the noise was too fucking much. So I had to get out of bed. I opened the window and poked my head out to see what this stupid commotion was about and I saw a hand, a severed hand, on the pavement below. It was twitching most vigorously, like as if it was still alive.*

– *And how did it get there?* I ask. My interest now aroused.

– *I'm coming to that bit*, he blurts impatiently.

– *A few yards away from the hand was a cop lying on the floor. He was kicking and screaming like a madman. It was his hand. And the place was fucking soaked in his blood.*

– *They could always use it to make black pudding*, I interject, – *Waste not want not, I always say.*

Azdine continues, – *An ambulance arrived then to take him away. And they wrapped up the hand and took it away with them as well. I suppose they did not want to leave it lying around for the dogs to eat. Then the ambulance drove away with the cop and his hand inside it.*

– *And they all lived happily ever after*, I add. – *Did you ever find out exactly what happened?* I inquire after a thoughtful pause.

– *No, Mr Fields of Athenry, best to keep your nose out of such things*, he asserts firmly.

A group of white men are playing an aggressive game of pool on the other side of the bar.

– *I know why you always have this long miserable fucking face*, Azdine volunteers out of the blue, – *It's that fucking police woman of yours. She is a nightmare for you.*

– *Keep it down*, I whisper, – *She is not a cop. She's just a civil servant who works for them.*

– *I don't know your technicalities*, he says, – *I do know she is no good. She is in too much control of you. You need an arrangement like the one I have with Alice. I go around whenever it suits. I bring a few drinks and some blow and stay for a night or two. She has a daughter. She might be convenient for you. She is seventeen. A nice piece of tight skin to brighten you up. She is a little insane. But she would be good for you.*

I tell him I will think about it, and immediately begin doing so.

Just then the white blokes' aggressive game of pool ceases any longer to be a game. They decide to instead solve their differences by thumping each other savagely with their pool cues.

I finish the last of my pint. It's flat. Time to go and snuggle up with my stale pornography; it's our last night together. Tomorrow, I move in with the aforementioned police woman and nights like this become the good old days.

The Last Man

Hedy Gibbons Lynott

For the umpteenth time he wonders about her. This woman who possesses his space. The way her hair licks at the nape of her neck, one little curl the opposite direction to all the others, so that he's tempted to reach out and flick it back into place. The soft bronzeness of the upswept sides, the slight bang. Heavy lids, wide-set eyes, and the curve of her mouth so delicious he frequently gives in to the urge to kiss its crookedness.

He pauses at the top of the black and white marble steps for a moment, gazing across the vast space, letting his eye run along the balcony, its soft arc against the sharpness of its surroundings. He always does that first thing, letting the space surround him, enjoying the sensation of floating at the top of those broad steps before descending their sharp zigzag through the glass floors.

Five years now she's graced this space, uplifted his mornings, haunted his evenings. Evenings full of dinners and handshakes and deals done and undone. Women who run their fingertips on his wrist, his arms, his cheek – if they can get close enough. Women who smile desperately across tables laden with New World wines and orange roughy harvested from the mid-Atlantic seamounts.

He descends the stairs, smiling back up at her as he does so, and crosses the wide expanse of chequer-board in the centre of the hall. It is good, he thinks, to have this solid black and white under your feet. It cost a fortune to install, soaring up through the middle of this glass pyramid – but then what are fortunes for, in the end?

He didn't need the Committee to tell him that those stairs were an anachronism in such a building. He knows what they think: 'Yantl is getting on a bit. Losing it'. His body still looks great. He likes to exercise on rising, and the slow-release chip implanted two years previously ensures he stays at peak functioning. He gives a small shrug. It seemed such a good idea at the time – and the Committee insisted. The women like their man vigorous, particularly Clarissa. Like most of the women, she still hopes.

His glance up to the end of the balcony is just in time to see the sun pierce the lightbox and bring the bronze curls to dazzling life. She floats there, ethereal through the layers of glass, smiling. Greeting him each morning, alone all day waiting for his return. Waiting for his caress on the nape of her neck, the light touch of his lips at the corner of her mouth, the faint warmth of his temple as he briefly touches it against hers. He passes through the doors that slide open at his glance.

He'd insisted the glass in the building be clear, with that in his penthouse a smoky black. Sometimes when he is in his living quarters and they are illuminated from inside, he can feel her gaze, especially when whatever woman is spending the evening reaches for him. Those times he finds himself turning from that woman towards *her*, enjoying how the smile that lingers is the one that started when he first gazed at her.

Yantl stops running. Through the ripples of low tide something gleams dully. He moves to the water's edge, glancing along the empty beach, not that he expects to see another human being. Nobody comes here. Nobody has for a long time. Once, on evenings like this, the place would have been thronged with people: fathers and mothers pushing buggies, power-walking women, neighbours stopping to chat, small clusters of men laughing at their own jokes. That was before the sea thundered in and tore huge chunks of concrete from the land, threw them out there somewhere, side by side with the enormous granite boulders. Sometimes he wonders if the granite still glitters pink underwater, the way it did when there were rosy sunsets. Out there, under the heavy grey waters, the great promenade.

He bends down to take a closer look, squinting against the low light. A head? Surely not. Not after so long. Small waves wash away more sand. He drops to his knees, reaches for a large shell, trying to scrape the sand away. But the shell is old and brittle and fragments into tiny shards between his fingers. Half in and half out of the water, oblivious to its cold wetness, he begins to tear at the sand with his hands. Water pools into the hollow as he works, soaks his threadbare pants, sand flying either side of him. And then he's running his fingers over the emerging head, along the seaweed hair. Silky. Alive. The most alive he's encountered in a very long time.

On the flat expanse of wet sand, breath rasping, he catches a glimpse of his own reflection, jaw taut, eyes sunken. Her can feel his body temperature dropping. It isn't safe to stay in one place for so long. But the eyebrows under his fingers arch gracefully, the nose must have been small and straight and fine. He traces the delicate jawline, imagining her lips with a trembling fore-finger.

He's shaking now, from cold or anticipation he isn't sure. He doesn't care. His glance flickers out across the empty water. No longer any boats, no rust-coloured sails, no hills rising purple and silver from the endless expanse of grey. And then he bends again to wedge cold fingers under the head, bracing himself, feeling the strain in his gut. And she comes free.

He lifts her. He thinks she might be smiling as he brushes the sand out of her ears and eyes and traces again the curve of her mouth, a quirky mouth. Definitely. Her voice would be low and husky, maybe have a lilt in it. He cradles the head in his arms, looks quickly along the coast. The great rocks are empty. No movement apart from the water. He's been out far too long, the light deceptive, the still air beginning to freeze around him, and the tide on the turn already meeting behind him.

Pushing himself to his feet, sucking the thin air, he tucks her inside his threadbare fleece. They haven't yet sanctioned new clothes for him. Then, holding her against his heart with both hands, he staggers up the beach. Half-way up he risks a quick look down at her, savouring the faint warmth of her against his chest. When it comes, the sound of his voice is cracked with lack of use, a harsh whisper in the biting air: 'you must have been a beauty'.

GORTNAGONE

John Walsh

It was the sports field behind the house that clinched the deal.

'There'll be no more houses built while that field's there', John Redshaw reassured Ian, as they stood looking out at the goalposts and the white line markings. Redshaw was a lanky, 'God bless' kind of man, zealous about selling. 'Eighty-seven homes, not one more nor less. Take my word for it, Ian, Gortnagone is one of the soundest investments in the city'.

Ian spent his evenings in his sound investment staring out of the master bedroom at the Gaelic footballers priming their muscles, at the greyhound trainers in their shiny tracksuits and spotless runners, and listening to the gangs of youths who gathered in the field after dark with their Bulmers and Bull. The next day he binned the empty cans they lobbed over his wall. If he tried to do anything about it, they would make his life hell. He knew that.

'Did you hear them at it last night again? The racket they were making. An' the filth those louts throw into your garden. Somebody should do something about it'.

Ian didn't know his neighbour well. She'd been there before him. How long he wasn't inclined to ask. She was a bit odd. Not only that she kept her curtains closed, day and night, but all the screaming he could hear through the block wall that separated them. Mostly it was the daughter and herself. The teenager retaliated to the mother's outbursts with a volley of high-pitched squeals, followed by a regular sequel of door-slamming. This kind of energy coming at him through the wall wasn't good.

'I don't think there's much we can do about it', he said to his neighbour. 'It would only make things worse if they found out you complained. Anyway, who is there to complain to?'

Maura was on her knees weeding her scrimpy patch of flower bed along the low red brick wall. She soothed her back with the palms of her hands and gasped as she raised herself. 'Somebody should do something, I said. I didn't say that somebody was me'.

The gardening clothes that Maura wore fell loosely from her as she balanced herself. Ian caught a glimpse of flimsy lace bra and a flicker of white breast.

'For god's sake, don't look at me like that'. Maura waved the trowel at him. 'If I don't do this, nobody else in this house will. And if nobody complains about them louts soon, things are only going to get worse'.

Ian stood at the window staring down into the back gardens, uneasy strips of green slotted in between the breeze-block walls. The builders had dumped all their waste into them, buried it under a pauper's layer of topsoil. By some miracle the grass still managed to push its way through, first of all patchy, now after a few cuts it was knitting into tight mats. His needed cutting again. Maura's was a mess. Wild, overgrown, dried-out and clumpy. She must never have done a thing with hers and now it was too late. He wondered what 'nobody else in this house' meant. Was there a father for the angry daughter? Of course there was – there had to be – but was he still there? Somewhere on the other side of the wall, behind the closed curtains in one of those rooms? Ian laughed to himself, tapping the wall as he went down into the kitchen. A pot of tea was what he needed.

The sound of the doorbell startled him. It was already getting dark. There was no light on in the hall or in the front room. No one could know he was there. He stood behind the kitchen door and wondered if he should open it. Again the bell rang. Then thumping on the door. Ian opened the kitchen door and switched on the light.

'Who is it?' he shouted from behind the closed door.

'It's me. Maura! There are noises outside. Open the door for god's sake'.

The minute he opened the door she pushed past him into the hall.

'What noises?'

'Out the back. On the other side of the wall. Animal noises. Groaning, wheezing. It's scary. Can't we do something?'

'Do something?'

'See what it is. There must be something out there'.

'Jesus, Maura, at this time of night? I'm not going out there'.

Maura sighed and came closer. 'You don't have to go out', she said in a kind of whisper. 'Just be a man and take a look'.

Ian could feel the heat of Maura's body. She stared at him, drawing him in, as if he were on a hook.

'Ok', he relented. 'Let me turn out the lights'.

He edged past her in the narrow hall, feeling the touch of her breasts on his chest. Maura looked at him, exciting and confusing him.

'Don't make a sound', he told her.

His throat was dry. Then he reached around the kitchen door and switched off the lights. Maura followed him over to the patio door and stood beside him as he flicked the lever and rolled the door back softly. Immediately they heard the sounds – eerie, desperate moanings.

'Get back', he whispered, pushing Maura away from the door. He eased the door shut and clicked the lock. 'We're not going out there. No matter what'.

'But what is it? What are those noises?'

'I don't know. I don't know'. Ian wished she would forget about the noises. 'Come upstairs. We can see out from the bedroom'. He didn't wait for her reply. He knew Maura would follow him.

At the bottom of the stairs Maura hesitated. 'I can't go up there in these'. She looked down at her high-heels.

'Well take them off, for god's sake'.

Ian realized then that he'd never seen Maura in a dress and heels before. He was sure he could smell perfume. 'Why have you got them on anyway?'

'I was out'. She looked at him as she kicked off the heels. 'I just got in when I heard the noises. I need to get out every now and then. Out of that house. What about you?'

'Jesus, Maura, now is not the time for … Just follow me and keep quiet'.

Ian led her upstairs and into his bedroom. She kept close behind him as he went to the lace curtains and carefully drew them apart. There were people on the other side of the wall, gathered around the nearest goalpost. They had ropes slung over the goalpost middle bar on which they were heaving up and down a dog, a large dog, its front paws tied to the ropes pulled tight over the bar. The dog moaned in pain as it was raised and lowered, its front legs carrying the weight of its body.

'The cruel bastards', Maura hissed. 'What are they doing that for?'

'Shssh!' Ian demanded. 'Get back. Don't let them see us'.

'But why are they doing it?' Maura whispered.

'I don't fuckin' know why they're doing it. It's their fuckin' dog. As long as it's not me, or you. Now get back'.

Ian sat on the bed. Maura bent towards him.

'We have to do something. We can't let them torture the poor dog. It's not right'.

'Jesus, Maura. Cop on. There's nothing we can do'.

'You mean you're going to let them do this and just do nothing?'

There was a long, piercing howl from the dog, then a heavy thud. They listened and heard a voice.

'Dump the bitch in the cart. Let's get the fuck outta here'.

Ian rose and went to the window. Through the opening he watched the gang head out across the field, pulling the dog behind them in a shopping trolley. Then it was quiet again, almost as if none of it had happened.

'They're gone', he said.

'An' what was it all for?' Maura asked.

'How do I know? I can't read these sick weirdos' minds. I don't know what goes on in them. I just don't want them coming after me, or you for that matter'.

'You're not much of a hero, are you?' Maura said, cornering him with her look.

'Oh for christ's sake, Maura! Who needs heroics? Going out there to let them kick the shite outta me instead of the poor dog. Is that what you call being a hero? I wouldn't stand a chance. An' do you think it would end there? No way. Now, can we go downstairs again? '

She pushed past him without saying anymore and hurried down the stairs. At the bottom she picked up her shoes and went to the door. As she opened the door she turned around.

'Enjoy the rest of your evening, Ian', she said. 'I'm sorry if I disturbed you'.

Without letting him answer, she slipped out.

Ian's hands were shaking as he clipped on the security chain. At times like this he felt he needed more than just a cup of tea.

'I'll open the side gate', Maura told him. 'You can bring the mower through there. That's great. Just give me a second. I'll come round'.

Ian stood at the closed front door, wondering if it made any sense what he was doing. Why did he feel he had to make up to Maura? Ok, he felt sorry for the dog, but his own skin was more important to him. Maura had kept on about it, the poor animal, the louts that were torturing it should be the ones strung up. It sent shivers down his spine.

He could hear Maura moving about inside, seemingly not in any rush to open the side gate. He took a few steps across the small path in front of the big window. The closed curtains hung unevenly. Ian leaned forward and tried to peek in through the gap that was left. Everything was dark. He moved in closer, straining his eyes, but just as he thought his focus was adapting, he heard Maura opening the side gate. Ian hurried away and took up position at the lawn-mower.

'Are you sure that'll do the job?' Maura mustered the lawn-mower that Ian had inherited from his mother. 'Looks like that thing's seen better days'.

'It's a tank of a lawn-mower', Ian patted his mother's lawn-mower, determined not to lose his patience again. 'Don't worry. There's a knack to it'.

'Do you need any help?'

Ian took a deep breath and ran through his serenity mantra. 'I don't think so'.

He wheeled the lawn-mower through the gate and into the backyard. Maura closed the gate behind him and went back into the house. He could see her watching him from the kitchen window as he adjusted the blade for the high grass and primed the motor. To his relief, three pulls on the starter cord got it going. He swung the mower out into the grass, tilting the front end high and easing it down slowly again to slice into the thick clumps.

It was murderous work.

The blade hacked at bits of blocks the builders had only half-buried and chipped at broken tiles that had been let fly from the roof. A rusted galvanized can was severed to smithereens by the thrust of the spinning blade. Ian manoeuvred the mower across the garden, letting it roll forward, then swinging it back quickly each time there was a clank or a crack from something underneath. In the corner near the back wall the blade hammered with a thud into a raised sod and the motor died.

Ian knelt down, tilted the lawnmower on its side and started ripping the wiry strands of grass that had got tangled around the blade. They were as thick as cord, hard to break off. The blade had left a gash underneath the sod, from which fresh, clean soil spilt out.

Ian spotted something in the soil and reached over to pick it up. The feel of it made him drop it back again. He wiped his hand clean on his trouser leg and looked down at what was lying in the soil. He reached over, picked it up again. It felt cold. With his finger he poked the dirt off it, then, glancing at the kitchen window, he stuffed it into his right trouser pocket. He could feel it fall against his thigh. Reaching a hand into his pocket, he tucked it into the cloth that he kept for wiping the mower's dipstick.

Then with the toe of his boot he kicked the sod back into place, covering up the gash that the blade had made. He bent over the mower and pulled the starter cord. There was a hoarse rattle as the mower burst into action again. Ian swung the mower around, manoeuvred it away from the corner and went on cutting.

'That's thirsty work. I've brought you some lemonade'.

Ian jumped when he heard Maura behind him. He let go of the lever and turned around. 'I'm nearly done. Thanks'.

He took the iced lemonade and drank it back.

Maura watched him.

'Where do you want me to dump the grass?'

'Just leave it', Maura told him. 'I'll put it in the bin and the council can take it away. Just leave it', she insisted.

'Right, I'll finish up then'. They faced each other as he handed her back the empty glass. Ian felt the weight in his right pocket. 'I won't be long'.

'You've done a great job', Maura said as she looked over her garden.

Ian nodded, then bent down over the mower, pressed the oil bulb and pulled the starter cord. He swung the mower around to go over the front strip again. Maura walked back towards the house. At the noise of the mower behind her Maura turned around, looked at him, just as Ian veered off to the left.

Back in his kitchen, Ian dug into his pocket, took out the cloth and let the content slap onto the glass top of the kitchen table. Then he sat down to study it. As far as he could make out it was an ear, probably a right ear, with a distended lobe, part of which had already been eaten away. With a delicate touch of his fingers he turned the ear over. The cut at the back had been precise. Ian wondered if the mower had done it.

'Jesus!' he said aloud and glanced at the kitchen wall. 'Jesus!' he whispered to himself. How had it got into Maura's garden? Was there more? And what was he going to do with it? He thought of dumping it in his bin or, better still, in one of the trash bins outside Dunnes or Aldi. Or burning it in the fire. Burying it in his own garden was not a good idea. But just dumping it didn't seem right, it seemed inhuman. He rubbed his chin, feeling the day's stubble.

Ian sat at the table, every now and then turning the ear to examine it from a different angle. It was clearly a human ear, no doubt about that. How long it had been where he had found it, there was no way of telling. They had experts for these things. The evening darkness settled in around Ian, without him really noticing.

A rattling at the front door startled him out of his concentration. There were a lot of noises as if someone was trying the door, trying to open it. Ian felt frightened. Images of the gang with their large dog flashed through his mind. Had he been seen at the bedroom window?

He got up and went out into the hall. Someone was at the letter box, trying to push something through. At this time of night? Ian rushed to the door and pulled it open.

'Maura! What the hell are you doing?'

Maura jumped in shock. Her hand was on a box that was stuck half-way into his letterbox. She looked at him without saying anything.

'Maura, *what* are you doing?'

'I wanted to give you something', she stammered. 'For all your work. Just a small thank-you'. Ian stared at her as she pulled the box out of the letterbox. 'I made some fudge. Here, these are for you'.

Ian reached out his hand to take the box from her. He realized Maura was wearing her dress again.

'I made them myself', she repeated as she let go of the box.

Ian held the box in his hand now. Though it was hard to be sure, he thought he could smell perfume. 'Is there alcohol in them? I can't eat them if there's alcohol in them'.

'No alcohol', Maura told him. 'It's my own recipe'.

'My god, Maura. You gave me a fright. I thought it was some of those louts from the other night'.

'I'm sorry. I didn't mean to do that. You didn't do anything, did you?'

'No, of course not. But it's late. You know ...'

He wasn't sure what to say.

'I'd better go', she told him. 'I'm sorry if I scared you. I hope you like the fudge'.

Ian waited till she reached her own path, waved, though she probably didn't see him. He locked the door and clipped the security chain into place. Back in the kitchen, he took the box to the table, opened the gift wrapping and tore it off. He eased the lid off. The home-made fudge were arranged neatly in three rows. He picked one from the second row and bit into it. It tasted creamy and rich, with a slight after-taste. He swallowed it and picked out another. It tasted different, an after-taste he couldn't quite place. The third was creamy again, with raisins he thought.

As he savoured it and swallowed, his eyes fell on the ear beside the box on the table. He looked at it with a strange feeling, a feeling of almost certainty.

He knew now it was a man's ear, a man whose daughter's teenage squeals sent an energy through the wall that wasn't good for him.

THE WOMEN OF CONG

Elizabeth Power

Beyond the fire of this Shaman's Circle in Brazil, beyond the dancers in trance, the women of Cong come down the hill and lean against a rusty old gate.

'Dance with us?' Sorcha asks.

I take her hand and start to spin. The drums pound, accelerate and gather in a cacophony of wild fire beats. Tempo, the Goddess of Time, with her pincer hold on past and future, joins the dance. I swing anti-clockwise; once, twice, thrice into their past.

Tara lies on the floor of the cave in a pool of blood.

A woman at her side is watching a spider scurry along a rock.

I confront her gaping stare.

'There are heroes in this story', the woman says, 'but few of them are human'.

Her nod is a sharp bow to the ground.

An ancient memory stirs in my body. It is my story to retrieve. My story to record. My story to heal.

I prepare to return.

It is the Autumn Equinox in the sixteenth century and the beginning of new things.

'We are going to create a new time', Rhona begins, 'and reverse what is happening to women and the Earth. Our connection to the Earth is being severed. Our knowing is ignored. We are becoming the servants of men. We are not servants. We are creators and have been always. We have called you women whose babies are due, to come and give birth in the cave where our mothers and grandmothers gave birth. We will begin by connecting with the ancestor energy stored in the walls and stones. You know what happens here has impact far beyond this place'.

Women stand with protruding bellies, or curved bellies or their pregnancy just becoming visible. They nod and smile at Rhona's words, glad to be here and part of this powerful ritual.

'What happens after the births, Rhona?' Aoife asks, easing her bulk from a boulder.

'We will return to the Stone Circle and lie on the Earth. She will hear the beats of our hearts. She will also hear our prayer for the future. The cords will be blessed. We will bury these with a power so strong it will change the direction for women. It will be our way of saving the Earth. Shall we begin?'

The women gather in a circle. Their voices rise and fall; their chant comes from walls around them. The song strenghtens, weakens, rises in sweetness and resounds against the stones. The chant drones on. Soon they are in deep trance and ready for the evening ritual ahead. They move around their autocracy to prepare. Some tend a fire near the entrance. Hot stones are taken from the flames and pushed into a water pool at the back of the cave. Others put food out for the night ahead and gather in small groups to share news from their communities.

Evening sunlight bounces off the walls and lights up ice sculptures on the cave's arched roof. Snakes, dolphins, phallic shapes, faces and bodies emerge and glisten. At the back of the cave a river pounds over a bank of pink rocks. Further over it slows to a gurgle before making a deep exit to the right.

At the back of the cave, two young girls, Mór and Sorcha undress and slip into the heated pool.

'Soon it will be my turn', says Sorcha. Her legs kick the warm water and she strokes her first soft swelling. She, too, will birth in this cave where bats fly low at dusk, as they do now.

'Oh Sorcha, can you wait that long?' Mór replies. She leans back against a rock and watches the water swirl over her plump body.

'Yes, I can. Something is bothering me though', Sorcha says straightening up. 'I don't understand my mother's anxiousness when she opened the Circle. Rhona is becoming like the old women who gossip and fret over nothing'.

Mór nods towards the two women tending the fire.

'Look at Aoife and Win over there with their heads bent together. That's all they do now. Whisper and look about them as though someone will leap out of a bush and strike them'.

Sorcha threads the water with her hand and listens to her friend speak her thoughts.

'The future is with us, not with those old women whose breasts are empty and whose wombs no longer bleed. Perhaps they are jealous of our bleeding, our young skin, our round tummies? I'm not concerned with their talk. I am Christian but I'm free in my belief. What if I still practice the old religion? What if I take their healing potions? If it's what I need – that's what I'll do'.

Sorcha nods her head lazily and closes her eyes again.

'Witches! witches! witches! who would lure men to make them pregnant and then kill the baby boys. That way only women will control the future', Aoife pauses and throws another lump of wood on the fire. 'That's what they call us. That's what they say we do'.

'Surely old age has taken my sharpness', Win replies. 'Kill the baby boys? What kind of nonsense is that?'

'It's what they believe'.

Win throws back her head and snorts. 'We have enough to worry about without this. There is still no sign of Ivy. She should have been leading the Circle tonight. I've been up at the house. Nothing is touched. Where did she go?'

'She wouldn't have left without telling us', Aoife replies. 'She wouldn't have left without saying goodbye'. She straightens her back and shakes off the fear that is turning her old bones rigid.

'It's the odd looks we get', Win says. 'A feeling you're hated. I'm too old to know this much of it. The Christian women say we rear the children without God, without religion or a spit of water on them. They say we women don't know our place. That our bad blood is seeping through the lines'.

'I can see lights over the hill', Aoife interrupts. 'Good. More are on the way. I'll put those pheasants on the stones to cook'.

'They're a good way off yet', Win says, turning from the entrance to see who is making a familiar sound.

Grainne is already in labour. When the pain flows she grunts and leans her weight on two women. When it stops, she straightens, yells a joyful cry. Sooner than expected, she is ready to give birth. The rest gather around her and begin to sing and clap. They are in high spirits, knowing the birthing is coming fast. Soon her baby, a boy, slips into a midwife's waiting hands. They begin their song of welcome and its old sound reverberates around the cave. They ask the stars and the moon to welcome him. They call the women and the men of this land and the spirits of the stones and the spirits of the trees to welcome him.

Rhona is the first to hear the sound of horses. She looks up and sees the lights approaching the cave. Something in the shape of the group bothers her. Word had spread about this ritual. They had expected a crowd but this is too many. Her eyes meet Aoife's puzzled gaze as she turns to face the mossy incline. Men, carrying fire, descend to the entrance. It is rare to see men come to the cave during birthing. Unless they're called. Unless there is a threat to their loved ones. Why are they here now? And why are the women, the Christian women following behind them? Rhona's heart begins to pound.

She moves forward and stands in front of the women. Padraig uses his shoulder to push his way to the front of the crowd. He is a small man whose thin face is drawn and cold. His eyes fix on the ground in front of her. She's known him all her life, but he frightens her now, standing there silently looking down.

'Goodnight to you, Padraig. What do you want?' she asks, keeping her voice steady. 'What are you doing here at this late hour?'

'We have been watching you all. For some time. We know what you do'.

'What do you think we do?' she asks.

'Few enough boy children coming from this cave. We're here to put an end to your killing'.

'Killing? Those rumours? There is no truth in those

rumours. Look', she says, pointing to the midwife who is washing the newborn baby in the river beside them. 'See, Grainne has just given birth to a beautiful little boy'.

His roar comes from deep in his belly. 'She's drowning him. She's drowning the baby boy'. He moves forward so those behind him cannot see.

'Get that boy. Go on', he shouts.

Three men rush forward. One grabs the child from the midwife's arms and calls a woman waiting behind him to come forward. He thrusts the child towards her.

'Take it. Go on now', he says, pointing to the entrance. The baby is carried up the mossy bank of the cave.

Grainne tries to rise from the ground. She grabs Padraig's leg.

'My son, what are you doing with my son?'

'You murdering bitch', Padraig roars. His knife is out and he runs a long blade through her body.

'My son. My boy', she says into a second of silence before women shriek and run in all directions.

Aoife and Win lunge forward with burning sticks towards Padraig. In an instant two men on either side of him run their knives through the women. They drop where they stand.

The crowd spreads out and block the entrance.

'Do it', Padraig roars again.

The men advance into the cave with their bushals lighting the darkest recess.

At the other side of the cave a woman has moved into the centre. It is her turn to birth. She is held by two women as she squats and bears down. Tara, the women call out over and over. The baby moves closer to life. Tara takes a deep breath, gathering her energy for one final push.

'What is that sound? Screams? Is someone having a

rough birth?' she asks, distracted. Shadows flicker on the wall behind her. Shadows where there should not be. She is in too much pain to turn and look. Suddenly the women holding her are gone. A man shoves her to the ground. She recognises her neighbour.

'Conal', she exclaims. 'What are you doing?'

'Leave me be', she screams as he pulls her clothes up and runs the knife down her length.

He cuts deeper into the placenta, reaches and pulls the baby back up from the birth canal. It is a girl.

Tara screams a single, desperate, shrillness.

He holds the baby up for the others to see.

'Look what I have. Another one of them', he shouts and spits on the ground.

The baby gives a faint cry. She has life. He walks towards the entrance and throws her blood-covered body into the fire.

Tara's breathing is coarse and guttural. She crawls towards the fire, towards the entrance, towards her baby. She reaches the triangular-shaped stone and exhales a loud sigh.

'The stones will hold all I am', she whispers.

Outside is a rustle. The caw call. The cry of Raven.

She speaks her last.

Ah, raven croak. I'm coming.

Padraig starts to laugh, a loud raucousness. Others join in. There is relief now. How easy all this is. The girls and the dead babies are thrown in the fire. The women standing at the entrance move forward to take the boys who have breath.

'Let's finish and be gone', he says. 'Get the rest. We don't want any alive'.

Rhona is thrown against the rocks and Padraig drives a knife though her body. As she lies there, her eyes fall on

Sorcha who has made her way towards her mother. One of the men digs a knife deep into her daughter's belly.

Drip. Drip. Drip.

The screams have stopped.

The crowd leaves.

'Oh Sorcha, I cannot reach you to hold your hand', says Rhona, but the words hang between them. There is no sound.

From the corner of her eye, she sees a woman standing in a doorway in the cave. The woman is dressed in black. She puts her two hands on the doorframe.

'What deed is this? Whose deed is this?' the woman roars.

She exhales and insects scurry from her breath. They move over the floor of the cave and begin their work. A small brown spider drops a thread from Rhona's hair and swings down its length. She follows its movement with her eyes. The spider spins and stretches on the thread until it reaches her daughter. The moon colours the silk blue as it winds around a strand of Sorcha's black hair.

There is so much blood between the placentas and the women's blood. They watch it ebb into the river. They watch it seep into the earth. They watch their blood flow away and their lifeforce with it.

Spiders continue with their work, weaving a web of silk between them. The women who had prayed together, loved the earth together, now prepare to die together. They do what they spent their lives doing. They join their souls together. They connect those souls to the walls and stones in the cave. They will stay here until their ritual is complete.

It is the end of the twentieth century. In the Shaman's Circle in Brazil, I sway to the fire beats of the drum and begin the transformation. My tongue swells with exquisite intoxication. I thrust and hiss as my body seethes its way through the earth floor. I am snake filled with love for the Earth. I lick its dry crust, run my tongue over rough tree bark and suck its wood into my mouth.

I have what I need to complete their work.

Back in the cave in Cong the air bristles as though it has goose pimples. My body, channelling their old energy, braces in a rigid seizure. A wind shoots through the entrance and whips the soil from under my feet. Struggling to keep my balance, I make out Win's outline standing beside the rocks. Her face is a whimsy, but her voice is clear and strong. The other women gather beside her. She speaks.

'From our time to yours, four hundred years later, we give this story to you. We are an ancient fragment of memory that resides still in your wombs. We're back to tell you women what you've lost'.

Her voice is dreamy now.

'We are the keepers of the knowing of women. How long. How cold. How lonely. But we waited here, knowing women in the future would seek us out when we were needed most'.

'What happens here has influence far beyond it', the woman with spider breath reminds me. 'Begin your work', she commands.

I breathe the fire of the thousand Brazilian drum beats around the cave walls.

I lick its cold ice.

Water pours down the wall.

'It is done', she says in awe.

'It has begun', she shouts to someone I cannot see. 'The ice is melting. The Earth's healing has begun'.

MURDER AND SELF-HARM

James Martyn Joyce

I suppose, for me, this one started out in rain. Cloaking rain, trickling into conch-like ears, insinuating rain, you know the type I mean: that tangle of swirl-rain that mats the thinning hair of the town's men waiting for the quickened chance to shamble home to their hunger-filling meals and their thin wives.

It was on such an evening that I stopped, teased for a minute by the shifting wind, to adjust my dripping collar at the candle shop on Igoe Street and overheard the voices sheltering in Parslow's Paints next door.

'She's playing them like fools'.

'Fools? We were always that'.

'Anywhere there's even the sniff of a woman'.

'Ah yes, my own tale too, but I'd still have bet against Jack Bodkin'.

'He should have left the married ones alone'.

'Bloody hell! Was he mad to bother with The Ouncel's wife?'

Someone joined me in the doorway; a streaming soul from The Cottages, a grey rag to his purpled nose as he sneezed, his face losing all composure when he recognised my uniform. I had to move along then, stemming the talk from the adjoining doorway as I passed.

'Good Jesus, there's himself! Did he hear us, do you think? Did he?'

The whispered gasp carried on the wind as I tramped towards the Starman Cafe and my tea, the one drawback of not having even a thin wife to go home to.

Now, who do you think runs a small town? There's a question. Sometimes I ask it for fun at seminars and such, just to hear the familiar answers. I watch the smug faces of my assembled colleagues and I listen to their offers. The Town Council, with its circling, grey politicians, they always get a mention. Sometimes the big businessmen with their meetings and their golf in the suburbs, yes, they often get the nod. The churchmen, slit-eyed, reptilian, with a foot in either camp, they get so many votes as well.

But me, who do I think runs a small town? Simple, one man can run a town. But he must have the balls to pull the strokes, to take the power to do this, the guts to wait, the leverage to ease the players into position, move the pieces here, put the pressure there. That's why when it comes down to it, I run this town.

The story of Jack Bodkin intrigued me. He had the artist's pull. I'd heard the whispers, The Ouncel's wife spread out wide like a full sail, Jack at the helm steering her to port. I'd heard the tales, the rumours and the whispered wish but always second-hand.

And anything that involved The Ouncel drew my full attention. After all he was a powerful man and not one of mine. No, not one of mine. He should be kept in check, it's always better when the edgeways deals go through the blender. That's me, except The Ouncel never liked to share. Did his deals beyond my reach, never touched the goods, he paid his men to do all that. I'd dropped the hints, made the pointed point, but he just was not a sharer.

And I hated his wry smile along the street, a swagger, flashing his good suits at me but still a dealer, still a pimp. That could be contagious, next thing every gimp and wideboy is giving you the hand-off. No, I couldn't let that happen. No.

Adequate, that's the dinner at the Starman Cafe, filling but not fulfilling, a bit like riding Mrs Hand, does in a pinch but lacking in reality. I talked to Skooner in between the mash. Yea, he'd heard that Jack was at it, bringing her to Dali's place out along the road. Dali didn't mind; he was an artist now as well, he had reinvented himself, got the name changed. He used to be Joe Daly, fixing cars, now he was all blowtorch and bottled gas, carving skeletal shapes out of bare metal, and his studio was in town. Anyway, he let Jack use his place, he was never there, well seldom, but he wasn't beyond a sneaking peek if he came back early.

He told the Bookie what he saw, that's the Bookie pushing pie just along the counter and the Bookie, well he told Skooner. Anyway Dali was wide with admiration. The Ouncel's wife, fine woman, redhead, full bush, moaning like a slow train, spread out under Jack and him standing sweat-licked as a Trojan, eyes tight and pumping 'til his bellow sent Dali running to the shadows, afraid to come out again until well after they'd both gone.

The trigger pulled, that's what I wanted, and so I took the scenic route: a picture postcard from The Louvre. I'd had it for years and now I typed a little note. 'You're not the only artist with a brush', and dropped it to The Ouncel at his new address since the wife had tossed him out.

In the end I nearly missed it when Jack Bodkin and The Ouncel had at it in the street. Blood and teeth, knees and bits of rock, torn clothes and faces pulped to mush and the crowd getting bigger all the time.

I sloped in at the outskirts, collar up and cloth cap down, in at the finish like a pit bull terrier. Jack should have had him, landing rib-benders like that and The Ouncel a snotted mess against the Stop'n Shop wall. But then, it's never, ever over and The Ouncel caught him with the 'brass'. He must have had the 'knuckles' in his pocket, caught him on the up, side of the head with a dead sound that filled the street. Jack keeled like a felled tree, out as the lighthouse, but The Ouncel wasn't done. That sweet kick must have busted Jack's jewels clear to next September and the crowd sweeping in to tear The Ouncel off.

I slipped away myself then, flagging down the patrol cars to tell them to forget it, no one to arrest, the pawns were moving now, all best settled by itself.

Jack was a hospital case for a week, sitting on a ball of air up there in the medical ward, his mouth wired shut and sucking shit through a big fat straw. I looked in just for the fun, knowing he'd give me the frosted eye.

'Fell down'. He mumbled as best he could with all that medical shit done to him, pulling the hospital gown around him, one bloodshot eye to evening news.

'Are you sure?'

'Yeah, I'll be out Monday', and he closed the good eye and rested on the pillows, his gears in the air with the pumped cushion lifting him higher than the mothers in maternity.

Then I thought I'd give The Ouncel a courtesy call, ready for the 'fuck you' and I wasn't disappointed. Hard as hell on a cold morning.

'Arrest me if you like', was what he said, his face still mushed up. 'And fuck me if you're able', and him standing there, light-like, on his shag carpet.

'I can wait, he'll be out Tuesday', was all I said.

'Unmarked car'. That must be the funniest phrase in any police textbook. I never use them myself, every dipper, drunk, pimp, skimper and sheep salesman, not to mention the few serious criminals we have, know them better than we do. No, I keep a little secret weapon for these careful days, the little moped with the blacked-out helmet. That's the boy, never stands out in a crowd, no one notices one of those things above another – just keep the plates switched and who's the wiser? I keep it locked away for these occasions. Someone reported it stolen about two years back and I found it myself right there on Igoe Street, still ticking over, so off I rode and I've had it ever since.

'Would I be in time to visit Mister Bodkin?' I asked on the phone.

The nurse was most helpful, I'd have to hurry. He was due to check out at three. Saw him myself from down the line of cars. He was walking kinda careful, kinda John-Wayne-like and bandaged like a mummy. The taxi driver gave him the several-times-over before holding the back door of the cab wide so's he could come down real easy on his busted undercarriage in the big back seat. Took him straight home and judging by the curtains straight to bed. But gingerly!

The cobwebbed rain was here again, drifting in along the bay, clinging to the church spires, soaking into gables, easing under slates, hanging in the ear cavities, dripping onto bony shoulders encased in dampening greatcoats, sheltering in wet-tiled doorways.

The buzzer on The Ouncel's apartment was one of the newest types, but still all hiss and pissing sounds like phoning in from Neptune.

'I have a few more questions', was all I had to say to the door camera after waiting in the dripping shadows for an hour to make sure he was alone. He met me at the door in a great suit. The helmet shook him though, rain-pearled, hanging on my arm like that, but he never blinked even when I put the sawn-off to his forehead, the rough-cut barrels digging in his flesh.

'Quit pricking around', he said, sure as anything. That was the bit I loved, the final move, checkmate, except The Ouncel would never mate again.

'They'll blame Jack'. I whispered. His eyes crinkled.

'He's still in hospital you fool. T-U-E-S-D-A-Y, remember?' Then he heard the snick, taking up the slack the gun-boys call it, one of them told me once in the cells how it could freeze a room to hell, the tiny grate as the trigger pulls.

'M-O-N-D-A-Y', I said, spelling it out for him as his head decorated the long apartment wall. Krakatoa in a shiny suit, expensive that Italian stuff.

It's the cleaning I hate the most, so the trick is not to do it on the double. The disk from the CCTV machine, a quick wipe to the buttons, just in case, and the helmet on and out of there. This was the quality high; if no one heard the shot I was home, if not exactly dry. I waited in the shadows for a time and no bother, no police cars, no sudden moves, so straight along to Jack's place easing the lock with a banker's card.

Banker's card? I'm always telling people at the neighbourhood watch meetings how the banker's card is the house-owner's worst enemy and I always get one 'Jim citizen' up to try to slip the lock on some handy door and they always fail. And I turn brandishing the card and I say 'but in the hands of a career criminal this card can have you inside in no time'. But I never, ever show them, they must believe. I can't be admitting that I know so much about these things.

The lock slipped with a razor snick, chain hanging so no need to use the cutters. Stairs dead ahead lit by the big fanlight and I could hear the bastard snoring, still it's better to check the other rooms just the same.

I remember once on border duty stopping an active member in the street. Done to the nines and dressed to kill. I pulled her in a doorway, quick frisk, ripped handbag, and her spit dripping on my cheek.

'Fuck you!' she hissed. 'Fuck you! Who do you think you are?'

So I leant in close, slipped my knee in her crotch, the easy touch.

'I've been where you live', I whispered. 'Wore my gloves searching it. Saw your mother, blear-tears on her wrinkled jaws mumbling in her gums about the new republic. I saw all that, I smelt the scabies on the sheets, the drag of dirt along the stairwell wall. I've been in your life. That's who I am'.

It hit her hard, face breaking, crumpled lip.

I thought of her then when I saw the rooms. Nothing much to this life, all his energy went in to The Ouncel's wife. Some woman that.

He was face up on the crumpled bed, mouth slack as the wires would let him. I was a ghost skipping then, a wraith kneeling as I leant across him, my wild stare to his closed lids, my lips pursed as I eased a wisp of breath about his eyes and he turned rough-mumbling, swatting at the air, still asleep, his face sagging to the side.

I placed the handgun on the grey pillow, easing the hammer back to the tightened click. C-L-I-C-K and his eyes really opened, wide: a difficult way to die, eyes-sideways, looking down the black uncomprehending O of a barrel vomiting flame and the end like a cinema gone black, leaving the darkness deeper than before.

His fingers wrapped easily around the butt, he made no objection, not even when I slipped the blood-smeared sawn-off down behind the old bureau and checked the handgun for position.

I hate funerals. But when it clears a caseload I can be accommodating. I could stand back now and make sure the calls went right. I was in the clear, the big guns from the Park happy it was just a love feud, murder and self-harm, their investigations done, no trace on the guns, no prints but Jack's.

'Grand old town you have here', one of the 'good suits' quipped the morning of the post-mortem.

'We do try, we really do'. I nodded and I meant it too.

Funerals? Who can tell? I stood near the back. They're nearly always the same, some serious tears, some pretend crying, maybe some eyeing-up and a lot of ticking off, debts met and bills paid and, if you're lucky, just a little real grief. Yes, death can be a stickler for the protocols.

The widow looked well in black, sleek, tight about the hips, like a second skin. I was thinking of the Starman Cafe when I pushed to touch her hand. I had to smile, Dali was right, a fine woman that. Fine woman.

'Sorry for your many troubles ma'am'.

'So good that you could come', she smiled, and her eyes weren't really red-rimmed after all, just deep and kinda grey and sliding upwards into mine. I could smell real cooking.

Death at a Funeral

Micheál Ó Conghaile

It would have been ridiculous for Eamon Bartley to stay ensconced in his coffin any longer. He couldn't anyway. He was far too good to have died. Every one of the merry mourners at the funeral were praising him – praising him up and down and back to front and top to bottom and arse to elbow – even those who hated his guts once upon a time; those who had it in for him due to some old dispute; those who cursed him roundly and fucked him from a height; those who didn't talk to him for yonks; those who crossed the road to avoid him, or looked right when he was on the left, or who stared at the ground if he was all around them. Every man jack of them praising him with gusto now. They were mourning him and mourning him and mourning him, they sure were.

'Eamon was all right you know, the poor fucker'.

'The whole town will miss him'.

'You could depend on Eamon, a sound man'.

'The poor soul, God love him'.

'He was kind and helpful to everybody'.

'He was all of that and more, even if he wasn't the full shilling'.

'Too true'.

'You never said a more honest word'.

'Absolutely'.

Eamon suddenly began to think that he'd be a proper fool to remain dead in his coffin any longer. Not one minute longer. Neither right nor proper nor appropriate. Besides it would be wrong to these good, heartbroken people gathered around him. Maybe I'm confused, he thought to himself, or maybe I'm not the same person I was ... in which case it wasn't me who knocked up Micil Bawn's young one at all; or broke into Mary Andy's shop and made off with two thousand euros, or nicked the sugar lumps from the priest's tea the day he was around for the stations, or who crashed into Martin More's nice new car without tax or insurance, or who fire-bombed the co-op's offices when they sacked me, or who broke into the police station looking for my hooch which the bastards swiped ...

With one vicious smash he crashed up through the brown coffin lid. Sat up. Straightened himself as straight as a bamboo cane in a teacher's hand.

The mourners woke up in consternation from muttering their prayers. Some of them jumped out of their skins, and into others'. A few of them gawped. Others seemed to run off in four directions at once, as if they were doing a set-dance mixed up with a waltz. The rest of them froze like icicles on a cold March day.

Eamon Bartley Coolan looked around him. And then looked slowly around him again in silence from person to person. His head and shoulders were barely up over the edge of the grave. He was grinning all over. A grin that grew until it went from ear to ear. A big, broad, stupid crescent grin.

'Aren't you all happy that I'm alive and kicking again?' he said, buddy-like and up-beat. Then he stopped, expecting someone to say something, anything, even a stutter. But there was no answer, not a word. He broke the silence again.

'Look, even though I liked the other life better than this miserable vale of tears, I just couldn't not come back, you missed me so much. You are all so nice, so straight. Too straight and honest really. I was really touched the way you all said nice things about me, praising me to the skies. Every single one of you. And I felt such pity for you. Your wailing and weeping would make the stones themselves burst into tears, and that's why I, that's why ... Hold on a minute! Is something wrong? Why are you all so quiet, gawking at me with your big wide eyes? Do I detect some misgivings now that I've thrown away the shroud? I mean, come on, it's a bit early for me to die again, isn't it? Begging your pardon then, my friends and companions and brothers in Christ, but am I allowed to stay just a little bit longer, to live just a little bit more? Am I?'

Nobody answered him at first. Nobody spoke. They stood around like statues, like telephone poles, like stiffened stalagmites. The priest. The undertaker. The doctor. The workers. His widow. The local petty politician who turned up at every funeral with his wet handshake. Relations of all kinds. Some who had never been heard of, others who denied having anything to do with him. Toddlers and raggy urchins. Teenagers. Neighbours. People from the town. From the hills. The odd person that nobody knew ...

'I drank fifteen pints at his wake. I'm telling you. Fifteen bloody pints. I never sank my moustache into so many creamy pints, the very best of pints, for the sake of a scrounger who never spent one cent on a drink in his life, nor on anything else either until he died. Don't let him spoil our day's boozing now. Believe me, he doesn't deserve to live ...'

'I was certain he was dead. Absolutely sure. Didn't I feel his pulse? I put my hand on his pulse three or four times, and I felt his heart, his ... No sign of life whatsoever. One hundred per cent sure. I'd be able to recognise a dead man rather than a live one any day before anyone else ... I have years of practice ... Think of my reputation, my good name, my professional record. I'm telling you, he doesn't deserve to live ...'

'The coffin is ruined anyway. Whoever heard of a second-hand coffin? And it smells. His name and date of death finely and clearly engraved on its brass plate, all arrangements on the news and in the papers. It's not as if it could be used again. You couldn't flog a pine overcoat that somebody had already worn. It would be unlucky, unhealthy. Think of the risk. Even a live person wouldn't be happy to sit in a second-hand coffin, never mind a second-corpse coffin, never mind a dead person. For God's sake, he doesn't deserve to live ...'

'He never voted for me. Never. Not once. The Bartleys always stuck with the other crowd, they didn't change over when others did the time of that bother about the potholes and the water. When I think of all the cars we sent to bring him to the polling booth on election day. Total waste of time. Election after election. And he never once voted for me, after all I did for him. And I don't suppose he's going to change his mind now with another election coming. On mature reflection, he doesn't deserve to live ...'

'He was a nasty bastard anyway. Frightening the shite out of me on the road coming home from school. Trying to scare me. Acting the eejit. Talking about ghosts, and hobgoblins, and fairies, all those silly things that aren't there anymore. Telling stupid stories. Acting the real prick. He bullied me often enough. I used to dirty the bed, not sleep at night, and have nightmares because of him. When you think about it, he doesn't deserve to live ...'

'I put ten euros offering on his altar. Ten euros, boy, I did, I'm telling you. I sweated blood and tears for those ten euros, and yet I gladly offered them up to the Divine Lord because he answered my prayers ... that I wouldn't see him sneaking past my door again. He was a right one ... and may God grant that he never comes snooping around again. If I had to offer another ten euros on his altar I'd be completely bust. No way! If you ask me, he doesn't deserve to live ...'

'He was a liar. A consummate, irredeemable liar. Pretending he had snuffed it. Making fools of people. Drawing attention to himself. Throwing shapes. Acting the big cheese. Trying to show the world that we in this town are only stupid pig-ignorant blubber-brains. Well, he has another thing coming. He doesn't deserve to live ...'

'I came all of seventy miles to be here at his funeral. Seventy long Irish miles, neither give nor take an inch or a half-inch. My health isn't good, you know. I'm ailing myself. I've put my life in danger by coming all the way here just to see him laid out. So I could see him stone dead before my very own eyes. I just had to. Ok, so I had a face on me and we weren't talking for a long time, but I wouldn't give the satisfaction of not coming to his funeral. Seventy miles, despite my bad health ... my rheumatism, varicose veins, blood pressure, weak heart ... despite my ... Ah, what the hell, he doesn't deserve to live ...'

'I'd put a bet on with the bookie. Quite simple really. Five thousand euros. Five thousand euros that he wouldn't make it to the end of the week. Jaysus, I'd lose everything.

My house, my car, my ex-wife, the whole bleeding lot. Keep the final curtain down until next week and I'll have claimed my money, and I'll have made it sing. No doubt about it, he doesn't deserve to live ...'

'It's not him at all. It's some kind of evil spirit, some kind of malevolent changeling that causes havoc if it doesn't get its own way. It's not of this world at all, I'm more than certain of that. How do we know that it's not the devil incarnate in some kind of disguise? The spawn of Satan. He was always an Antichrist. He hasn't come back for our good, I'll tell you that. He doesn't deserve to live ...'

'Pretending all the time that he was a bit simple. A bit gaga. Nobody at home, like. I suppose he thinks now we believe he was so simple that he couldn't tell he should stay pegged out the way he was, like any decent corpse with a wisp of sense. Like any decent corpse with any respect for the unfortunate creatures he'd left behind. Himself and his stupid, inane, asshole simplicity. A bad bastardy ball-brained bollux. Let's be fair, he doesn't deserve to live ...'

'I'll never get the widow's pension. Fat chance as long as that fat turd is around. I'll be disgraced and mortified again, like the last time when he shagged off and they called me the "live man's widow". We can't let him get away with it again. It would be appalling, unjust. He's a cheating lying deceiver anyway – letting on he was dead, the little shite. That was below the belt. The lying scumbag. He got his just desserts. If he crapped out as cold meat, let him stay crapped out to push up daisies like any half-decent man. It's bad enough when someone is a sly chancer in this life, but when they come back from the dead to be a sly chancer again, it's ten times worse. We've yapped on long enough about him. He doesn't deserve to live ...'

'I got to him just in time. Just in time to anoint him. I wouldn't have, of course, if I hadn't left my fine dinner to go cold on me. I certainly wouldn't. And he wouldn't have made his last sincere confession if it hadn't been for me. A true and genuine confession from the bottom of his heart ... real soul-searching stuff. When he was fading away and his breath coming in short wheezy gasps, I said the Act of Contrition right into his ear. I did, I did that. And before my prayer could go through his thick head and out through the other ear – puff! – he popped off. Croaked. Out for the last count. But it didn't matter, I had forgiven him all his sins, even the very worst of them, every single one of them – and I can tell you they were many and varied ... robbery, calumny, lies, cursing and swearing, blasphemy, lechery and whoring and whoring and lechering. Not to mention all the newfangled sins he had deliberately learned from the New Catechism. I'd be here until morning or beyond. By the time I was finished with him he was ready to go; as ready and as steady as a strong stone bridge, and maybe he was halfway across it on his journey to paradise if the fool had only kept going. The next time, yes the next time, the unfortunate man may not be half as prepared. Maybe he'd be caught off-guard, on the hop. And as regards the altar offerings, they were the biggest that I have ever seen for a deceased man in this diocese. He must have been held in the greatest respect, or the greatest disrespect as the case may be, and people were relieved to see him gone. All those tenners, and twenties, and even a few fifties – and the mass cards! Hundreds of them with a tenner stuck in them all. Enough money for half the devils in hell to buy their ticket to heaven. I'd never be able to give them all back, never. I've already booked two fortnights in Bangkok, put a fat deposit on a new car. And why not? An extension wouldn't be good for him anyway. More time would be bad news. I'm only for his own good. His soul was as pure and as scrubbed-clean as the new marble on a memorial monument. He wouldn't be half as ready the next time – that is, if there is to be a next time. He couldn't possibly be as prepared as he was, or his soul as ready to meet his Maker. I mean, if I was to be called out again to anoint him, I couldn't really be expected to ... I mean, how could I believe that kind of a call. Once-bitten twice-shy and all that. He'd be the worst for it, he'd be the one to suffer. Another sackload of sins accumulated, one blacker than the other. God's will be done. We're only for his own good. In the name of God and of His Blessed Mother, and for all our sakes and the sake of all the saints and the suffering holy souls in purgatory who are in torment, but most of all for his own sake, I have to say to you ... that ... he doesn't deserve to live ...'

'He doesn't deserve to live ...'

'Do away with him ...'

'Send him back to where he came from ...'

'Finish the job ...'

'Good riddance ...'

'For once and for all ...'

'For ever and ever ...'

'Amen'.

They beat his legs. Broke his bones. Twisted his arms. Tortured his limbs. Split his skull in two places. They smeared blood on his face, on every part of him. Tore out his hair. Ripped out one of his balls. Bruised him black and blue with their boots and kicking. Stabbed him with knives, stabbed him anywhere they could find unstabbed flesh. Children spat and snotted at him ...

Then they blessed the body.

Translation by Alan Titley

THE AMBUSH

Aron Costello

Galway City, 1978

In a cool, dusty attic atop a large house on the northern end of Threadneedle Road, James Fahy and his grandfather Robert sat hip-to-hip on a mound of cushions, laughing over old issues of *Mad* magazine. They had been in the attic for over an hour before the first stinging twinge of arthritis seized Robert's left hand.

Robert grimaced.

'Granda? You ok?' James' expression was all circles of worry; wide, china-blue eyes, o-shaped mouth, pale, moon face registering something akin to panic. Robert managed a comforting smile, astonished, as always, by the fierce love he felt for the boy.

'Right as rain, Jimmy', he replied. 'A blink-and-you'll-miss it spell, they happen all the time. Listen, you keep on reading. I'll look for another pile of these gutbusters'.

James giggled through his hands, 'ok, Granda'.

Robert stood, straining to keep his wrinkled face serene as another hot dart of arthritis enfolded his right hand. He nudged his spectacles along his nose and trudged across the room, scanning the shadow-strewn boxes and humps. To his right, he spied a sheaf of magazines rising from the pools of bric-a-brac like a pagan pillar. Robert angled towards them.

His shin connected with a stack of hardbacks, spilling them noisily across the floor. Fresh pain lanced his ankle. Robert hissed and swore under his breath.

'Granda?' James called.

'No probs, Jimmy. Only knocked over some books'.

'Ok'.

Robert bent gingerly to pick up the novels, smiling when he saw the titles, *Sister Carrie* and *Serenade*. He'd brought them (and virtually everything else in this attic) over from America when he had finally moved home, ten years ago.

It was then that he spotted the slip of yellow paper, curling out from the pages of *Double Indemnity*.

Robert took the book, opened it, and unfolded the piece of paper. It was a front page from *The New York Times*, dated 23 March 1928; the headline a garish, fitting reminder of that blood-drenched era.

> *DONOVAN GANG MASSACRED*
> *FIVE OTHERS FOUND WITH BODIES*
> *STOLEN CASH STILL NOT RECOVERED*

Robert Fahy eased himself onto a creaky chair. He rubbed his forehead gently, even as his hammering heart sped up inside his ribcage; even as a hot, uncomfortable tingling, far worse than the blasted arthritis, raced along his spine and into his ribs. Suddenly, the attic was too small. The air was too thick, and the day was too bright. Words …

sounds ... images ... his memory had erupted like a bloated pimple, spewing forth a noisome discharge of violence and mayhem and murder.

How long had it been since he'd even thought of that terrible day?

Twenty years? Twenty five?

And now the memories were back to haunt him.

Robert Fahy remembered.

Sitting in a corner booth of Magliore's café, trying to ignore the slick coat of sweat that covered his upper body, 22 year old Robert Fahy lit his seventh cigarette of the morning and sipped his lukewarm coffee.

The sweet strains of a Gershwin tune issued from the radio Magliore kept dangling over the cash register. Robert focused on the melody, hoping it would calm him, soothe the jangling and jumping of his nerves. It didn't. Blaine was late.

Outside, West 57th Avenue bustled and shone. Bent coppers walked their beat; twirling billysticks washed clean of skin and hair only minutes before. Ruff-tuff-creampuffs played Penny-Ante outside the stores and barbershops. The young women wore frilly hats and blouses or daring knee-length skirts. The young men pretended not to notice, straightening their ties and combing imaginary hairs off their suits.

None of this concerned Robert Fahy. He cared little for 'Society', and even less for its laws. Prohibition was a joke: he knew the location of four Speakeasies within two blocks of this café. He had a teaching qualification, but he hadn't found much use for it yet. As for dames, he was good-looking, picking and choosing as he pleased.

The Gershwin song finished. The newscaster announced an overnight shooting in Glory Falls, a fire in Atlanta and another possible sighting of the Donovan gang.

Robert drained his coffee, doing his best to look unconcerned. But it required a superhuman effort. He was, after all, an unofficial member of the notorious crew.

The Donovan gang had carried out a daring bank robbery in Queens the week before, escaping with a million dollars. Five people had been killed in the crossfire, including a cop and a blind woman. The gang had immediately gone to ground. Since then, the heat – and public clamour – had been tremendous.

'Six days have passed since the robbery', the Newsie was saying, 'and still the authorities have no leads as to the whereabouts of Carl Donovan and his gang. Eyewitnesses state that the gang has seven members ...'

'Eight, as a matter of fact', Robert said, and then shut up, cursing under his breath. One stupid quip like that could earn him a police grilling.

He had met the gang only once, at a meeting where he outlined the information he had worked so hard to get: Carl Donovan, the psychotic, grey-eyed mastermind; Lane Rhack, Donovan's devoted second-in-command; Jack 'The Brain' Irving, who had quit Harvard Law School in his final year to lead a life of crime; Russ Ford, the burly, monosyllabic getaway driver; Al Kinsey, who sported two long-barrelled .38s in underarm holsters; Sam Wilcox, the quiet Canadian who didn't speak two sentences in a day; Tom Gatlin, fast approaching his seventies and labelled 'the ol' campaigner' by Donovan; and Leon 'Eyeball' Jarwin, who sported a mottled scar along the right side of his face.

A professional crew. Ruthless. Determined. The kind of men who populated normal folks' nightmares ...

When Robert felt the tap on his shoulder, he almost cried out. He turned, and Blaine was standing there, Fedora tipped at a jaunty angle. Blaine's suit was pearl-white silk. His spats were gleaming.

Blaine slid into the opposite seat and signalled Magliore. 'Coffee, Mo'.

Carefully, unhurried, Blaine took a packet of Camels from his breast pocket and lit a cigarette with a gold lighter. He took off his hat and placed it on the table. He smoked his cigarette, feigning interest in the street.

Robert didn't say a word. He knew about this man's mind games. Toying with people was a speciality of Blaine's; when he wasn't setting up meets – like the initial one between Robert and Donovan – or acting as a conduit between the underworld and 'respectable' citizens.

Only when he had finished his cigarette did Blaine finally look at Robert. His lips stretched in a cheery grin. Robert thought it was the fakest thing he had ever seen – the smile of a corpse, caught in rictus.

'Our mutual friend isn't happy with the information you supplied', he began. 'It wasn't as accurate as promised. A cop died, as you know'.

The first icy finger of concern caressed the bumps on Robert's spine. Struggling to keep his voice even, he said, 'He can't pin that on me. His guys got too trigger-happy'.

Blaine looked pained, probably because he was used to not being interrupted. 'All the same, our friend thinks your cut should be squared away some. Say ... twenty five thousand'.

Robert snorted. 'You've got to be kidding. I risked my neck getting that info. The deal was for one hundred grand, remember?'

'The boys have decided to go their separate ways, in the interests of safety', Blaine went on, ignoring Robert's objections completely. 'The cuts will be divided tomorrow at 9am. The Maywood district. Same spot you met our friend to discuss your involvement. 'Course, you could argue things out with *him* if you wanted'. Blaine seemed amused by this last.

Magliore arrived and set a cup of steaming joe on the table. Blaine nodded, took it, sipped it.

Right away, Robert knew he had been bracketed. He had no leverage and nothing to bargain with. He had, in fact, been rendered useless the moment the robbery took place. His job was done, so why should the Donovan gang care for an unemployed Mick teacher in way over his head? To them, he was nothing more than a loose end.

And argue with Carl Donovan? Given the man's fearsome reputation Robert would sooner take a straight-razor to his own face.

Seventy five isn't too bad, he thought. You're lucky to get a single dime, considering who you're dealing with. Seventy five can bring you a long way. Take it, and get out of this city as fast as you can.

'Ok', Robert said at last. 'I guess seventy five will do. I'll be –'

Blaine's laugh – a short, sour yip – cut him short. 'You misunderstand me, *pal.* When I said twenty five, I meant twenty five. That's what you'll get – not what'll be taken from your cut. Got it?' A huge grin spread across his face, and his eyes shone merrily. Robert had to restrain a sudden, overwhelming urge to pick up a knife and thrust it into Blaine's face.

Jesus. Jesus Christ. Twenty five. After everything I did ... everything I risked ... twenty five.

Blaine slid out of his seat, and placed the Fedora on his head. 'Like I said, argue it out with him if you want. Be seeing you ... sucker'.

He left the café without another word.

For the next hour, Robert sat in his seat, silent, not moving a hair. Magliore approached at one point to ask if he needed a refill. When he saw the blank, empty look in the kid's eyes, he changed his mind.

Just before 11am, Robert placed a nickel beside his cup and left the cafe. He knew exactly what he had to do.

The afternoon sunshine streaming through the study window illuminated the left profile of Phillipo Toscani's pockmarked face colouring his red beard golden. As Robert finished speaking Toscani leaned back in his chair and laced his thick fingers together. He looked utterly thunderstruck.

For a few moments, the only sounds in the study were the tock, tock of the grandfather clock in the corner and the squeals of Toscani's children – Robert's cousins – in the garden outside.

'So let me get this straight', Toscani said finally. '*You* were the one who supplied Donovan with the juice on that bank they hit. Any chance telling me how you did it?'

'Sure. Patience. Luck. A very stupid female teller. And Rico Fontane'.

Toscani appeared even more astounded, if that were possible. '*Fontane?* That snitch from Hackensack? I thought he was hiding out in Canada'.

'Exactly'.

'Mother of God', Toscani scratched his beard, 'and everyone had you figured as a fag schoolboy'.

Robert shrugged, uncaring. Since the age of eight, his position within the family had been that of a virtual outcast. He was a 'cold fish' in the words of his late father – brooding, distant and prone to bouts of sullenness that could last for hours or days. Nobody had ever been able to figure out his unwillingness to mix with other kids or his fondness for books.

Reverting to his mother's maiden name after his father's

death from cancer five years ago had only pushed him further from the fold.

In his teens, Robert had inadvertently discovered that his respectable 'Uncle Phil' was a second-echelon mob member. The affable giant sitting five feet away owned judges, fixed fights, took payoffs … and occasionally 'pushed the button' on people.

As if reading Robert's thoughts, Toscani sighed. 'You don't know what you're asking me to do'.

'Phil, please don't think of me as some long-lost nephew come looking for help. What I've outlined is a simple business proposition'.

'"A simple business proposition?" Listen to the kid! You only want to ambush the most feared men on the eastern seaboard!'

Toscani took a cigar from the box on his desk. He didn't light it – simply held it in his hands. Enunciating carefully, as if he were addressing a troublesome child, he said:

'Look, Robert. I know you're intelligent and all. I was proud when you landed that teaching diploma. Everyone was, the whole family, regardless of what was said and done in the past. But this ain't no exam in no hall. You want me to help you knock off a bunch of grade-A hardcase fruitloops. I've met the whole bunch over the years, and there's not one of 'em that wouldn't kill you for looking at 'em sideways. I even know Carl a little. I say 'a little' because I doubt if even that bastard's mother knows what she gave birth too. I watched him try to jam a pool cue down Webber Smith's throat one night. A bunch of us were in this hall over in Harlem – I'm talking *years* ago, now – and Carl accused Web of cheating on the game. There wasn't even any money involved. Carl held Web on the floor and tried to ram this cue into his throat. Web was thrashing around, coughing up blood, trying to call for help. But none of us would help. Because nobody wanted to cross Carl. Not then, and *definitely* not now'.

Toscani bit off the top of the cigar and spit it into his palm.

'Christ in a sidecar ... it gives me chills *talkin'* about the guy'.

Robert nodded, unperturbed. 'If you come in, you keep sixty percent of the take', he said casually.

'Bullshit', Toscani replied, his voice slightly unsteady.

'I'm serious. Six hundred grand, to you. Only *you* pay the Triggermen'.

Before Toscani could answer, Robert went on: 'It'll work, Phil. If we keep our heads, and if the men you find are any good, it will be over in five seconds. The cars stop on open ground ... the gang step out ... and *boom*. That's it'.

Toscani opened his mouth.

Sensing victory, but knowing a final push was needed, Robert continued, 'I'm not stupid, Phil. But you know what else? I'm not scared either. I know who we're dealing with, sure. But I never would have come to you unless I was sure this thing would work. It will. And you *know* it. I want my fucking money'.

Toscani stared at Robert uneasily. He had never seen the kid act this way before.

It was peculiar ... but for a moment he had felt like he was in the room with ol' Carl Donovan himself.

What kind of thing is that to think about your dead brother's son? Toscani thought. A boy who's about to make you very rich.

Toscani assembled four men before 6pm that evening, refusing to divulge any details of the scheme until everyone was together in his study.

Present were Malt Fairlacke, a part-time grifter and member of the SouthSide rackets; Dan Elke, a Waldheim Way hitter with a reputation for being fast; Hank

Carpenter, a good-humoured Bostonian who, like Al Kinsey, carried two guns, his being Silver Colts; and Sly 'Fluke' Luka, a Mexican who had once escaped a seven-strong hitman team.

Toscani had chosen well. The men's shirt collars were frayed and their shoes too shiny. It was obvious, despite their arrogant posturing and suspicious glances at each other, that they needed money, and fast.

When the ambush (and its targets) were outlined, there was a marked reaction from everyone present. Fairlacke's mouth dropped open. Elke's sallow scowl turned cheesy. Carpenter smiled and folded his arms, bemused, as if somebody had told a funny joke and he was dying for the punchline. Luka's ratty features folded in mock horror.

A short argument ensued. Both Luka and Elke told Toscani flat out that they weren't interested. Fairlacke seemed troubled, giving no definite answer. Only Carpenter prudently elected to remain silent.

When Toscani told the men they would each receive fifty grand for their services, all argument ceased.

8:55am: The Maywood District

The five-storey building was deserted and crumbling – a towering, concrete skeleton, identical to the eight buildings surrounding it. Eighteen similar areas lay dotted around New York City, abandoned, devoid of life, save for the plump rats that whispered trails up the creaking stairways and cast elongating shadows on the walls.

The six men waited in position on the ground floor next to two large, shattered windows. They were standing thirty feet from the only road through the area with every gun trained on the spot where Robert had met Donovan, one month ago. If the Donovan gang decided to go to a different meeting point – or not come at all – then the ambush was off, and the money gone forever.

Robert glanced at the men standing beside him, Fairlacke and Luka. Luka's palms were practically dripping sweat. He kept touching the barrel of his rifle, as if it was a magic totem that could somehow shield him from harm. Fairlacke licked his lips constantly, angling his tongue up and down and left and right. On the far side of the room, Toscani stood with Elke and Carpenter. Toscani glanced at Robert and winked, but he didn't smile

Robert studied the weapon he held, one of his uncle's Berettas. The gun felt strange in his hand, in spite of an hour-long practice in the woods behind Toscani's house yesterday. He knew he should be scared stiff – should, in fact, be pulling out his hair in terror at the thought of what he was about to do. But he felt calm.

More than calm: he felt nothing.

The six men had stayed in Toscani's house the previous night, reviewing their plan from every conceivable angle. Toscani requested a makeshift diagram of the area, which Robert dutifully drew.

When it came time to select weapons, Luka and Elke chose rifles from Toscani's arsenal, but everyone else opted for their own handguns.

'Shit', Carpenter commented drily, 'at that range, it'll be like shooting fish in a barrel'.

At one am, Toscani finally stood, stretched, and said:

'Ok. The moment of truth, gentlemen. Call 'em'.

'Jarwin', said Elke. 'I've a score to settle with that lowlife'.

'And me with Cole'. This from Carpenter.

Luka hesitated, then said, 'Wilcox. For old times' sake'.

'Irving', muttered Fairlacke.

Toscani nodded, satisfied. 'I'll take Kinsey. How about you, Robert?'

Robert said, 'since nobody's said so, I'll have Donovan'.

He waited for one of the men to crack wise, or snicker.

None of them did.

Wise, Robert thought. Very fucking wise …

A distant, rumbling drone stirred Robert from his reverie.

The sound of approaching cars.

The Donovan gang were coming.

Two vehicles – Ford Convertibles, red and blue – came into view at exactly the same moment. Both entered the area from different directions and drew towards the building. Black plumes of smoke jetted from the red car's exhaust.

The cars covered the final few yards, slowed and stopped … exactly where Robert had said they would.

Irving and Gatlin were the first men out of the Fords. They opened the trunks and took out a battered suitcase.

The other six members of the gang got out, stretching, lighting cigarettes. Each and every one of them looked exhausted.

Carl Donovan stepped into view last. His grey eyes glinted coldly in the morning sunshine.

'Jesus, look where they have it stashed!' whispered Luka, pointing at the suitcases.

'Quiet!' Toscani hissed. 'Get ready!'

Six palms tightened on stocks. Six thumbs curled around triggers.

Donovan surveyed the barren area, taking a swig from his whiskey holder. The rest of the men stood in a loose circle, ragging Gatlin about cheating the splits.

Now that things were at an end, Carl Donovan finally allowed himself to feel a sense of relief. In spite of the relentless police pursuit, he and the others had managed to stay hidden. In a matter of minutes, they would split up, for good. None of them could ever meet again.

Fine with me, Donovan thought. Sooner I get rid of this goddamn baggage, the better. Argentina, here I come.

'No sign of that Irish kid, Carl', Jarwin said, stroking the scar on his face absently.

'Fuck that Mick', Donovan growled. 'If he shows, he shows. Anyway, you know what to do'.

Jarwin spun the chambering of his .32. 'Yes I do'.

'Ok guys', Toscani growled from his perch. Closing one eye, he leaned into his riflesight. 'On three. One ... two ...'

'Come on Jack!' Donovan suddenly barked at Irving. 'I want to get out of this shithole! What's taking you so long?'

'Yeah, Jack, what's the hold up?' Lane Rhack echoed his boss.

Irving waved a hand, yawned, and said, 'Yeah, yeah, I know, but –'

'THREE!'

The morning's silence was shattered as a multitude of gunshots pierced the air.

Elke pumped five bullets into Jarwin's chest, dead-centre. Jarwin flopped about like a puppet and sank, gargling blood, to the ground. He never knew what hit him.

Carpenter took half of Ford's head off with his first shot. Ford pitched backwards, brain matter filling the air in a thick, pink mist. A second shot went through his open mouth, exiting his skull in a spray of teeth.

The first two rounds fired at Wilcox missed by less than

an inch, spanging off the red Ford's fender. Wilcox reached for his gun, and was blown over the bonnet by Luka's third.

Irving was shot four times in the stomach by Fairlacke, but somehow still managed to stagger three yards to the left, shrieking, holding in his intestines. Fairlacke's next two bullets mushroomed through the top of Irving's head, spinning him around in a bloody swirl.

Toscani fired at Kinsey's heart, confident of a one-shot kill ... but instead of falling, the man flew backwards, sparks jumping from his body.

'Goddamnit!' Toscani cried as Kinsey rolled to safety behind the blue Ford. Incredibly, the bullet had ricocheted off one of his revolvers.

Robert fired three times. His first shot starred the windscreen of the blue Ford; his second blew it in; and by the time he had fired his third, Donovan had leapt to cover.

All of this happened in less than five seconds.

Rhack and Gatlin scrambled to cover behind the red car; Donovan and Kinsey behind the blue.

'Christ, who the hell is that, boss?' Gatlin shouted over the gunfire, struggling to free his weapon. His white hair seemed to be standing on end. 'Cops? Drake's crew?'

'Who gives a good goddamn!' Donovan roared in return. 'Nail those fuckers! Ground floor window, building dead ahead!'

Dash fragments, pieces of metal and glass sprayed from the Fords as a fresh barrage was unleashed upon the four remaining men.

'Don't let them break!' Toscani shouted over the tremendous roar. 'Keep 'em there! They ain't got a chance!'

Slugs blasted out sprays of cement and tore by his face. The explosive whine and snarl of firing ripped at his ears, making them ache. Toscani had never been in battle, but he was pretty sure this was a fairly accurate representation.

The cars' tyres blew in.

Headlights imploded.

Seat cushions spun away.

The red car's gas tank erupted in a guttering whoosh of flame, roasting Gatlin. He screamed and scrambled away from the firestorm, into the hail of lead. He was cut to pieces in seconds.

Then there were three.

Robert felt bullets whizz past his ears and nose. They actually made a sound, a highpitched *ziiinnnnnnng* noise.

A round nicked his left sleeve. Plaster and grit struck his cheeks. He fired blindly with the Beretta, aiming in the general direction of the cars, and pulled away from the window a millisecond before Fairlacke's head snapped back. Fairlacke hit the dirt, convulsing, a red spray arcing from his throat. Luka spared the body a token glance – the others never even looked around.

'We've got to run for it!' Kinsey cried, blasting away with his good .38. 'There's too many! We're dead if we hold!'

'So we gotta kill the sonsabitches!' Donovan answered, wiping blood from his left temple. 'Right, Lane?'

'Yeah, Boss!' Rhack roared, and let out a delighted whoop. He reloaded his Smith and Wesson, the hot, empty shells branding crescent moons into his fingertips.

The fusillade continued. Carpenter stood, boldly framed in the window, firing both his Colts empty. He ducked, dropped to reload and sprang up again with lightning speed, like a monster jack-in-the-box. He was hit in the shoulder and went down, moaning.

Rhack felt a burning sensation in his midsection. He had just enough time to see that his stomach had been torn open by a stray round when he was struck in the throat. Rhack pitched over and drowned in his own blood ten minutes later, long after the ambush had ended.

A bullet-riddled door spun away from the blue car, landing beside Kinsey. Kinsey stared at it, eyes wide and bulging ... then dropped his empty gun, grabbed the door and raced across to the adjoining building, using the door as a shield.

Donovan watched, stunned, as a shower of bullets careened off the steel – as Kinsey crossed the open ground without getting so much as a scratch.

Kinsey was five feet from safety when one of Carpenter's bullets shattered his right ankle. He went sprawling. The shredded door cart-wheeled away, and Kinsey wriggled and bucked as a dozen slugs tore up his skinny body.

There were five or six more scattered shots, and then the gunfire tapered off to nothing.

Donovan watched Kinsey fall.

He looked around, dazed, hearing the final echoes recede into the distance.

None of this made any sense. Five minutes ago, everything had been roses. Five minutes ago, the world had been his for the taking. The future lay bright and shining, all debts squared, all ties cut. Enough cash to do anything, anywhere, with anyone. A dozen ideas for a dozen new jobs. South of the Border.

Now everyone was dead – all his men, every last one. Lying sprawled around this horrible wasteland, looking like badly-used mannequins splattered with ketchup.

Donovan looked down, and saw one of the suitcases in the dirt. There were a cluster of exit wounds on its right side. He leaned over, clicked the locks – Irving and Jarwin had never had time to open them – and took out his lighter.

Jesus H Christ, he thought, flicking the flame. Did that Mick teacher set me up?

Robert was still gaping at the shredded remains of Kinsey – the man had either been incredibly brave or incredibly foolhardy – when he spotted Donovan, a vague hump behind the blue car. He drew a bead with his gun and got ready to shoot.

A moment later, Toscani coolly put three rounds into Carl Donovan's head.

The five men trudged across to the smoking, mangled remains of the Fords. Elke led the way, rifle pointed dead ahead. Carpenter was next, muttering about his shoulder. Toscani and Luka brought up the rear, along with Robert.

Robert hung back, nursing a phony bruised ankle. When everyone was directly in front of him, only yards away, he stopped, pointed his reloaded gun and fired.

The calmness descended as he shot Elke – the only one with a weapon drawn – in the head. Carpenter was next, the bullet snapping his lower jaw like a wishbone. Luka managed to raise his rifle before he was hit in the throat.

Toscani whirled about, black fury stamped on his face. Two bullets tore open his gut, and he collapsed.

Robert walked around the fallen men, looking for signs of movement. Only Toscani was still alive, gasping and shuddering pathetically.

Not too bad, Robert thought, smiling. Looks like that

practice yesterday was worth something after all.

He trudged over to Toscani and pointed the Beretta at his head. There was a single bullet left in the gun.

'You … you little shit', Toscani wheezed. Blood poured from the corners of his mouth and pooled beside his ears, turning his red beard dark-brown. 'I helped you … risked everything fuh-for yuh-you … we all did …'

'You didn't risk *anything* for me', Robert said. 'You did it for the money. That's all. Same as the rest of these creeps'. He laughed, and shook his head in wonderment. 'As if I was going to give up a dime of my money, Phil. See, there'll be nothing for you. Not one red cent. I was the one who earned that money. Not you. *Me*'.

'Robert … Robert, listen to me … listen to your Unc –'

A final gunshot, ratcheting and bouncing off the empty buildings like cannonfire at dawn.

Robert wiped down the Beretta and placed it in Carpenter's hand.

Then he locked the suitcases, grasped their handles, took a deep breath and ran.

He ran, his long legs carrying him across the empty landscape towards the last building on the left. Parked behind this building was a green Packard. He had parked the car there the previous day … right before his meeting with Toscani.

And as he ran, two words played over and over in Robert's mind, like a record stuck in a groove:

It worked! It worked! It worked!

Robert Fahy began to laugh.

Black turned to grey, and gradually to white.

Sounds came in … colours …

The room solidified before his eyes.

He looked around.

He could hear a young voice – what was his name? John? James? – calling out, but the voice sounded far away, like an echo from the bottom of a vast dungeon.

But this wasn't a dungeon.

No; it was an attic.

The attic.

Yes – he was sitting in the attic, and James was calling.

'Dinner! C'mon Granda!' James was hopping about impatiently at the top of the stairs. 'Mam said I could have chips!'

'Coming, Jimmy', Robert said. 'Be down when I finish here'.

'Jeez, you been there for the last twenty minutes!' James said and descended the ladder.

The newspaper clipping was still gripped in one clenched fist. Robert studied the headline again.

DONOVAN GANG MASSACRED
FIVE OTHERS FOUND WITH BODIES
STOLEN CASH STILL NOT RECOVERED

An acrid taste lined Robert's throat; a bitter bile born of memory. He wanted to retch. His stomach wanted to revolt, perhaps spewing the last dampened ashes of horrible fate out of his system.

Instead, he ripped the cutting to shreds.

He had been young … and foolish … and vengeful.

'All in the past', Robert Fahy whispered. 'A long time ago'.

He steadied himself against a table, took a breath, and followed his grandson downstairs.

That night, the dream returned.

In the dream, Robert Fahy went back to the site of the ambush. He returned in the very car he had escaped in – a green Packard.

As the last light faded from the sky, Robert parked on the spot where so much death had occurred.

Getting out of the car, feeling his joints flare and wail in agony, Robert heard a noise.

He turned, and saw thirteen pairs of hands break through the surface of the ground.

Robert watched, mouth agape, as the men he had led to death clambered out of their mass grave, their clothes awash with blood and dirt. They shambled towards him, a dreadful, tottering collection of white-faced spectres. Each still bore the terrible wounds they had suffered. Ford's face was practically gone. Donovan had three holes in the centre of his head. Worst of all was Toscani – his mouth stretched into a silent scream, his silver eyes gleaming with unimaginable fury.

Robert staggered against the Packard, holding up his hands in supplication.

When the corpses were bare inches away, a figure stepped out from behind the car, toting an arsenal of guns. It was the young Robert Fahy – tall, and proud, regarding the dead with unconcealed disdain.

'Well, I was the one who earned that money', young Robert said. 'Not you. Me'.

He sprayed the corpses with bullets again, obliterating them.

As a downstairs clock chimed 4am in a Galway house, Robert Fahy slept easily, with a smile on his face.

JANE AND DICK

Gerry Galvin

There was an A&E crisis that morning: an unidentified
woman, barely alive, thirtyish, Jane thought. Hard to say
exactly because of the poor wretch's condition. Blood
seeped through the blanket a passing motorist had draped
over her as she lay mangled on the Tuam Road before he
called emergency services. Jane, with one of the interns,
hoisted her out of the ambulance on to a hospital gurney,
through the lobby and, as fast as they could, wheeled her
to surgery where senior medics were already gloved,
masked and ready. Jane knew the score, she'd done this so
many times: the horror of multiple injuries and
undignified death was nothing new to her. She boasted
that the daily carnage she witnessed at St Peter & Paul's
had no effect on her. 'You know the old saying about
ducks and water. Well, that's *moi*!'

But for some reason this one was different. Maybe it was
the woman's age, around the same as herself.

'You ok?' the intern asked, as they reported to the front desk.

She was shivering in spite of herself. 'I'd kill the fucker who did that', she snapped.

'Don't make it personal, Jane. We just do our job. Ok? Anyway the guards got him, he'll be charged with drunken driving'.

At thirty, Jane had begun to foresee a life on the shelf, punctuated, if she was lucky, by one-night stands on the way downhill to prissy spinsterhood. She was not happy. The prospect of being old and alone terrified her. What she remembered of her father before he disappeared was not nice, and her mother had drugged herself to death before she was supposed to be old. Jane didn't talk about her past; it made her dumb; dumb and angry. And it was so boring: every second Tom, Dick and Josephine had a lousy childhood. No big deal. She feared drink because of what her father did to her when he was drunk and yet she drank. The merest reference to drug abuse on radio or TV evoked memories of her mother's decline from adoring parent to a quivering, deceitful wreck of a woman who lost all her capacity for virtue of any description. By the time she overdosed in the park Jane had long since disowned her. And yet Jane smoked and coked with the best of them. Hospital parties were as much drugfests as booze-ups. That was the way it was. You went out to dinner with some smartass, know-all doctor because it was what nurses did. When you couldn't stand the sight of him after a couple of bottles of wine the only way you could tolerate sex was to get as high as a kite. Then you might as well be fucking a corpse.

Men in general disgusted her and yet she couldn't keep away from them. The last guy she dated disappeared without a word and before that, well, Tommy was before that; the less said about Tommy the better. After he moved in with her it was all rows, rows, rows, heated and physical. For a while she quite enjoyed it: a kind of argy-bargy high, with occasional fists flying. She gave as good as she got. In the end she battered him with a cast-iron frying pan. He never learned to respect her space and when he came back from a night on the town with his mate Zak, pissed as newts, that was the last straw. Zak, like a scampering puppy, fled from her rage. Tommy followed, blood streaming through his fingers, holding his head, screaming at her as he stumbled down the stairs to the street. 'Fuck you! Stuff your apartment! You're a crazy bitch, you'll kill somebody if you're not careful!'

She felt like a character out of Mills & Boon: 'an edge had entered her soul'. In the pubs and clubs she found herself anxiously scanning the crowd, clenched hand on glass, fixed smile. Almost painful to look at the morning-after creases by the sides of her mouth and the purplish shadows under the eyes. She avoided the image in the mirrors that pursued her all over the hospital where she worked. What she saw or thought she saw in those invasive reflections suggested a body displeased with itself.

'Janey baby', she instructed herself as she came off duty the day after the trauma of the dying woman. 'It's time you had a proper mister to look after you'.

She'd spied Dick a couple of times, once with another woman in a pub. Big, muscular, with a good-natured face. She could have sworn he gave her the eye on the way back from the loo. Then when she spotted him on his own in the club she arranged to bump into him. Beer all over her, him all apology morphing to opportunism. Men were so see-through.

'Have to make it up to you, buy you a beer to drink for a change'.

She let herself laugh at his brass neck, encouraging him.

When Dick first noticed her in the pub he felt a flash of recognition. Not of her beauty – she was not beautiful – but something about her presence held him, an animal quality that aroused him from a distance, capturing his attention as if he alone interested her. Through the bar noise and fumes he noted her looks: the wide eyes, large nose and riveted smile. Close up he experienced it again, more powerfully, this magnetism that pulled him to her.

On their second date she let their bodies take over. He was artless and crude, but she felt a need in him, a boyish dependence that lit some atavistic spark in herself, along with the realisation that this might be as good as it got and she could make something of him. Her predatory instinct recognised a soft centre.

'I've met him', Jane told nurse colleague Anne, the only one she had any time for. 'The guy I told you about, not quite the man of my dreams but working raw material'.

'Dick?'

'Every bit of him', Jane replied and they doubled up.

'He's a mechanic, a bit rough', Jane said.

'Nobody's perfect'.

'But this guy I know I can manage', she replied, nodding in agreement with herself.

'Do I have to remind you, Jane, for Christ's sake? You said the same about the other guys, even Tommy!'

'Tommy Murphy was a shit!'

At face value Dick was no match for Jane, but guilelessness gave him a free pass through so much of her snide comments, and when she mimicked his accent he laughed it off. Beneath the big softie exterior lay a quiet determination and a capacity for unselfish love. It might have been his intuition of the lack of love in her life that drew him to her in the beginning. He couldn't verbalise it but he was familiar with the feeling of one hurt heart responding to another. Unlike Jane, he'd had a father he trusted. His mother's bouts of depression impacted less on all three of them because Dad was always there, a constant support. No matter how far she receded into her illness her husband stood by, attentive and caring. Eventually he was rewarded with a recovered woman who was able to return the gift of care in the year before the cancer took him. Tables turned; she grew in strength as her husband's ebbed away.

A couple of months into the relationship Jane surprised him. 'Let's get hitched, Dick'.

'So soon?'

She wouldn't let it go. 'We love each other, don't we? Why wait, what are you afraid of?'

'Nothing, I'm not afraid. I think I love you but do we know enough ...?'

'*I* know enough', she told him. 'And anyway I'm pregnant'.

Cornered and honourable, he gave in and they were married soon after. Jane wanted to get the legalities done with and would have had no formal celebration were it not for her new mother-in-law's insistence on making a fuss. She cooked a roast beef dinner for the wedding party of six, including her sister May who lived nearby, Dick's best mate from Faherty's garage and Jane's bridesmaid, Anne.

It was fine for a while. Dick moved from his mother's into Jane's apartment. He worked six days a week at the garage and she was able to cut down her hours at the hospital as the pregnancy progressed. She cooked, cleaned, did the laundry, including his oil-stained overalls, three times a week. They went to the pub on Friday nights, made drunken love into the early hours, slept late Saturday and chilled out on Sundays. Mr and Mrs Wilson. Dick was so happy, soft and lovey-dovey.

The pregnancy was difficult, morning sickness and back pain. She thought of it, considered all the possibilities, but abortion wasn't on if she wanted to hang on to Dick. The prospect of a child made him behave like one. Every Friday he came home with some ridiculous anticipatory toy: dolls, cars and footballs to fuel her resentment. He'd feel different if he had to carry the bloody thing for nine months.

A few weeks into the pregnancy, before they were able to determine the sex of the child, she emphasised her preference. 'It better be a girl'.

'Boy or girl, I couldn't care less as long we get a healthy baby'.

'Stuff the footballs, Dick. I don't want another man in my life'.

She was tetchy at work, barking at patients. Matron suggested a break. 'Why not, Jane, you're due maternity relief soon anyway. We can manage. I've spoken to the boss and he's sure it's better for everyone'.

'Fuck them', she remarked to Dick. 'They just want to get rid of me'.

'Nonsense, you've been there forever'.

'This is their chance, believe me, they can't wait to see the back of me'.

Next weekend she refused to go out.

'Look at me. I'm not fit to be seen anywhere. This thing has taken over'.

'It's ok, darling', Dick said, trying to cheer her up, 'we'll iron out the bumps together. Wait till I get my hands on the little brat'.

He attempted to pat her tummy and she pushed him away. 'Take your fucking hands off me'.

'Ok, ok, Jane. This is a tough time for you and I don't want to make it worse. You just take it easy and I'll work harder for the three of us'.

'Bloody right', she snapped. 'And you can wash your own disgusting overalls as well'.

She got up late, shuffling round the apartment, half-dressed, hugging herself, watching TV in the afternoons on a diet of peanut butter sandwiches. Dick's dinners became microwave afterthoughts. He put a brave face on it, took to buying lunch at the takeaway next to the garage. He bought her flowers and chocolates. Once he suggested they go to a movie. 'George Clooney's in it'.

She turned on him, snarling. 'Look at me! Look at me, dickhead! Do you really think I want to be seen like this?'

He felt like telling her to mind her language and just getting the hell outta there for a while, let her soak in her own juice. Instead he asked, 'Are you taking the pills, darling?' The doctor had prescribed a mild sedative. Opening wide her arms, spreading her legs, she pushed her distended belly at him. 'There's no pill to fix this'.

It's the pregnancy, he consoled himself. She'll be fine when the baby comes. He remained hopeful and this hope spilled over into happiness when their son was born. Now they could work together as a family.

She was having none of it. Dick christened the baby Danny, after his own father, when Jane refused to discuss the subject. 'Call him what you like!'

He pleaded with her, urging her to see a counsellor. 'You've had a hard time, you need support'.

No go. He took a month off work, did all the chores, fed the baby. Jane's involvement was intermittent, grudging, unpredictable. Their parroted reactions evolved like a play with a familiar script. When he tried to touch her she recoiled, hissing distaste, her body tutored for avoidance of any contact with his.

Back at work again, he dashed home every evening to be with his family. Danny's chuckles at the sight of him made up for Jane's increasing hostility.

'She'll come round, give her time', he reassured his mother when she expressed concern. Something was going on unseen but decidedly obvious to the older woman.

'I don't like it Dick. She's not the same person since you married her. I don't like it one bit. The way she looks at you gives me the shivers. I don't like it'.

'I love her, mum. Funny I know, but I really do', he said with a wry smile.

Twice in one week Jane was not home when he got in from work, Danny asleep in his cot. She refused to discuss or explain.

'Jesus, Jane, what about Danny?'

'What about him?'

'Here all alone, anything could happen'.

'You're here!'

'But ...'

'Oh, piss off', she snapped, banging the bathroom door behind her.

She was not sleeping well and it was getting worse. Her recurring nightmares climaxed in wailing pain that petered out in bouts of sobbing. One night Dick lay tense in the bed listening, counting her small sobs: one, two, three, four, five, six ... every twenty seconds repeating themselves. He got out of bed and tiptoed to the armchair under the window where a bar of moonlight angled through the window like a spotlight. He sat in silence, listening, counting the seconds between sobs, watching her heaving chest beneath the bedclothes. He sat there, docile and bewildered.

Next week, same again. She would not talk except to show revulsion.

He confided in his mother who offered to take Danny.

'Only for a while, Mum, until we sort things out'.

'For God's sake, Dick, be careful'.

When he returned to the apartment Jane was waiting in the kitchen, backed up to the sink, officious, hands behind her back. When she spoke the words came out slowly, deliberately, like a teacher inflecting to a recalcitrant student.

'WHERE THE FUCK IS HE?'

Arms opening wide in conciliation, he moved towards her. 'Jane, darling, let's ...'

She charged at him, exposing the knife. In the split second before he evaded her repeated lunges he glimpsed the dark animal that had first attracted him; nothing sexually arousing now in the hate-filled, screwed-up mask rushing at him. He had the presence of mind to grab a tray for protection. The knife penetrated the thin wood, piercing his shirt, drawing blood as he fell beneath her weight.

The social worker was solicitous but direct. 'I'm sorry, Dick. If she won't talk to me I can't force her unless you press charges'.

In spite of all, he loved her still, the desperate love that wouldn't let go. Desperation decided him. A fresh start.

Jane was not in when he brought Danny home. He tried calling her, letting her number ring and ring. He called Anne at the hospital.

'I haven't seen her and, Dick, to tell you the truth I don't want to see her, not at work anyway. She made such a scene here last week. I can't go into it now but she had to be forcibly removed by security'.

'Mummy will be home soon', he whispered to his son who was already sleeping. He waited. Two hours, three. Eventually he fell asleep on the couch. He dreamed of Jane, the laughing girl in the nightclub. He was laughing too, their delirious bodies melding together, laughing, laughing, laughing. He sat up with a start. The laughter was real and present, Jane's laughter. In the bedroom, Jane, laughing but not funny. The same knife, the carver. She wielded it two-handed above her head, over the cot. His rugby tackle whacked her against the bedroom wall but she held on to the knife, slashing at him. Untouched, Danny slept while his parents grappled on the bloody floor.

After that, downhill. He talked to the Gardaí. It was no longer advisable to have her anywhere near Danny. Through the free legal aid scheme Dick engaged a lawyer. Jane was interviewed by a psychiatrist whose wordy diagnosis seemed to indicate a personality disorder of some kind: '... with a capacity for violence', his report stated.

With great reluctance the eminent medic agreed to Dick's request for a personal appointment to suss out at first hand what he really thought about Jane's likelihood of recovery. If he could meet the man, Dick's optimism reasoned, he would have a clearer picture and that could only lead to a satisfactory outcome.

Dr O'Mahony, the psychiatrist, a dishevelled man in his sixties, peered at Dick over a pair of thick spectacles perched on the tip of his Roman nose like a second pair of eyes. The pose unnerved Dick to the extent that he was unable to verbalise the elaborate hope that had built up in his head. He sat as directed and listened.

'Jane Wilson, ah yes, a most unusual case, quite rare in fact, in some aspects quite rare indeed. The deterioration in this young woman's condition has been remarkably swift, quite extraordinary. She seems beset with deep-seated inner conflict that probably stems from childhood trauma. There's an amount of re-constructuion going on, dramas re-enacted in her subconscious, some of it imaginary and manifest in this conflicted behaviour, with which you have become familiar, I gather'.

Again the doctor cleared his throat. I hesitate to be prescriptive, Mr, ah, Mr ...'

'Wilson', Dick proffered.

'Ah, yes, Mr Wilson. Your wife, in my opinion, suffers from anxiety-driven anti-social behaviour due to a profound lack of childhood nurture. From the sessions I have had with her it would seem to be clear that her family of origin was itself a damaged entity'.

'Not enough love', Dick heard himself say.

She received a six-month custodial sentence. As she bent to enter the rear of the Garda van outside the court she must have sensed Dick's presence in the small gathering on the pavement. Pausing, looking in his direction, picking him out, their eyes met. She raised her handcuffed wrists in a parody of prayer, mouthing a silent threat: you're next, it said, as clearly as if she had screamed into his ear.

Granny urged him to get a gun for his own protection.

'For our sake if not your own. She's evil, Dick. You don't know what she'll do when she gets out. She blames you for everything that's wrong with her and she resents Danny being with me'.

'No, mum. I can look after myself. If it makes you feel safer, get Dad's old army piece down from the attic'.

Ever since his father died, Dick had allowed his mother to take on his apprehension and now, inevitably, without a thought, she accepted as hers the fear and loathing of Jane he could not face. Cemented by a survivor's grit, her love for son and grandson hardened to hatred of the woman that threatened them.

Dick and Danny, Granny and Danny, Dick, Danny and Granny. Months of relief and hope renewing. Dick delivered Danny to his mother each morning and collected him in the evening on his way to and from work. Sometimes when Danny was happily asleep in Dick's childhood cot (which Granny had recovered in a trawl through her attic) he stayed overnight in his old room.

'You look more and more like your dad', she said to him at breakfast one morning.

'And everybody says Danny is the dead spit of me when I was his age'.

A loving smile lit up her face. 'If he has his dad's big heart he'll have little to fear'.

'He has his mother's temper'. The words had escaped him before he knew it. That bubble of normality they had reclaimed was easily punctured by inadvertent reminders that the future had Jane in it.

He went to the prison every Sunday afternoon. She refused to see him. Every Sunday he asked that the same message be passed on. 'Tell her I'll be back again next week'.

'A nasty piece of work', the warden told him. 'Take my word for it, Jane's a very disturbed woman. I don't like to admit it but prison is not doing anything for her in the way of rehabilitation. Some of our inmates, a minority I'm glad to say, are like that – they thrive on badness. She's in with a rum crowd, Dick. Move away. Go somewhere where you and your son can have a normal life without her'.

'I'm prepared to give her another chance. She's still my wife, Danny's mother'.

'Up to you. It's merely my duty to warn you. Maybe you should put off any definite decision until she's released in a few weeks on parole'.

For the first time Dick began to consider the warden's proposition. Too early to let his mother in on the idea of a move, but at some point she would have to be consulted. He had nothing definite in mind. It was far too early for that, but in the balance between his wife's credible threats and his son's safety there was only one possible conclusion. He wondered who he might talk to – his boss, his mates at work – anybody to give an objective opinion. He couldn't think of anyone. Apart from his mother, the only other person he had been able to confide in was Jane.

The evening news left him in no doubt.

'... two female prisoners on the run ... guard shot ... stolen car ... do not approach ... armed and very dangerous ... Charlene Mary Grogan and Jane Catherine Wilson ...'

Jane Catherine Wilson, his wife, the criminal on the run.

He left Danny with Granny and drove back to the apartment. Where else would she go?

Granny, with Danny in her arms, watched Dick rush to his car. Her cry, 'Be careful, Dick', he couldn't have heard over the screech of tyres as he accelerated out of the driveway. She held the baby closer, took him back into the house, fed him, held him, listening to his contented gurgles until the bright eyes quivered shut and his little head drooped. If he was true to his usual pattern Danny could be expected to sleep for several hours. Then she called her sister, Dick's auntie May, asking her to look in on Danny within the hour.

'I'll stay the night if you want', May suggested, as Granny knew she would.

'I shouldn't be more than a couple of hours but don't wait up just in case I'm detained. I've made the bed in the spare room'.

After a check on the latest local radio news she had a quick shower, dressing as though for a walk in the country. One more peep in the cot, a noiseless, pursed kiss conveyed by fingertips to the child's forehead and she tiptoed out of the room. Her aging Volkswagen purred into life as soon as she turned the ignition key.

A Garda car pulled up as Dick parked outside the apartment.

'We'll have an unmarked car within sight for the next twenty four hours. If she comes here, we'll nab her'.

As he adjusted his cap his eyes never left Dick's and, with practised reassurance, confided almost casually:

'She'll be back inside in no time'.

Dick knew different. She'd try to get to the apartment alright but he did not share the Garda's confidence that she would be easily caught. If he could get to her before the police he might be able to talk to her, convince her to give herself up. Deep down, regardless of all that had happened, she had to know she could trust him. He let himself in, prepared to wait. She'd come and he'd be ready. He went to the cupboard for coffee. A jar of peanut butter sat open on the shelf where the coffee should be. Her peanut butter.

In the moment it took him to realise Jane was already in the apartment her reflection loomed out of focus in the window by the kitchen sink – his last sight of her. The bullets scattered his brains, peanut butter and shards of glass all over the kitchen.

She escaped through the kitchen into the garden and over the fence to the alley where Charlene waited at the wheel of a stolen car, looking scared as Jane hopped into the front passenger side.

'Now, drive, to the lake!'

Granny's instruction from the back seat brooked no indecision, supported as it was by the fierce-looking, antique military weapon she shoved into the back of Jane's neck. Charlene took off, terrified.

'Drive', Granny repeated, 'drive, you bitch, drive!'

ARLEN HOUSE
Ireland's Leading Publisher of Short Fiction

GERALDINE MILLS
Hellkite (2014)
The Weight of Feathers (2007)
Lick of the Lizard (2005)

ÓRFHLAITH FOYLE
Somewhere in Minnesota (2011)
Clemency Browne Dreams of Gin (2014)

ALAN MCMONAGLE
Psychotic Episodes (2013)

AIDEEN HENRY
Hugging Thistles (2013)

JAMES MARTYN JOYCE
What's Not Said (2012)

EILEEN CASEY
Snow Shoes (2012)

NUALA NÍ CHONCHÚIR
The Wind Across the Grass (2004/2009)
To the World of Men, Welcome (2005/2011)

VALERIE SIRR
The Beautiful Rooms (2014)

DEIRDRE BRENNAN
The Banana Banshee (2014)

PÁDRAIG Ó GALLACHOIR
Porto (2011)

SÉAMUS Ó GRIANNA
The Lights of Heaven (2006)

MÁIRTÍN Ó CADHAIN
Dhá Scéal : Two Stories (2006)